To: Ma.

Great friends from way back in the good old days. My very best to you both!

Dan Drew

Blue Ridge Justice

a mystery for Lynchburg's finest

Dan Druen

AuthorHouse™
1663 Liberty Drive, Suite 200
Bloomington, IN 47403
www.authorhouse.com
Phone: 1-800-839-8640

This book is a work of fiction. People, places, events, and situations
are the product of the author's imagination. Any resemblance to actual
persons, living or dead, or historical events, is purely coincidental.

© 2007 Dan Druen. All rights reserved.

No part of this book may be reproduced, stored in a retrieval system, or
transmitted by any means without the written permission of the author.

First published by AuthorHouse 6/25/2007

ISBN: 978-1-4343-1423-9 (sc)

Printed in the United States of America
Bloomington, Indiana

This book is printed on acid-free paper.

ACKNOWLEDGMENTS

This book is dedicated to my Grandfather, Radford W. Childress and to the men and women who served and to those presently serving in the Lynchburg Police Department. The task of being a policeman is sometimes under appreciated, but when one stops to think about it, without their dedication there could be chaos.

My Grandfather's career with the LPD spanned just over 40 years from 13 Feb 1890 to 1May 1930. He dedicated those years, along with his compatriots, to providing safety and security to the citizens of Lynchburg.

* * * *

This book, like the others, would have never been completed without the help and devotion of my family and friends. Special thanks go to: my daughter, Ann who designed the cover and made this manuscript work; Mike Glass whose guidance and knowledge of police work kept me on course; Colonel Charles W. Bennett, Jr. who granted me permission to use the picture and badge on the cover; Joyce Maddox who graciously provided her professional comments, which insured a dumb fighter pilot's words made some sense; and finally to my friends and family who read the manuscript and added encouragement for me to finish this story.

FOREWORD

My Grandfather, Radford W. Childress, was a member of the Lynchburg police force from February 13, 1890 to May 1, 1930. During his active career, one incident stands out as an example of the danger policemen face. On March 29, 1920 he and Detective Arthur Mann located and approached a suspect reported to be a felon and wanted for questioning. As they started their questioning a scuffle ensued. During the melee the suspect pulled a concealed weapon killing Detective Mann and wounding my Grandfather. The suspect was apprehended a month later and executed for the murder. Police work was certainly a perilous calling, even in those days.

I was three years old at the time of his retirement and don't really recall the event. However, as the years went by, I do recall his continued association with the force. There were many evenings when he would be picked up for a night patrol by officer's on active duty who still held him in high regard. Smiling, he would almost bound into the front seat of the patrol car waiting beside the house. He would wave and off they would go. It was truly a mission of joy for him, but I am sure their efforts during the evening were in the best interest of safety and security for the public. Many times I would be awake and hear him return late at night. He always checked on me to make sure I was tucked in tight. It gave me a sense of relief and a secure feeling to know he was back home safe.

I can remember his service revolver, which he kept on a side table in the dining room. The gun appeared to be molded into its holster from years of being carried in his hip pocket. It didn't appear it could come out of the holster without a strong tug, but he once demonstrated to me how easily it would slide clear. He only showed me the gun one time and told me never to touch it. And I never did. Its location wouldn't meet today's gun controls to keep children safe from home firearms, but that was gun control in the early 30's, at least in our home, and it worked for me.

As the years have gone by I have always had strong feelings about the police and the dedication of policemen in particular. When I became commander of my first fighter wing in Kansas, one of my first priorities was to spend a large amount of time with the members of my Air Police unit. I told them 'Cop' was a good word in my mind and it was based on the memories of my Grandfather and his life as a career policeman. I stressed the point that they were the front line of action; they would be the first to arrive at the scene of any disturbance. I wanted them to know my thoughts about different situations, and how I thought they could influence the outcome. I expressed no hard or fast rules placed on their actions, but I wanted them to know they could make or break a happening by what actions they took in those first critical moments of any situation. I was never disappointed.

As my career in the Air Force continued and I was promoted to higher rank with more responsibility, I always made sure that our airmen, who wore the badge, received the highest attention in their efforts to provide top-level security. I have seen these stalwarts standing guard in sub-zero weather on our countries northern tier, protecting the perimeters of our bases in the heat and rain of Southeast Asia, and standing tall on the many isolated remotes around the world. If support isn't there, then it would have been impossible for them to sustain us in achieving our mission, which is to Fly and Fight.

The word police is defined in the dictionary as: 'The department of government that keeps public order and safety, enforces the laws, and detects and prosecutes the lawbreakers.' It is sad commentary that today in more than one locale some of our citizens don't respect the men and women who are duly appointed to protect them. To them, 'Cop' isn't an endearing term.

I would like to think that respect for these individuals is growing back to what it was in earlier years. To what it was at the turn of the 20th century when my Grandfather and other great policemen wore the badge. Let us hope so, because it has never been more important for safety and public order to abound in our country. We need to show the respect deserved, more than ever, for these dedicated people who are enforcing the laws and keeping our cities safe.

I salute them for making the police profession a lifetime work. Without such involvement by caring men and women, our world would be chaos.

CHAPTER ONE

The wide-open roar of the motorcycle made the quiet street a madhouse of sound. Rad Childers clung to the handles of the sidecar, which was attached to this maniac machine, as if his life depended on it, and it did. Rabbit Tankers, goggles pulled down snugly over his eyes, focused on the approaching curve. Actually, it was a dead end with only a small path leading off to the left. Ahead, the culprits were barely visible in the cloud of dust left by their battered Model-T as they raced to escape the long arm of Rabbit and Rad, the fledgling detective force of this small town on the bank of the James River.

Rad, a solid one hundred and ninety pounds on a six-foot frame, had been on the police force for nineteen years. He had followed in his father's career, which had been cut short after fourteen years. He was killed in the line of duty when Rad was only a young patrolman. Now Rad was one of two detectives on the active force of a small, hilly Virginia town nestled in the foothills of the Blue Ridge Mountains.

In fact, Hill City got its name for being perched on seven hills beside the mighty James River. Many said it was like Rome, built on seven hills, although the similarity certainly stopped right there.

Rabbit, a close friend, and also a longtime member of the police force, was the second member of this two-man detective squad. He appeared stocky in his five foot six inch stature, which belied the bundled energy surging in his powerful body. It became a well-known fact when they were new on the force, Rabbit would chase

1

the criminals down and Rad would lock them up. At least that's the way most of the stories went. Sometimes things turned out a slight bit differently. This was one of those times.

The morning had started out to resemble any normal late spring day in this part of the country. There were some wispy clouds in the eastern sky, but they didn't deter the promised warmth of the sun as it slowly rose to herald the new day.

Rabbit and Rad had met for breakfast at their longtime feeding place, Old T's, across from the Academy Theater. Old T's did most of their business during the evening performances of the theater, especially during the breaks between play acts. Every man in the theater would come across the street for a short beer or something else a bit stronger. Old T had rigged a bell in the bar area set to ring one minute before the next curtain was scheduled to go up. Didn't want the ladies to be by themselves during the first part of the next act or their men would have a hard time getting back for another libation during the next intermission.

Not everyone could get breakfast at Old T's, only those chosen few, and most of those were members of the police force. An occasional judge would be in attendance, but usually they didn't get up so early in the day.

Rabbit and Rad had departed for headquarters after three cups of coffee. They were strolling down Main Street, ambling past the various shops and stores, which weren't open at such an early hour. The clock on the bank showed the time to be six-forty. They knew every shop owner and were well known by them as keepers of the law. Many of these owners owed their well-being to these two officers. They were responsible for the apprehension of more than one thief trying to pilfer goods from many of these Main Street businesses. Most of the crimes had been in the category listed as minor, but it did give the merchants a feeling of having the law enforcement agency of Hill City on its toes.

Rabbit slowed and looked at his partner. "Rad, I'm still not used to these civilian duds. They make me feel like I'm not on the force anymore. You sure this is the way we need to dress to do our job?"

"If we are going to be detectives, we need to work in clothes that don't make us stand out as regular patrolmen. This is the way the big city detectives are attired when they are on duty." Rad brushed the lapel of his jacket, pleased that he had insisted on their new dress code.

"What did the chief say when you told him we'd be wearing these togs?" There was a pause when Rad didn't answer immediately. "You did tell him these are the clothes we're gonna be working in from now on, didn't you?"

"You let me worry about the chief. We've only been at it for a few days now. If this police force is going to have a detective unit, then we will look and act like detectives. We'll be what they call, 'plain clothesmen'. You got any problem with that?"

"Naw, I just would like to see the chief's face when he finds out we are his 'plain clothesmen'." Rabbit's eyes went half closed as he tried to imagine the event.

"Don't worry, he'll understand. It is the way of the future. There are a lot more things I need to talk to the chief about. Things that could improve the well being of every officer on this force. My father could've been alive today if only we'd been able to communicate better." Rad continued walking down the street toward the corner before his next comment, "And for another thing, I want you to meet Jay Stevens. He is a young man with modern devices, which will give us a chance to apprehend criminals in ways we've never thought of before. The force, and the chief in particular, need to understand just what's available to law enforcement these days."

They had turned up Ninth Street when Rabbit said, "I don't care what we're wearing or what has to be changed, I'm just hoping today will be slow. I'm needing to get the wife and kids over to see my older sister, Mary, in the worst way. She's been a bit puny lately. That is, ever since her husband died last month. My Bess plans to fix her up with some chicken dumpling soup and fresh made bread."

"I'm sure you will be able to get away early. We've been blessed lately. Nothing but a few robberies and those haven't been that difficult to solve. Seems the same people continue to do the same crimes. Now that they have been put away, our jobs should

3

be easier." Rad lengthened his stride as the grade increased going uphill toward police headquarters.

They were nearing the crosswalk at Church Street when the alarming sound of a klaxon filled the air, shattering the morning's peaceful calm. At first it was difficult to determine exactly which direction the alarm was coming from, but the clanging seemed to have its origin in the vicinity of Main Street. Of course, the bank on the corner of Eighth and Main had to be the source, no other system had as piercing a sound. Luckily it wasn't near a cemetery, the shrill sound could have awakened the dead.

"Rabbit, you hurry on and get a motorcycle with a sidecar from the motor pool while I run down and try to determine what's causing all the commotion. We could have a big problem on our hands." Rad was on his way down the hill as he yelled over his shoulder.

Rabbit bolted toward the police garage behind headquarters as Rad turned the corner of Ninth and Main. Once on the main thoroughfare it was evident the alarm was coming from the bank. No one was on the sidewalk immediately in front of the bank. In fact, the street was still empty of pedestrians and traffic. It would be at least another hour before any of the stores opened for business. Rad advanced cautiously toward the bank.

So, maybe the alarm in the bank had short-circuited, or perhaps some electrician was doing an early check on the system. Those hopes died however, when two men came running out the front door of the bank carrying two large money bags. One, closest to Rad's position, turned and fired a wild shot as both men raced away around the corner of Eighth and Main. Rad ducked into a doorway pulling his revolver to return fire. When he next looked out, the two re-appeared from around the corner of the building in a Model-T. One of the culprits was driving while the other was in the backseat with an additional person who appeared to be tied up. Rad fired two quick shots but he was well out of range as the car picked up speed heading toward the north end of Main Street.

It was only a matter of seconds before Rabbit came screaming around the corner from headquarters. In his haste, he was barely able to keep the three-wheeled cycle with its sidecar from tipping over. He pulled to a screeching stop as Rad pointed in the direction of the fleeing car.

Rad quickly ran around the rear of the machine and jumped into the small cockpit of the bullet shaped sidecar. He had hardly settled in the seat before Rabbit opened the throttle and was off in hot pursuit.

Speeds reached to near twenty-five miles an hour as the two pursuers dashed across the bridge over Blackwater Creek and up Rivermont Avenue. They barely caught sight of the escapees as they topped the hill heading toward the Rivermont Fire Station. Luckily, there wasn't any other traffic on the street as the two vehicles raced out the avenue.

The gradual curve near the intersection of Denver Avenue should have been easy to negotiate, but due to a small amount of dampness on the street's surface, the cycle slewed sideways as the speed increased. On the straight stretch before reaching Garland Rodes School, control of the cycle became more manageable. They caught a better glimpse of the Model-T as it passed the school, which meant they were gaining some ground on the bank robbers.

The robbers turned off the avenue toward the airport, or what was known as the airport. In actuality it was an open field where an airplane landed once in a blue moon. There was one small hangar with a worn windsock hanging from a corner. The entire structure looked like a steady wind could blow it over. Usually, there were two rickety biplanes inside, leftover relics of the war. They were mostly in some semblance of repair, nine times out of ten having to do with the engine. Occasionally some daredevil with a bright new machine would stop over for the night to give rides to those fearless few who thought aviation had a real future. Otherwise the field could have been better used to raise crops. Maybe one of these days aviation would be more than a way to thrill people, but the contraptions would have to become a lot sturdier before normal people went up in them.

Rabbit made the airport turn without difficulty, giving the cycle full throttle. The distance between the two vehicles was shrinking rapidly as they both raced down the street lined with some of the bigger houses in town. If they could keep up the speed, the detectives

5

were anticipating getting close enough to fire a few shots in an attempt to halt the fugitives. But, as luck would have it, the paved portion of the roadway ended. That's when the crash occurred.

Police Chief Dick Stoddard, a tall fatherly figure, was just walking into his office when his secretary said, "Councilman Brenner is on the phone for you."

"What could he want at this hour?" The chief ambled over to his desk, gently taking the phone from its cradle and saying, "What can I do for you on this fine morning, mister councilman?" The chief had had a few unpleasant words with the councilman on more than one occasion. But, since the police department came under the control of a special committee of the city council, the chief couldn't ignore Brenner who, unfortunately, was the chairman of that committee.

"Two of your men just passed my house heading toward the airport on one of your police motorcycles. They were going at breakneck speed, which only increases the sound made by that infernal contraption; it is enough to wake the dead. I assume they were your men, although they were in civilian clothes. Were they on official business or are they just out for an early morning joy ride? It hasn't been much more than a week ago since I called you about your officers disturbing the peace and quiet of our fair city, and for no good reason."

"If any of my officers were racing out by your house this early in the morning, they should have been in uniform and on official business. You know there is such a thing as 'hot pursuit'." He could almost visualize the councilman's rotund body, clad in his bathrobe, shaking by his phone.

"Well, it better be. I expect an answer and make it before noon when I get it." The councilman slammed down his phone. It was a sure thing the central operator must have received a deaf ear if she was still listening in. Most of the time you could count on the operators listening in, especially when there was a call to the office of the Chief of Police. Might be able to tip off the newspaper to a scoop and get a little money for their effort.

"Rachel, get me someone who knows what's going on in this department. Why two men in civilian clothes would be driving one of our motorcycles by the councilman's house at almost seven o'clock in the morning is beyond me. He doesn't even live on the main drag; however, his house is on the street leading to the airport. Why would anyone from our department be going to the airport? For the sake of the department, please let a major problem be the reason for their trip; I've had enough sarcastic comments from that chubby busybody. My only hope is he won't win again in the upcoming election."

Rachel, who wasn't bad to look at coming or going, was out the door of her outer office heading toward the desk sergeant's location before the chief had completed 'Get me someone'.

Rad leaned over towards Rabbit's ear, "As far as I know, there's no other way out from the path they are on. It dead ends at the railroad not more than a mile from here."

Rabbit only nodded, for unfortunately the motorcycle had just run out of roadway and was on unpaved ground. He was doing his best to make the unwieldy machine turn, but the skid was inevitable; they were headed directly into a large wooden barrier marking the street's end.

The heavy post anchored in the ground to hold the middle section of the barrier passed between Rabbit and Rad separating the sidecar from the motorcycle. Had it been one foot either way, one of the two stalwarts would have been doomed for sure. As it was, they each went their own separate way, although for the most part they were on unguided courses. The ground behind the barrier sloped away gradually for a hundred yards or so before sharply dropping off to a rocky creek below.

Rad threw up his arms to protect his face as leaves and small branches from the thickets slammed by his head. Rabbit had his goggles to shield his eyes, but the whipping limbs and twigs were doing a facial job that wasn't helping his complexion. Their separate paths through the tangle looked like two giant lawn mowers had cut parallel swaths in a mad dash to beat the other to the finish.

Their vectors sent them into heavy undergrowth, which blessedly slowed both the motorcycle and the sidecar. The undergrowth probably saved their lives, for had either of them gone much further from their stopping points; they would have soared off a cliff. This would have resulted in a freefall of several hundred feet, ending on the rocky bed of a small creek below.

Rabbit crawled away from the motorcycle and looked around for Rad. "Rad, where're you? You all right? I'm OK and thankful to be all in one piece."

"I'm over here. Part of this sidecar is wrapped around my ankle. See if you can help me get out of this thing." Rad was struggling to free himself as Rabbit made his way through the now battered down shrubbery.

Rabbit pulled part of the frame away from Rad's leg. There was a small amount of blood, but nothing to get excited about. Rad pushed against the other side of the small cockpit with his free foot, which gave him just enough leverage to wriggle free. When he tried to stand, he immediately sank to his knees.

"Rest yourself for a second and let me put a handkerchief around the cut on your ankle. Your circulation is gonna return in a minute or two. Your foot was pretty well cramped up by that rod from the frame of the sidecar. You should be able to walk soon and the cut doesn't appear none to deep."

"Thank you, Doctor Tankers. I hope your medical advice is better than your motorcycle driving." Rad's voice had a twinkle in it so Rabbit knew he wasn't really mad. "What we need to do is get to a telephone. If those three try to come back this way, we need some help and some transportation."

"Three?" Rabbit said inquiringly. "I thought you said two men came out of the bank."

"I did, but when they came back around the corner of the bank in the car, a third person was in the backseat and he appeared to be trussed up."

"Boy, that sure sounds odd."

The desk sergeant, Ben Martin, was breathless as he entered the chief's office. He wasn't used to the unexpected; excitement wasn't the normal thing in his daily routine. The man was nearing retirement and his weight had almost exceeded his days of service. From Rachel's excited comments when she arrived at his desk, he knew something was amiss. His face was flushed as he stopped in front of the chief's desk.

"What's up, Chief?" His words were interspersed with gasps for air in an attempt to keep from fainting.

"Councilman Brenner just called me about two people in civilian clothes driving one of our motorcycles past his home at breakneck speed. Do you know anything about it?"

"Yes sir, I thought you'd heard about the bank robbery."

"What bank robbery?"

"Well, sir, the bank on the corner of Eighth and Main was robbed just minutes ago and Childers and Tankers took off in pursuit. They were just coming up Ninth Street when the alarm went off."

"No, I hadn't heard about it. I am the chief you know. Seems someone would keep me informed. And, what's this about them being in civilian clothes?"

"Oh, they started wearing civilian clothes a day or two ago. Childers said that's what detectives wear. He said he was going to tell you about it when he saw you." Only a glare greeted the remark, so Ben continued, "The robbery just happened and I was just about to notify you."

"You were taking your own sweet time. Where are these, out of uniform, detectives now? Have we sent anyone to see how they are making out?"

Rachel entered the office and walked between the two men. "Chief, the president of the bank is on the line for you."

The chief grabbed at the phone as if it would bite him if he didn't immediately pick it up. He took a deep breath and spoke as calmly as possible, "Chief Brenner speaking."

"Chief, this is Jack Moorehead. I want the two men who robbed my bank brought to justice before this day is over and I want my money back." Moorehead, from a long line of Mooreheads with connections going back to the days of the Lynch Ferry, the very beginning of the town, never hesitated to demand immediate action.

"Jack, we are on the case and expect to apprehend the criminals before lunch."

"Well, I hope you are right. Crime in this town seems to be getting out of control. Now it's bank robbery. What can we expect next, murders on Main Street? There won't be anyone safe in their own homes if we don't nip this crime wave in the bud. Please tell me when my money will be returned." The conversation ended with a blank line; Jack Moorehead hadn't waited for an answer. He assumed all he needed was to make the demand and it would be taken care of.

The chief didn't take kindly to being the scapegoat of the town's elite, but he didn't let it get him down. His eyes sparkled as he said, "Ben, get a squad car out front for me. I'm heading out Rivermont Avenue, hopefully in the direction of the chase. Also, get on the radio and have any patrol cars in the vicinity check in by telephone. Tell them to head for the airport. We're going to need some help before this is over." Ben was out of the office before he received further instructions. However, the chief was still in mid-sentence, "Rachel, let Captain Snyder know what's happening so he can brief the morning patrols. He is an assistant chief so he should be able to contribute something to solving our problem. We want to get these criminals before most of the town wakes up. I'll call in by telephone once I find out what those two so-called detectives are doing. If the captain hears anything, he can give me a call on the radio and I'll react to his directions. One of these days we will have a radio setup where I can talk back to you, and it will be the envy of every police force on the East Coast when we get it."

"I'm sure you will, Chief. Seems I've heard Childers say something about achieving such a capability. I think he wants to talk to you about it." Rachel held the door for the chief.

"I have several things I want to talk to him about, and that isn't at the top of my list. If per chance he should make contact with you, tell him to see me before this day is over. Those two detectives have been difficult to pin down. See you later." Dick Stoddard winked cockily at Rachel as he nonchalantly placed his cap on his head. He then strode out of his office as if he were marching off to war.

With Rabbit supporting Rad, they hobbled toward the well-traveled pathway so they could be in position to cut off any attempt by the fugitives to retrace their getaway route. They were a bit dusty and rumpled because of the last few yards of their miraculous motorcycle ride. However, they were ready for action.

"Looky yonder," cried out Rabbit. A cloud of dust appeared over the small rise at the far end of the open area. "Could it be those robbers returning because they reached a dead end?"

"Get on the other side of the road, Rabbit. I'll stay on this side so if they try to get by us, we can catch them in a crossfire."

"It sure does look like they's coming back this way. That car is getting closer to us every second. You gonna be all right if I let go your arm?" Rad pushed Rabbit toward the other side of the path as Rabbit continued to talk. "I'll yell over to you when I'm ready."

Rad crouched on one knee; he had to because his foot wouldn't permit him to stand. He pulled out his revolver and replaced the two spent shells. He wanted to be ready with a full load if the criminals tried to crash through them.

"I'm ready and waiting, Rad," came the call from Rabbit. Rad could see him stooped over on the far side of the path, gun in hand. "Well, looky there, the car stopped deader than a doornail," came a surprised call from Rabbit.

Startled, Rad looked in the direction of the car and sure enough, it had halted about twenty yards short of their position. As he watched, a man got out of the driver's side and held his arms up in a sign of surrender.

"Don't shoot, I'm innocent." The man seemed to be shaking in his boots.

"Walk toward us slowly and don't try anything funny," called Rad. "We have our guns on you."

The man was obviously scared as he moved forward toward the two detectives who were now standing in the open. "Stop right there. Where are your two cohorts and where is the money?"

"I ain't got no money. Those two high-jacked me as I was coming out of my store; it's up on the corner of Eighth and Church. They tied me up and drove my car to the corner of the bank. I wasn't sure what they were going to do with me. They left me tied in the back of the car. It was at least ten minutes before they returned and drove off with me in the back. They held a gun to my head the whole way out here. When we got to the dead end of this path, they both jumped out of the car and started for the railroad tracks. By then, I was able to get my hands loose and drive the car here."

"A likely story. You stand still there now." Rad limped towards the car as he spoke. "What happened to them? They just up and let you go so you could return like nothing had happened?"

While Rad talked to the driver, Rabbit moved quickly and was beside the car before Rad reached the man. "Ain't nobody or nothing in the car, Rad. Looks like they skedaddled with all the loot. Those bags of money might be hard to drag along for very far. Should slow them down a bit."

"Like I told you, they run off when the fence stopped us short of the railroad. They had the moneybags with them as they went down toward the tracks. I thought they was fixin' to shoot me before they left, but they didn't. Last I seen, they was going up the tracks away from this place."

"Put the cuffs on him, Rabbit, and get him in the backseat. My foot feels good enough to drive. Let's get after those two before they are totally out of the area."

If it hadn't been for the residents of the last house on the street, the chief wouldn't have found the detectives before they renewed the chase. The people had heard the clamor of the motorcycle going through the fence and were standing in the yard when his patrol car passed.

Neither detective saw or heard the chief pull up. The Model-T was raising such a clatter; the noise level was well past the normal hearing range. The chief's driver, Patrolman Sam Whitman, blasted his siren as he pulled the patrol car beside the battered vehicle.

"What's going on here? Who's that in the backseat?" the chief was halfway out of the car as he spoke.

Both Rad and Rabbit looked around in surprise. "Chief didn't see you come up. He," nodding to the man in the back, "was in the getaway car with the robbers. He claims they high-jacked his car and then made their escape. He says they jumped out when they reached the dead end up ahead. He says he was able to get free and drive back here. We were just getting ready to head out and pick up their trail."

"Where's your motorcycle? You did have one, didn't you? And, what's with the civilian clothes?"

"We had a bit of trouble making the turn where the street ended. Rabbit will explain what happened later. Best we get after those two before we lose touch." Rad waved for the chief to follow as he stomped down on the accelerator with his good foot, which made the old car almost leap forward in an amazing burst of speed.

Rabbit leaned forward from the backseat and yelled to be heard, "How come you said I would explain about the motorcycle? You could have told him we were both lucky to still be alive and kicking, plus you didn't answer him about our clothes."

"Don't worry about it. Shouldn't take more than a couple of month's pay to get that machine back in some feasible working condition. You're lucky it didn't go over the cliff and down into the creek. Think what that would have cost you."

"I'm lucky it didn't go over the cliff? I'd say we are both lucky it didn't go over or neither of us would have to worry about its condition. But I tell you; I ain't paying for no motorcycle regardless of what happened to it. That wreck was in the line of duty and you know that for sure." Rabbit was getting red in the face trying to make his point. Rad couldn't hold a straight face any longer and started laughing out loud. It took Rabbit a few more seconds to realize his leg was being pulled more than just a little bit.

As the two cars pulled to a stop at the end of the dirt trail, they could see the railroad tracks were empty in both directions. No telling which way the bank robbers went.

"Did you wait long enough to see the direction they started in when they got out of the car?" As he spoke, Rad turned and grabbed the prisoner by the front of his shirt to make sure he made his point.

"Naw, sir. As soon as they left me, I wiggled loose and started driving back the way we had come from. If'n I had waited around, they might of come back and shot me."

"You said back there that the last you saw was them heading up the tracks. Did or didn't you see them depart?" Rad shook him firmly to make sure he was being understood.

"Well, I guess I did see them head in that direction." He pointed up the tracks, which would indicate they had departed west toward Forest.

Rad got out of the Model-T and moved over to the chief's patrol car, which had pulled to a stop directly behind the getaway car. The soreness in his foot was lessening so he made every effort to walk without a limp. He didn't want the chief to ask him why he was favoring one leg. "Chief, can you take this prisoner off our hands while Rabbit and I go after the two with the money? I'm not sure whether this driver is part of the robbery or not, but I think we ought to hold him till we find out for certain."

"Yes, we'll take him into custody. You two head up the tracks. I'll get to a phone and contact headquarters. We'll see if they can get hold of officers White and Johnson so they can cover where Link Road, Ivy Creek, and the railroad intersect. If the robbers get that far, they can cut them off."

"Can you get somebody to work down this way? Maybe we can trap them in between us."

"Don't worry, you get going. I'll make sure all the avenues of escape are covered. You and Tankers just get after them before we lose contact altogether, and when you find them, make sure to recover that money. I've already had a call from the bank president threatening me to get the money back or else." As Rad and Rabbit departed toward the tracks, the chief yelled to his driver. "Get that prisoner in the backseat of our patrol car and make sure he's firmly handcuffed to the handrail."

A pleading voice was heard to say, "I ain't no robber, I was kidnapped at gunpoint. All you have to do is call my wife."

Rad and Rabbit barely heard the chief's response to Sam as they proceeded in a northerly direction up the tracks.

Sam and the chief were headed back toward the paved road when the chief said, "Pull over at the drugstore when we reach Rivermont. I need to get on the phone to headquarters."

"Right, Chief. Look at this guy; he is shaking like a leaf. I don't think he had anything to do with those bank robbers."

"Maybe so, maybe not. We'll see when we can get all this stuff straightened out."

The store clerk was surprised to see the chief of police come running into his store. It certainly wasn't a usual sight, especially this time of morning. "What can I do for you, Chief?" When he saw the chief hold the fingers of his hand like a phone, he pulled the store's instrument from under the counter.

The chief clicked the receiver twice then waited for the operator to come on line. "Operator, this is the chief of police. Get me my office."

"One minute, please."

"Chief of police office. Can I help you?" Rachel's voice sounded clear as a bell.

"Rachel, listen closely. I need you to contact patrolmen White and Johnson. Tell them I want them to cover the north part of Link Road. Have them take Williamson and Patrick with them so they can patrol the south part of Link Road up to the railroad. I want all possible escape routes covered. I'm not letting those felons get away."

"Will do, Chief. Is there anything else?"

"Notify the newspaper to get a reporter and a photographer to meet me on Link Road. When we catch these felons, I want this city to know their police department is capable of teaching criminals this town isn't a good place to try anything. I'm also going to throw the headlines in Moorehead's face."

The chief returned to the patrol car with a few less worry lines on his face. "Well, we'll have most of Link Road covered before long. I don't think those crooks can get by us. Now, if our two detectives can push them into our net, we'll have them before noon."

"Don't worry, Chief, Childers and Tankers will probably catch up to those two before they can get far along those tracks. That Rabbit is one of the fastest persons I've ever seen and Rad is no slouch."

"Well, I hope you are right because if those crooks get away, we'll all be in trouble." The Chief looked at the prisoner in the back seat. "What is your name, anyway?"

15

"My name is Jerry Holden, and I own a store on Church Street, just up from the bank."

"Well, Jerry you will have to go with us for now. I don't have time to get you to the jail before we see an end to this fiasco." He sat for a moment before adding, "Let's get on out to Link Road, Sam, I'm anxious to get my hands on those two."

It was difficult walking alongside the tracks, especially with a sore ankle, but Rad wasn't letting his wounds slow him down. They had each taken a side of the tracks to walk along. Rad had stayed on the north side and Rabbit had moved over to the south side.

"That signal arm up ahead is in the open position and the light is green. Guess no trains have passed since those two struck out up these tracks. At least they haven't hopped a slow moving freight. If they had, they could be halfway to the next town by now." Rad slipped slightly in the gravel as he looked up at the signal.

"You OK over there? Don't hurt yourself this far from transportation, I might have to leave you for the buzzards." Rabbit chuckled at his attempted wit. Rad continued his steady pace by the side of the tracks without feeling a need to fuel Rabbit's sense of humor.

They hadn't gone more than three quarters of a mile when Rabbit yelled out, "Look down yonder on the fence. See that piece of cloth caught on the barbed wire?"

"Yeah, I see it. What do you think it is? Looks like a piece of canvas."

Rabbit was down the bank toward the fence before Rad could get over to his side of the tracks. Rabbit gave the small shard a very close look. He might appear at times to be somewhat clumsy, but he knew how to handle evidence. "Looks like we have part of a canvas bag. And looky here, here's a fifty dollar bill over here in the weeds. Reckon they busted one of those money bags gettin' over this fence."

Rad reached the fence and helped search around for additional money. "Look, here's another fifty and two twenties. They must have been in a hurry to keep on the move. Doesn't seem they took much time to make sure they retrieved all the money from the torn bag. Guess they stuffed what they could in the bag they had left and took off." Rad continued to look for more money.

"They took off over yonder." Rabbit was pointing over toward the bank that climbed on the far side of a small creek. "See where they broke that underbrush back as they scrambled up the slope?"

"Yeah, I see the path they made. You follow the trail while I leave a sign in case someone should work their way down the tracks in an effort to meet us. Hopefully, the chief has told somebody by now. I'll pile some limbs on this side of the tracks and make them in the shape of an arrow pointing in the direction we're going to travel."

"OK, I'll move on along and you can catch up with me. If I spot'em, I'll wait for you so we can make the arrest together. If they continue to bungle through this undergrowth like they have so far, they will leave a trail my mother could track." Rabbit was like a good hunting dog hot on a scent. He wasn't about to hit his point until he spotted his quarry.

"From their direction, it appears they may be heading for Link Road. Maybe they have someone waiting in a car for them there. I hope the chief has the area covered, or they could get away from us. Move out after them, but don't get too far ahead of me. Remember, they have guns and are willing to use them. I wouldn't want you getting yourself shot up. Then I'd have to leave you for the buzzards." Rad wasn't sure Rabbit even heard him. If he did, he chose not to respond to his humor.

"Mr. Moorehead, I appreciate you taking my call. I wanted to let you know the chief of police expects to apprehend the men who robbed your bank in a matter of hours. They already have one of the three in custody and we are in pursuit of the other two." Brenner's voice was at its official best.

"That's all well and good Mr. Councilman, but I'm more interested in getting my money returned. I told the chief I expected immediate action. You both can call me when the money has been recovered, otherwise, I have other important business to attend to."

"I just wanted you to know we are working hard to that end. We are leaving no stone unturned. As one of the outstanding citizens of our city, every effort is being made to protect your assets."

"Cut the malarkey, Brenner, and stick to your clothing business, something I assume you know about. I voted for you in the last election only because you were the better of two evils, which isn't saying much. And, if you don't show more support for the people who count in this town, you won't be around for the next term. I will see to it personally. Now get off my line, I'm a busy man." The line went dead, removing all doubt, even for Brenner that the conversation had ended.

Brenner turned to his secretary with a downcast look in his eyes, "I've tried to do everything possible for that man and all I get is 'what have you done for me lately.' And to think I was about to transfer my account to his bank. I won't be sorry if he never gets his money back. Check with the chief's office and tell them to make sure I'm kept up to date."

The secretary walked out of the councilman's office with a slight smile on her face. *Life was tough at the top, couldn't happen to a more deserving person.*

The going wasn't easy through the half-swampy, half-forested area. The only trees were spindly pines with heavy undergrowth making up most of the ground cover. Most of bushes contained briars, which caught on anything brushing against them.

The sun was well up in the sky by now and the temperature was starting to build. Their civilian suits weren't meant to be worn tramping through the woods. In fact, with their sojourn on the motorcycle through the fence, their trek along a major railway, and a stroll through what appeared to be unexplored territory, they couldn't have been clothed any worse if they had tried.

Rabbit's trail looked like a herd of cattle had stampeded their way through. Either the two robbers were charging ahead pell-mell without worrying about anyone being in pursuit, or Rabbit was making sure Rad would be able to follow without any difficulty. Most of the swampy ground had disappeared, so the firmer earth made travel easier. Rad felt he should be catching sight of Rabbit before he went much further. He had to keep up the pace; those two felons weren't in any better shape than he and Rabbit. In Rad's mind, they should be ready to give up the chase. Rad's ankle was beginning to swell and he wasn't sure how much more trudging through the woods it could take. How much further ahead could Rabbit be?

It was fast approaching nine o'clock when Rad finally caught sight of Rabbit. There was a small ravine between the two and it would take Rad several minutes to close the distance. He could see Rabbit standing by a lone pine with his hand up shielding his eyes from the glare. He looked like an Indian scout checking for smoke signals on a far hill.

Rad yelled out to him and waved to let him know he was finally back in contact. Rabbit waved back, then continued to look in the direction of Link Road.

Suddenly they both could hear the sounds of sirens blasting up ahead.

Link Road was congested with patrol cars and people. The chief had two patrolmen running toward the bridge over the railroad while two others were moving off the pavement toward a small stand of pines bordering the roadway. Before either group knew what had happened, two panting and bedraggled robbers stumbled onto the roadway.

Arms over their heads, they said, "We give up. Those two maniacs behind us have worn us out. Take us in."

The wail of the sirens spurred Rad forward the last few yards. He stopped beside his detective partner, "Why have you stopped here? What's all the commotion on the road up there?"

"I didn't have the strength to go on. You're not going to believe me when I tell you what just happened. Seems like our two fugitives stumbled out of the woods and gave themselves up before I could reach them. Now the chief has taken over the capture. All our efforts seem to have been forgotten."

"Did they get the money back?"

"Beats me; I haven't been able to get close enough to see." Rabbit just leaned against the tree, dumbfounded.

19

"They must have had the money with them when they surrendered. We didn't find any more of it when we were on their trail. At least I didn't, did you?"

"No, the only money I've seen is what we picked up back at the railroad tracks. And, that seems like years ago now."

The chief was striding back and forth, waving his arms like he was cheering for the home team to score some runs. The two bank robbers had been secured with handcuffs near one of several patrol cars, while two officers, guns in hand, watched their every move. Rad couldn't make out who the officers were, but they looked like Williamson and Patrick. Not far away were White and Johnson who were right in step behind the chief as he directed the remaining uniformed policemen to various tasks. Crowd control was the least of their problems, although there were a few civilians who had been attracted by the sirens.

Rad and Rabbit traveled the remaining distance to the roadway without being noticed. They stopped to brush some of the briars and mud off their clothes before making their way toward the chief, although their efforts really didn't help improve their appearances appreciably. Their snagged and tattered clothing would take more than a slight brushing to bring them to any semblance of normality. They would certainly stand out in the growing crowd, which was beginning to act as if they were at a carnival.

"I'm going over and talk to the chief, you coming with me?" Rad's voice was determined.

"You go right ahead. I still got to get some of these briars out of my britches." Rabbit slowly shook his head as he tried to assess the damage to his clothing.

A black Chevrolet with the top down came roaring down the roadway. It screeched to a halt inches from where the Chief had stopped his pacing. In the very corner of the windshield was a small sign with PRESS printed on it. Two people from the newspaper bounded out of the car, one with his camera posed ready to start taking pictures.

"Williamson and Patrick, get those prisoners over here so we can get pictures of their capture for the newspaper." The chief was guiding the cameraman by his elbow to the spot where he wanted the pictures taken. "We want to show the public how quickly our police force reacts to a major crime in this town. You two get on each side of the prisoners and look like you just put the cuffs on them. Hold up that bag of money, I want it to be the center point of the picture."

Before the cameraman could set up for his picture, the Black Maria drove up with its siren blasting. The growing crowd parted to let this menacing vehicle through. It pulled to a stop just ahead of the chief's car and suddenly became the center of attention.

Rad took this pause to quickly dash over to the chief. It would probably be his only chance before this impromptu ceremony continued. "Chief, what's going on? Rabbit and I chased these two so they could be apprehended. We should be the ones in the picture."

"Childers, I want our police force to appear like neat, clean-cut people. You two look like you were in a dogfight and the dogs won. Just look at yourselves. I've never seen such disheveled individuals in my life. Why, your pants have almost been shredded. We can't let our citizens think our police force is a bunch of rag tags."

"You would be a little unkempt, too, if you had chased these guys through what we've been through. Not mentioning the motorcycle accident, but slogging across hill and dale thickly covered with briars, as well as plodding in the swampy mud between here and the railroad would dishevel the best dresser in the world."

"Speaking of the motorcycle incident, just how did it occur? If it wasn't an accident, you two are looking at a pretty large repair bill. We'll take that subject up when I finish with the newspaper folks."

The chief moved away from Rad and continued with his involvement in getting the proper camera setting for the newspaper. "Make sure you let the good people of Hill City know we recovered the bank's money and it will have been returned to the bank before your paper goes to press."

Rad leaned forward to the chief, "Here's one hundred and forty more dollars of the bank's money we found back near the railroad track. We certainly want the bank to get back the entire amount stolen from them, that is if they know how much was stolen." The sarcasm went straight over the chief's head.

21

"Thanks, now get out of the picture before you spoil it." The chief was still urging the photographer to get more pictures as Rad walked back over to Rabbit's position.

The two desperados were being led into the Black Maria while the reporter continued talking to officers Williamson and Patrick. The chief was listening to their answers, there was no way he was going to allow them to freewheel their comments.

Rabbit leaned over to Rad and said, "You could've left out the part about the motorcycle accident. Now we are for sure into some deep trouble that's gonna cost us more money than we've got."

"Well, it won't be so bad after I explain to the chief how you were doing all the driving. And, you were the one who lost control and almost got us killed."

"Come on now, you know I wasn't trying to get us kilt. I was doing my duty. You're the one who told me to go get the motorcycle. I should have let you drive. Darn, and I thought this was gonna be a quiet day. Now I don't know how Bess is gonna get over to see my sister Mary." Rabbit was not only depressed, but he looked the part. Maybe the chief had been correct by not letting them be in the picture.

"Don't you worry. I'll explain everything to the chief. The accident was certainly in the line of duty and probably it won't cost you much at all." Rad had to look away to keep from smiling. But, when the words "cost you much at all" came out, Rabbit sank to the ground like he had been hit over the head with a baseball bat.

A long sigh was the only sound coming from Rabbit's crumpled position.

"Come on, partner, I was just kidding. If they try to make us pay for fixing that motorcycle, there is something wrong with the system. We'll be all right. Right now, we need to get some transportation and get on some better clothes. I must agree with the chief, we look like we've been run over by a fast moving train, and more than once."

Rabbit slowly got to his feet, "If we'd been in our regular uniforms, at least it would be the department's clothes we ruined. Those uniform pants probably wouldn't have snagged like these pants I have on. Don't know what Bess is gonna say. Now, I've got to buy me a whole new suit." Rabbit's face got even longer.

"Don't worry, my plan is to have the department pay for the clothes we work in. That's the way other police forces do it."

"Well, I sure hope you're right. But just remember, the chief just found out we don't wear uniforms anymore."

The door of the Black Maria was about to close when officer Sam Whitman came running toward the chief. "Chief, a call just came over our receiver from dispatch. There's been a shooting in White Rock. Could be murder, and it sounds like there's going to be problems. They want you to call in."

"My god, is there suddenly some type of crime wave starting in this town I don't know about?" The chief shook his head as if trying to bring some semblance of order to the recent turn of events. "Williamson, you and Patrick give your patrol car to Childers and Tankers. You can ride back to headquarters in the Black Maria and be sure you keep a close eye on these prisoners. This shooting situation in White Rock sounds like we're going to need the best we've got."

Pointing to Rad and Rabbit, the chief said, "It appears you two are going to have a full day. Please don't wreck this patrol car on the way to the scene like you did the motorcycle. Get to a phone as soon as you can and let me know what's going on."

"Don't worry, Chief, we'll be on it before you can snap your fingers. We'll call the desk sergeant when we can, but it would sure be nice if all our patrol cars had two-way radios. Any chance we can get them in next year's budget? I know a person who might be able to solve that problem for us."

"Even if we had the money, I don't know if two-way radios are even possible. No other force on the East Coast has that capability. But, you let me worry about radios and budgets. Now get on the way before I send someone else."

As the duo turned onto Fort Avenue with siren blasting, Rad said, "I'll help you make up a good story for Bess."

"Yeah, and you are the one who said we'd been blessed with only a few robberies lately. You had to open your big mouth." Rabbit still seemed a bit sullen when suddenly he yelled out, "WATCH OUT, that car coming around the corner almost hit us."

"Yeah, don't worry, I saw him all the way. He must have been going over 29 MPH when he came shooting out of that side street."

"We ought to go back and give him a speeding ticket. The roadways aren't safe anymore with these speed demons behind the wheel." Rabbit was still looking back at the intersection as he spoke.

Rad, concentrating on the roadway ahead, whispered, "You are probably right and if we weren't on our way to a murder scene I'd do just that. But remember, we're back on the first team, so hang on."

The siren made a wailing sound as the sparse traffic cleared in their path.

CHAPTER TWO

The small crowd gathered near the front porch of the low bungalow didn't appear overly agitated as Rad and Rabbit pulled to a stop beside the white picket fence bordering the residence. Their arrival was taken matter-of-factly with the exception of one woman who was visibly and vocally upset. Two men and a lady were attempting to quiet her without much success. Her sobbing could be heard above any other sound within miles. When she spotted the police car she started to move towards it until she saw two men in civilian clothes get out. Her confusion stopped her wailing, at least for the moment.

The two detectives moved through the gate towards the porch and as they approached, a tall man dressed in a business suit raised his hand as if to stop their advance. Rad brought his shield from his coat pocket before anyone in the group could say a word, "We're the police, what's going on here?"

The distraught woman burst forth, "Someone shot my husband and they won't let me in to see him." As soon as the words were out of her mouth the wailing started again.

"Can someone take her someplace where you can calm her down? We're never going to find out what's going on until she has been taken care of. Is this her home?" Rad was looking at the tall man who had held up his hand when they arrived.

"No officer, she lives four houses down the street. We'll see if we can get her home. You will be wanting to talk to her, won't you?"

25

The man seemed to be the spokesman for the group; at least he was the only person who was willing to venture any comments.

"Certainly we'll want to talk to her if her husband has been shot, but she won't be of any help to us until she becomes more composed than she is now. We'll also want to talk to anyone else who might know anything about this shooting. Now get her home and then come back so we can talk to you."

Rad motioned to Rabbit who had been looking around the outside of the house, "Let's go inside and see what we have here. We also need to find a phone. If there is a body, we may need the coroner. I can also update headquarters and see if they have any help they can spare."

"Yeah, we need to take a look at the crime scene before we know if there really has been a murder. That bunch on the porch must know something about what happened inside. You were pretty smooth the way you whipped out your badge. You got instant respect when they saw it."

"Let's pin them to our coat lapels while we're investigating. That way we won't be taken for something we aren't."

"Good idea, Rad. I'm liking this plain clothes stuff already." Rabbit moved ahead into the house, being careful not to disturb any possible evidence.

The darkened house smelled stale and rancid. The entrance hall went straight to the back end of the house where it opened into the kitchen. There were doorways on either side of the hallway about halfway down. One opened into the parlor, while the other appeared to be an office of some type. The prone body of a large man blocked its entrance. A dark spot beneath his torso attested to the fact that he had been shot, death had been swift.

"Well, I don't think this guy shot himself so I do believe we have a murder on our hands." Rad was taking a close look at the body as he spoke. "Do you see a gun any place? There doesn't appear to be one anywhere near the body."

Rabbit continued his search of the room but didn't seem to be finding anything of importance. After completing his tour of the office he slowly shook his head, "Nothing here that could be used as a murder weapon. I'll give the hall a good look-see, maybe someone dropped something when they were leaving." He carefully stepped over the body and turned to go down the hallway when the front door opened suddenly. Both men turned quickly at the sound. Peering around the door edge was the spokesman from outside.

"Hold it right there. Did you get the wife settled down?" Rad turned back to the body as he spoke.

"We finally got Maria, that's the wife's name, calmed down. She should be all right in an hour or so. I left her with two of her best friends, they will take good care of her."

"What is this man's name? Since you know the family I would think you would know his name." Rabbit pointed the eraser end of his pencil at the body while holding a writing pad ready to take notes on anything he said.

"He was Clyde Bishop and his wife's name is Maria, as I said."

"How about you? What is your name and what is your connection with the Bishop family?" Rabbit was asking the questions while Rad continued to examine the dead man.

"My name is Dave Stone and I'm Clyde's next door neighbor, or at least was his next door neighbor. Clyde worked at the bank down on Main Street. He was a teller in the one on the corner of Eighth and Main."

Rad had gotten to his feet to look the man straight in the eye when Dave said Clyde worked at the bank. "Apparently he wasn't at work today. Did he usually not work on Wednesdays?" Rad hardly paused long enough for an answer, "Are you aware that his bank was robbed early this morning?"

"No sir. I don't know nothing about any bank being robbed. Only thing I know is Clyde seemed mighty upset about something these past few days. But, I sure don't know what it was he was fretting about. Maybe Maria might know."

"Well, thanks a lot for what you did know Dave. We'll be talking to Mrs. Bishop soon as we finish here. Now if you will move back outside, we will wait for the coroner to arrive to take care of his body." Rad nodded to Rabbit as they started to move towards the front door. They had just stepped onto the porch when a young boy came running up.

"Sir, sir, the radio in your car been calling for Rad Childers. That you?"

"Yes, that's me. Is there a phone anywhere nearby?"

"There's one in the house across the street. I'm sure they will let you use it."

"Rabbit, you see what else Dave knows, and I'll call in. Probably the chief is wanting some news on what's going on."

Captain Winston, the other assistant chief, came barging into the chief's office just as the chief was hanging up his phone. He had his forefinger raised and his mouth partly open. With his five foot, six inch frame and his dark unruly hair, he appeared more like a schoolboy who needed to find a bathroom quickly, rather than one of the top men in the police department. "Chief, I've got an idea which just might solve some of our problems with the councilman. I know he's been pestering you from time to time, and now he's got his dander up about this bank robbery. We could...."

"Winston," the chief cut in, "all I need is for you and Captain Snyder to mind your normal duties and let me work on the special things. If you would spend more time worrying about the basic needs of the department and less out at the country club with your fancy friends, maybe the entire force would run smoother. The councilman has had his dander up long before the bank was robbed and if it wasn't the bank, it would be something else. So, for the last time, leave the things that don't concern you to me. When I want your input I'll ask for it."

Rad was solemnly shaking his head as he came back across the street. "Well you won't believe what just happened. The chief needs us to find out why we can't have two-way communications in some of our patrol cars. Wants us to get on it right away. He said he was tired of waiting to hear from us by phone."

"Didn't you tell him we were right in the middle of the murder investigation? He should remember, he sent us out here. He must be going daft. Although there's not really much sense in us hanging around this place, at least not until we can speak to the widow. None of these people seem to have any knowledge of what happened."

Rabbit was tucking his small notebook back into his coat pocket as he spoke.

"You are right." Rad looked around to make sure they hadn't missed anything important. "The chief also said the coroner had been notified. We will wait until he comes then we can be on our way. The patrolman who just arrived can guard the scene until we get back. Maybe that will give us time to look into the radio problem on our way back to headquarters. Remember the person, Jay Stevens, I was telling you about him when the alarm went off this morning?" Rad looked at Rabbit questioningly.

Rabbit didn't have the look of complete recognition, but he nodded his head in the affirmative and said, "Yes, but what does he have to do with anything?"

"He might have the answer to many of our dilemmas. We'll stop by his place and see what he has to say about communications and two-way radios in particular. He also might have some other ideas which could come in handy." Rad paused and smiled more to himself than to anyone else.

"Here comes Red in the coroner's wagon now, lets show him the body and be on our way." Rad and Rabbit greeted Red on the front pouch of the small bungalow like long lost friends. They didn't get to see the coroner too often; there weren't that many murders in Hill City.

Red was his usual solemn self with a clump of red hair poking out from under his old battered fedora. "Hain't seen you two in a spell. Where's the body?" Red was a man of few words.

"He's inside about halfway down the hall. Come on, we'll show you." Rad and Rabbit led the way through the door stopping at the prostrate body.

After a quick examination Red looked up and said, "Looks like a single bullet did it, and I don't think he lasted long after the shot was fired."

"We haven't found a gun, as yet. You probably won't run into one either, but in case you do, save it for us. I assume you will give us a call as soon as you get some particulars."

"Shore will." And with that Red turned to the task at hand. He was alone in his world and didn't even notice when Rad and Rabbit left for their patrol car.

Rachel's voice had not yet reached the shrill level, "I've told you for the last time, Detective Childers isn't here." She took a deep breath. "I expect him back before three, but if you are in a hurry I may be able to get a message to him." Rachel's voice returned to its calm and accommodating style, but deep down a sense of foreboding had entered her mind. The individual on the phone projected a tone of panic and she was wishing Rad had been here to take the call.

"If you will leave your name and number, I'll do my best to see that he gets the information." Rachel was running out of patience even though she knew it could be something important. Finally, and much to her relief, the caller gave her his first name, John, and his address. He told her if she didn't get the message to Rad before six o'clock tonight, it might be too late.

"Too late for what?" Rachel was hoping to get more information now that she had a place the caller could be contacted. "What is your phone number? You only gave me your address."

"I'm calling from a different location than the address I gave you. I will be at that address by four o'clock this afternoon and I need to talk to him in person." The caller paused as if trying to think of anything else he needed to add. Rachel thought for a moment he had ended the conversation, but she could hear him breathing. Then he blurted out, "You just tell him I need to talk to him personally, that's all I can say now. Good bye," and the phone went dead.

Rad pulled the patrol car up to a long, low building which resembled a small warehouse. The front of the building had a small door and window beside a larger door that slid up when it opened to allow vehicle size items to be brought inside. The side yard adjacent to the building was filled with various pieces of rusted car bodies and other discarded items, which looked as if they should have been sent to the rubbish heap long ago.

"Oh good, it looks like Jay is home," Rad seemed pleased.

"How can you tell? This place looks like something left over from a garbage collector's convention. Which piece of scrap does he use for transportation?" Rabbit shook his head in disbelief.

"I'm sure he has a use for it all, come on and we'll knock on the door."

Rad had just gotten out of the patrol car when the sliding door on the building started to move. It made the sound of two metals grating together which produced an ear splitting shriek a hundred times worse than chalk screeching across a blackboard. As it agonizingly rose, feet and legs began to appear from inside the building. There smiling, when the door had completed its tortured journey, stood Jay Stevens.

"I'm certainly glad to see you, Detective Childers. Is this your partner?" Jay said, while extending his outstretched hand towards Rabbit.

"This is Detective Tankers, Jay. I've been telling him about you and how I hope you can help us." Rabbit and Jay shook hands as they all moved further into the building.

"Boy, you sure have some weird looking contraptions in this place." Rabbit's mouth hung open as he stared from one thing to another. "Do any of them work?"

"Some do and some don't, but about them later. What can I do for you?"

"Well, we have a communications problem to start with. As you may know, our patrol cars have radios, which only receive. There is no way to transmit. I remember you telling me about an experiment you were working on concerning two-way communications." Rad's voice ended on a hopeful octave.

"As a matter of fact, I believe I have perfected such a device since we talked last. Haven't been able to give it much of a practical test, but I sure would like to give it a try. Trouble is, I haven't had the ability to get a moving station to test it on."

"I can believe that from the looks of some of the vehicles in your yard," Rabbit injected, as he continued to poke around the warehouse.

31

"How would you like to use our patrol car as a test vehicle?" Rabbit's head spun around when Rad mentioned using the patrol car.

"That would be fine, but it would take me a day or two to install my equipment in your car. We can use the base station I have here," Jay pointed to a bench, which held a formidable- looking radio contraption. "It could be set up almost any place as long as I can position an antenna on some high ground. A tall antenna will give us enough range to meet your city-wide requirements." Jay's face gleamed with the thought of getting a real test for his experimental gear.

"We will drop off this patrol car later this evening and you can get started. We'll need a rush job, maybe overnight if at all possible, because I don't think we can sell the chief on having one of his prize cars out of commission for very long."

Rabbit put his hands to his head, "I don't think we can sell the Chief on even one hour. Who's going to tell him? ...You?"

"He's the one who wants two-way communications. You can't get it without some downtime on the equipment. And, yes. I will tell him... if I have to." Rad turned to Jay who was already itemizing some of the parts he would need for the installation of a transmitter.

"How much will this contraption cost?" Rabbit directed his question to Jay. "You will need that Rad, when you tell the chief all about this grand idea." Rabbit looked a bit smug as he spoke.

"Well, I thought I would let you tell him when you go to explain how you wrecked one of his motorcycles. I'm sure you could hide the cost of the transmitter in the repair bill for the motorcycle."

"Now, Rad Childers, you know very well I ain't planning on having to explain to the Chief how that motorcycle got damaged. It was in the line-of-duty and that should be good enough for him." Rabbit was starting to get red in the face.

"Just kidding, don't get so defensive," Rad grinned as he winked at Jay.

"We can worry about the cost later. I've got most everything I need to make the installation. Just get me the car as soon as possible and maybe I can get the job done overnight." Jay's smile attested to his can-do attitude.

"We'll get you some money for this, but at this moment I'm not sure where it will come from. There is supposed to be some type of fund for this kind of expenditure. I'll talk to Captain Snyder, he might be able to help us." Rad paused and then said, "As a matter of fact, Jay, you can have the car now. Rabbit and I will walk back to Main Street, its only a mile or so from here."

Rabbit's face showed more than surprise as he spun around at Rad's comment. "I don't know why we need patrol cars. All we've done today is walk through the woods and now you want to walk to town. Might as well be back on the beat."

The White House Restaurant wasn't very crowded when Rad and Rabbit walked in wiping their brows. Most of the lunch business had dwindled and only a few of the hangers-on still lingered over an additional cup of coffee. Rad and Rabbit went straight to one of the back booths usually reserved for regular customers. They passed Gus, the proprietor, on the way and immediately asked him for two tall glasses of water.

"You and your ideas about walking from that junk yard to Main Street. It must have been five miles if it was an inch. I'm beginning to wonder about your judgment." Rabbit gulped down the water as he spoke, almost choking on his words.

"You needed the exercise. And furthermore, if we plan to get that patrol car back tomorrow morning with a transmitter in it, Jay needed to get started on the installation immediately."

"I just hope it works when we get it. Maybe the chief won't be so upset if we can give him a new toy," Rabbit took a breath from his water intake. "Well looky here, the pretty lady we all know and admire is coming through the door."

Rad turned in time to see Rachel headed in their direction. It was easy to tell she was on a mission, but you had to admit, it was fun watching her in full stride. She bounced in all the right places.

"I'm certainly glad I found you." She slid in next to Rad and took a sip of his water without asking. "Where have you two been?"

"We've been out for a before lunch stroll. The big oaf you're sitting next to wanted to work up an appetite so we hiked from some

33

dump yard about halfway between here and the city limits." Rabbit was still wiping perspiration from his forehead.

"The chief called us off the murder investigation to look into getting two-way communications in a patrol car. So, we left our patrol car with an acquaintance of mine who thinks he can put a two-way radio in it by tomorrow morning." Rad brought the water glass to his lips as soon as Rachel put it down.

"Well, it's lucky I found you. A very mysterious caller was trying to get in touch with you. He said his name was John and here is his address. He wouldn't leave a phone number." Rachel retrieved a slip of paper containing the address from her purse. "He said he needed to talk to you in person before six o'clock tonight."

"John, the name doesn't ring a bell with me, but maybe I'll know him when I see him. He didn't say why he wanted to see me, did he?"

Rachel shook her head no, and then added, "He sounded very weird to me. His voice sent cold chills up my spine. If you plan on going to see him, please be careful," she shuddered and moved closer to Rad. "Oh, and there is one other thing. The chief and Captain Winston had a few words this morning. The chief told him to attend to his regular duties instead of worrying about what the chief was working on. He said he should spend less time with his country club friends, and more on his work. I thought it odd to hear the chief comment on Winston's off-duty time."

"As far as I'm concerned, Winston hasn't done anything to help better the force. He has hardly spoken to me since he became an assistant chief. On the other hand, Captain Snyder seems to be a team player."

"That goes double for me." Rabbit stopped drinking his water to make the comment.

"Just thought I would let you know what I heard in the front office. Are we going to have any lunch?" Rachel reached for the menu as she settled herself into the booth.

"As you mentioned earlier, maybe Snyder would be the one to talk with about the motorcycle, plus getting any money for a transmitter installation. He is a can-do person and seems to want to help." Rabbit's comment caused Rad's eyebrows to rise.

"We'll contact him as soon as possible. We need all the help we can get."

Suddenly they all realized Gus had been standing patiently by the booth for a good minute. "Are you three ordering lunch, or are you waiting for the evening dinner special?"

The sergeant on the front desk frantically hit the hot line button to the chief's office, "Chief, Mr. Moorehead is on his way in to see you."

Sure enough, when the chief looked out his office door window the overly pompous bank president was striding down the hallway wearing an insidious smile, which gave away the treachery of his visit. He tapped on the office doorframe with his polished cane handle even though the chief was beckoning for him to enter.

"Please come in and have a seat, Mr. Moorehead. What can I do for you, now that your stolen money has been returned? I told you on the phone we would apprehend the people responsible and we did it in minimum time."

"You are a man of your word, chief. However, I'm not sure we caught the correct people."

"What do you mean? We caught the two men red-handed with the moneybags in their possession. My officers saw them come out of the bank. We thought the other person in the car was part of the scheme, but it turned out he had been kidnapped so they could use his car. As far as I am concerned, we have our bank robbers behind bars where they belong."

"Regardless of what you think, chief, I want to see these men before any final charges are filed. I talked with Captain Winston about my visit and he said he could arrange for me to go to their cell. I also want him to accompany me when I talk to them."

"I don't know what Captain Winston has to do with any of this, Moorehead, but I would like to remind you I'm still running this police department, not you or Captain Winston." The chief was beginning to get a little hot under the collar. "There is no earthly reason, in my mind, why I should allow you to talk to these men. So, as far as I'm concerned, our conversation has ended."

"You may be running this police department for now, but I'm not sure you will still be in this position of authority when the upcoming election is over. Your situation could become very untenable from what Councilman Brenner tells me. He seems to think Captain Winston might be a more productive person as chief of police in this city. You can put that in your pipe and smoke it." The bank president slammed his hand down on the chief's desk and stood up.

"Well, until that day comes, you, Councilman Brenner, and Captain Winston can be concerned about the future. I will operate on the present. You do know your way out, don't you, Mr. Moorehead?"

The bank president's stride down the hallway towards the front of the police department was impressive. If he just hadn't stumbled when he went through the outer door, his departure would have been monumental.

The chief's blood pressure had barely gotten back to normal when Rachel stuck her head around the door. "Mr. Charles Worthington on the line for you, Chief."

"I wonder what the senior partner of the shoe factory wants with me? I've had about all I can stand from these pillars of the community for one day." The chief took a deep breath as he slowly picked up the phone. "What can I do for you, Mr. Worthington?"

"Chief, I just wanted to call and congratulate you and your police force for their quick and efficient work today. I know some of my erstwhile friends like Joe Brenner and Jack Moorehead can't appreciate what you are doing, but there are others of us in this community who value your efforts."

"I thank you for your words, Mr. Worthington. And, you are correct, some of your friends don't agree. In fact, Mr. Moorehead just left my office."

"Well, Chief, I'm sure he is under some additional pressure. You can understand his concerns when he's just had his bank robbed. I'm going to be with him tomorrow, I'm sure he will feel different by then."

"I hope that is the case. Thanks again for your call, we are always here if you need us." The chief's look of amazement was directed at Rachel, who was still standing in the doorway.

"Chief, we need to get together for a drink sometime soon. I'll give you a call and we will set a date. Congrats again, I'll be in touch." The phone went dead.

As the chief hung up his receiver, he looked again at Rachel. "Well, that is one for the books." The chief spoke so softly Rachel had to move closer to hear him, "It is surprising, but comforting to know there are some of the more influential people in this town who appreciate our work. I was beginning to think the entire town was against us. Maybe there is a light at the end of the tunnel after all."

"Chalk up one for our team, at least one of the muck-de-mucks is on our side. One never knows, there could be more on our side." Rachel's comment drew a smile from the chief. Something she hadn't seen for most of the day.

Dusk had come on rather rapidly. "I thought this was supposed to be a short day. Here it is dark already and we're still trying to track down some clues to what happened over in White Rock. At least we didn't have to walk out here. Does the chief know we have another patrol car?"

"I didn't ask him. We needed transportation and we are on official business to see what this mysterious caller has to say. When we finish here, we'll call it quits and return the car." Rad pulled the patrol car into the curb near the street corner.

The weather-beaten stucco house sat back from the street, so the street lamp on the corner cast a shadow over the front of the building. No lights were visible from the front but there was a sliver of a ray coming from the back of the house. Rad knocked on the door.

After a long minute a rather tall man opened the door. A small lamp down the hall was the only illumination and it wasn't casting off enough light to clearly make out the man's face. He looked familiar but in the dimness Rad couldn't place him.

"We are here about a call someone made to our office. The man who called said his name was John," Rad held his badge up so the

37

man could see it. "The message said we needed to be here by six, there was no way we could make that, but here we are now."

"I'm the one who called, Detective Childers, my name is John, John Butler. You may not remember me, but you and your partner arrested me for running a little whiskey about two years ago. I don't hold a grudge; in fact if you hadn't taken me in, I might be dead today. So I feel as if I owe you one. Won't you come in?"

"We'll stay here on the porch and talk." Rad turned from the doorway, then suddenly snapped his fingers as a look of recognition came across his face, "Oh for sure, I remember you now. Your wife was about ready to tee off on you with a baseball bat. Rabbit grabbed her before she could complete her swing. Remember it, Rabbit?"

"Yeah, she was sure a big woman. If she had hit you with that bat your brains would've been spread over the best part of this county. She was still trying to get at you when we hauled you off. Where is she now?" Rabbit's smile was more from pity than amusement.

"She went back to North Carolina, thank the goodness. I'm blessed she decided she wanted a divorce and wanted it to be final before I got out of jail. That woman was half crazy; I don't know why I ever married her to begin with. What happened was, she was drinking most of what I was supposed to be delivering, and that caused the problem. When I told her she would have to lay off the sauce, or the moonshiners would want my hide, she decided to beat them to it. Don't know what was in that stuff, but it sure brought out the devil in her. That's why I'm beholden to the two of you."

"Well, I'm glad your troubles have been solved and I'm glad we helped in some small way, but why did you need us to come out here to tell us? You could have waited until you got us on the phone. Plus, you told the secretary we needed to get here by six o'clock. What's so all-fired important you had to see us tonight?"

"After I got out of jail, I went to find me a respectable job. I got one with the shoe factory and have been there ever since. However, the other day I heard some people talking about some money that was going to be available for the right person. Seems they were looking for someone to strong arm a few people. Since I had been on the wrong side of the law once and I ain't little, they came to see me. They was looking to have someone go over and beat up some people from a bank. They didn't want them killed they said, just bent slightly. The why, I never did learn. I knew it weren't for me when I found out exactly what they had in mind. When I told them no, they didn't say another word to me."

"What bank did these people work for?" Rabbit had moved closer to the conversation.

"I don't know, but just before I went on my lunch break today two big guys came by my department and said they wanted to talk to me. Said they would be by tonight to have a little chat. That's why I called for you. I'm thinking they might think I know something about what's going on."

"What is going on?" Rad leaned back on the porch railing.

"I don't know a thing except them asking me to strong arm some people and I turned them down. I been clean since I got out of jail, and I don't want to do nothing that will put me back. But it seems to me something funny is going on."

"You may be correct, John; we've had a bank robbery and a murder all in one day. That even seems funny to me. Could I use your phone?"

"It's down the hall, be my guest."

Rad's call was quick and it wasn't long before he was back on the porch. "Keep your nose clean, John, and if someone tries to push you around, let us know. Here is our direct line phone number." He and Rabbit waved as they departed.

It was quiet back in the patrol car as the two detectives sat for a moment. The day certainly had contained more than the normal run-of-the-mill activity. In fact, there had been enough action to fill an entire month period.

"Do you think John's comments tie-in at all with the bank robbery or the murder? Don't know why anyone at the shoe factory would be involved with either." Rabbit slowly slid down in his seat as he spoke.

"After what's gone on today, I wouldn't be surprised at anything. Maybe tomorrow will shed a little light on things. Oh, by the way, we won't have our two-way radio ready as planned. That call I made was to Jay. He said he was having some difficulty getting his rig to work properly. Said it didn't have anything to do with the patrol car so we could come pick it up if we needed it. He'll let us know when things will be ready for installation. So we might as well get the car before we turn in."

"You bet, this way we won't have to tell the chief we have one of his cars tied up on a whim. We can spend most of the day trying to explain the other things he has listed against us, like motorcycle wrecks and civilian clothes."

Rad turned the ignition key and pressed the starter, the continual grinding noises from under the hood weren't the usual clamor associated with smooth running engine sounds. The gas gauge told the story; it registered "E", for enough.

The two detectives looked dejectedly at each other and spoke as one, "Looks like we have a short night stroll before we turn in."

CHAPTER THREE

The crack of a single bullet was almost eardrum shattering as it splattered against the wall directly above the rounded counter. In fact, the projectile had only been inches from being at head level of anyone sitting at the bar. The first reaction of the occupants was surprise, but with the realization that one's life had just been placed in danger, the bartender and his two customers dropped to the floor. Their only problem now was the plaster raining down over their heads. A belated tinkle of glass attested to the fact the shot had to have come from somewhere outside the room. The remnants of the broken glass windowpane left the telltale evidence.

Jack Moorehead, the president of the bank, was first to speak, "What in the 'Sam Hill' was that?"

In a grating voice, Charles Worthington, croaked out, "I think somebody just fired a shot into the bar and the bullet didn't impact very far from where we were sitting." He slowly got to his feet on shaky legs.

"Homer, did you see who fired that shot?" Moorehead's voice wasn't much firmer than Worthington's.

"No sir, Mr. Moorehead. I might have seen something flash from outside near the parking lot, but I'm not sure. I know there weren't any golfers on the first tee cause I was looking that way." Homer was still crouched down behind the bar. "Maybe I'd better call the police."

41

"Let's get out of here, Charles, before anyone calls anyone. I don't believe there will be a board of governors meeting today. Not after this. I know for sure I'm not staying around for one."

Charles was already moving towards the door as he said, "Me either, Jack. We can discuss our little problem later."

"Homer, when the police show up, don't tell them about Mr. Worthington or myself being here when the shot was fired." Moorehead placed a five dollar bill on the bar top to back up his request.

"You can count on me, Mr. Moorehead. Mums the word." The color in Homer's face had come back to normal as he swept the money from the bar.

The club manager, who was at a full trot, met the two men at the barroom door. "What in the world happened in there? Sounded like a shot from where I was in the building. Was anybody hurt?"

"You can get the story from Homer, he's calling the police. I suggest you postpone the board meeting and as far as you are concerned, we were never here. Understand?" Moorehead mustered up his sternest glare.

"Whatever you say, Mr. Moorehead. I'll let you know when we can reschedule the meeting. Glad you or Mr. Worthington weren't injured." The manager only paused long enough for the two men to pass before he continued into the barroom. He found Homer hanging up the phone and waited for him to speak.

"I told the police about the shot being fired into the club. They said they would get someone out here as soon as possible and not to touch anything until they arrived." Homer had a satisfied look on his face as he talked to the manager.

"Did you see anybody or anything before the shot was fired?" The manager was looking up at the chink in the wall where the bullet had impacted. He was trying to visualize an imaginary line from the hole to the broken windowpane.

"No sir, but that bullet didn't miss hitting Mr. Worthington's head by more than a few inches. Don't know if someone was gunning for him or not, but if he was he didn't miss by much."

"Things are getting pretty bad when someone starts shooting into our club. I hope this doesn't get out or we may have a few cancellations from some of our more squeamish members. Oh well, we'll leave the place as is until the police arrive. Can you set up a bar in the ballroom? We'll have to operate from there until after the police arrive. Then you can clean up in here after they are finished." With that the manager headed for his office with his head down. That was all he needed, one more difficult happening added to his already busy day.

When the manager cleared the door, Homer shrugged and mumbled an incoherent oath under his breath. *It seems like it is always something that adds to my workload without any extra pay. At least the fiver from Mr. Moorehead will help. Now, where is the trolley cart to move these bottles to the temporary bar?*

The patrolman guarding the White Rock crime scene slowly got up from an old rocking chair as the two detectives approached the front porch. He looked tired; it wasn't the most desired job to be put on guard duty.

"Anything been going on, Robert?" Rad shook hands with the patrolman as he asked the question.

"Not a thing. Ben and I traded off since you left yesterday. He said nary a soul came around and I ain't seen nothing either."

"Why don't you go get yourself a cup of coffee? Rabbit and I will be here asking some questions if we can find the people we want to talk with."

"Thanks anyway, the wife brought me a thermos of coffee and a sandwich. I'm just fine. How long we going to have to secure this place anyway?"

"Hopefully we can finish up here before the day is over. We'll let you know."

As they entered the house, things hadn't changed very much since their last visit. Of course, the body was gone and there weren't any people gathered on the front porch. But, the house still smelled stale and rancid and the bloodstains remaining by the office door attested to the fact someone had come to no good.

They had finished another thorough, but fruitless, look around when Rad said, "I guess we should go and see if the wife of the

43

victim will talk to us. She should have calmed down by now." He was moving towards the front door as he spoke.

Rabbit, also moving down the hall, said, "I hope she will be a bit calmer than she was yesterday."

Before they could reach the door it opened, revealing two men and a woman. They were standing in the glare from outside the doorframe and at first neither Rad nor Rabbit could make out who they were. Robert, distinctive in his bell shaped patrolman's hat spoke before anyone else. "These folks say they need to talk with you detectives. OK to let them in?"

"Sure, it'll be all right."

Stepping further into the hall the woman said, "We saw your patrol car come up and thought you might want to talk to me. I promise I will be more cooperative today." It was the wife. "You can call me Maria and this is Mr. Williams. He claims he saw a car leave from the back of the house soon after the shot was fired." Her voice was very smooth and controlled. She was taller than she had appeared yesterday, at least five six, which was tall for a woman. The little they had seen of her was when she was bent over in a sobbing stance and being supported by her friends.

"We are glad to see you, Mrs. Bishop. We want to express our deepest sympathy at your loss. We hope, with your help, we can find out who shot your husband. We have a few questions if you feel up to answering them."

"That's why we came up so you wouldn't have to search around for us." She had come a long way since yesterday when it appeared she had been very close to a nervous breakdown.

"Let's go into the office so we can sit down and be comfortable." She didn't look down as they stepped over the bloodstains. When everyone was seated, Rad said, "Whose house is this anyway? We understand that you live a few houses down the street." Rabbit had pulled out his pad and was starting to take notes.

"It belongs to Mr. Will Sutter. He and my husband were in a small business together and worked out of the office here. Clyde used to come up and work even when Mr. Sutter was away. That was the case yesterday. Sutter had gone on a trip to Richmond and wasn't scheduled back until the weekend."

"Why wasn't your husband at work? Didn't he have a regular job at the bank?"

"Oh, yes, he was on regular with the bank. He had taken a couple of days vacation. He had been extremely despondent for about a week and I had urged him to take a little time off. I was beginning to worry about his health. I hadn't even wanted him to come up here to this office but he insisted, so I stopped complaining."

"Do you happen to know why he was so despondent?"

"I'm afraid not. I wanted him to go see a doctor, but all he said was, 'I never thought it would come to this.' Just what that meant is beyond me."

"Did you know the bank had been robbed yesterday morning?"

"No, I didn't learn about that until late in the day. It wasn't until after I had calmed down that my friends told me about the bank. Maybe if Clyde had been there he could have stopped it. He was one of the main tellers, you know."

"Or, he could have been shot, those fellows did have guns. I guess either way it wasn't his day." Maria Bishop looked down in her lap and twisted her handkerchief. "Sorry, I didn't mean to sound morbid, Mrs. Bishop." Rad coughed to hide his embarrassment. Quickly changing his position he looked towards Mr. Williams, "So you claim to have seen a car speed away from the rear of this house shortly after the shot was fired?"

"Well, I didn't actually see a car speed away, but I did see a car parked behind this house before the shot and it was gone after the shot was fired." Mr. Williams who had been sitting quietly while Rad had been questioning Mrs. Bishop now appeared to fidget nervously in his chair.

"And, just what is your connection to this area. Do you live anywhere nearby?"

"Yes sir, I'm a neighbor to the Bishops. I live on the other side of the street across from them. I was taking a shortcut between the houses when I heard a shot, or what I thought was a shot. I continued on home, I didn't want to get involved in anyone else's problems. My wife was one of the ladies who went over to be with Mrs. Bishop after she came home. When she returned I told her what I had seen and heard, that is about the car and the shot. She insisted I tell you people when you came back. That's why I'm here now."

"OK, Mr. Williams. Why don't all of us go out back and see if that car you saw left any tracks. Rabbit, get Robert to come with us. If we find anything, we'll need him to guard it. I don't think we need to worry about the inside of this house any longer. Do you?"

"I agree, we covered all we need inside. I'll fetch Robert, and meet you all in the back." While Rad and the two others lingered in the office, Rabbit moved quickly. He was at the back of the house with Robert before the others arrived.

When Rad, along with Maria and Mr. Williams, came through the kitchen door, Rabbit said, "Look over here, Rad." He was pointing towards the side of the house. "See those tire tracks, they're plain as day. Is that where you saw the car parked, Mr. Williams?" Rabbit was pulling his pad out to make a sketch of the tire print.

"Yes sir, that's right where it was," Williams voice sounded a little more confident now that he was outside the house. He was getting ready to add something when a young tow headed boy came round the corner of the house.

"Detective Childers, someone is calling you on your radio again asking you to call headquarters." The boy was smiling from ear to ear.

"You the same lad who told me about the radio call yesterday?"

"Yes sir, I been listening for you."

"Well, thank you. We're going to have to get you on the force if you keep taking messages for us." Rad dug a coin out of his pocket and gave it to the young lad. "Here, take this nickel and get yourself a coke."

"Sir, you can use the phone over in my house again. When I grow up, I'm going to be a policeman."

"And you'll make a good one I reckon." Rad turned towards Rabbit, "I'll be back in a minute. Maybe after you complete your sketch you can find something to cover up those tracks. We don't want them being erased before we can get back and recover them." Rad went around the corner of the house heading towards the house across the street to make his call to headquarters.

Rabbit turned to Mrs. Bishop and Mr. Williams, "That should be all we need from you right now. We appreciate you coming up when you saw our car. We'll be looking around here a bit more before we leave. When we can piece some of these things together, we'll let you know. In the meantime, if you think of anything else that might be important you can reach us at the police station. If we aren't there, please leave a message and we'll get back to you as soon as possible."

Rabbit was back by the patrol car when Rad came across the street. "There may be some other clues near those car tracks. Want to take another look back there? I put a piece of wood over the tracks and told Robert to make sure nobody tampered with them."

"What happened to Mrs. Bishop and the man who saw the car? Did you tell them we might need to talk to them again?"

"Yeah, they said anytime we needed them they would be available. I told them to call if they thought of anything new." Rabbit started in the direction of the backyard.

"Hold it, you won't believe what the chief has ordered us to do, and it has to be done immediately." Rabbit only shrugged. "Seems someone fired a shot into the bar area at the country club and he wants us to find out what happened. I told him we were on this case, but he said to put it on hold and get going. I wonder if he realizes someone was shot dead out here?"

Captain Jordan Snyder entered the chief's office without knocking. Rachel hadn't been at her desk to announce him so he felt at ease in making an immediate entrance. He couldn't have been more wrong.

Looking up from the papers on his desk, the Chief growled, "Why do you think I have a door on this room, Captain? It's because I expect people to knock before barging in. Think you can remember that the next time?"

"Sorry, Chief, I didn't realize I was intruding." Jordan didn't let the chief's outburst interfere with his purpose of being there. "But, I do have something we need to discuss. Are you aware that Childers and Tankers are being assigned other minimum tasks, which are interrupting their investigation of the murder in White Rock? Can't we get some other officers to run errands for whoever is diverting them from their main duty?"

"It might be of interest to you that I have been the one tasking those two freewheelers. They get on one case and spend all their time on it. It's about time they did a little something more for this department than just what they desire." The chief shifted in his chair and only raised his voiced slightly; "I will continue to give them additional duties whenever I feel like it. Is that understood?"

The air in the room suddenly got very chilled. Captain Snyder wasn't sure what to say next, he already had his foot in his mouth and it was difficult trying to talk over the sole of his shoe. "Well, that is something I didn't know. Would you share your motives for giving them so much grief?"

"Captain Snyder, you will no doubt be an asset to this police force, much more so than our other assistant chief who appears to be more interested in politics and rubbing elbows with the high muck-de-mucks in this city. I don't feel I have to explain my actions to you, but if you must know, those two detectives are capable of carrying a much greater load. I'm pushing them to find advancements that will increase the ability of our force to better serve this community, particularly in the long run. I won't let them flounder, but they belong to a handful of people who can give me the results I want."

"OK, Chief. If that's what you have in mind. I'm glad to hear you don't intend to drive them under. I just hope you know what you are doing. Regardless, I don't withdraw my request for additional manpower. We need it and I expect to continue to work for it."

"Your interests are noted, Captain. Now, if you will get out of my office so I can continue my work, I will be most grateful." The chief's eyes went back to the paper on his desk and there was no doubt in anyone's mind the conversation was over.

As Jordan walked past Rachel's desk he was pleased to see she had returned. He contemplated stopping to pass the time of day; she was the best looking person in police headquarters. However, on second thought, it might not be the most prudent thing to linger immediately outside the chief's office door. He felt he had accomplished the main part of his mission so it would be best he stayed on the move. Also, the taste of shoe leather still lingered in his mouth. So much so, he only nodded to Rachel.

She seemed somewhat surprised when Captain Snyder only gave her a brief glance. She sensed he had paused ever so slightly, but that could be only her imagination. She couldn't blame him for not being more cordial with the chief's last comment ringing in her ear.

The country club was impressive to Rad and Rabbit as they strolled in through the front entrance. As they proceeded towards the rear of the building, heading for the bar area, it wasn't hard to notice that most of the windows facing West looked out on a sprawling green expanse. It was the only golf course in the surrounding area and barely two years old. Many of the members had only recently taken up the game; however, it was growing in popularity throughout the Blue Ridge area. The two detectives only knew it was played with some sort of club and a small white ball.

The bar was located in a rotunda overlooking the first tee, which was adjacent to the member's parking lot. Many times the patrons in for an early eye opener before lunch had made it a tradition to comment on the abilities of the knicker clad participants. It was a lot easier to criticize than to execute. Today the place was vacant. The bartender who opened the room for them looked a bit ashen.

"You look familiar to me, Homer? Have we met before?" Rad lingered long enough to take a closer look at the bartender.

"I don't think so, sir. I try to stay away from the police if at all possible." He moved quickly into the room in order to get away from other probing questions. "You can see up there on the wall where the bullet hit, and the window over there," he pointed to the broken pane, "is where it must have come from."

"You let us figure out where it came from. Who was in here with you when the bullet hit the wall?" Rabbit was pointing his pen at Homer like it was part of some kind of projectile.

"I was all by myself. I was just setting up the bar for the afternoon crowd. Also, there was supposed to be a board of governors meeting later in the day." Homer's voice was sounding firmer now that they were in the barroom.

"If you were alone, how do you account for those two partially filled glasses there on the bar? It looks to me like you had a couple of customers who undoubtedly left shortly after the bullet hit the wall." Rabbit was at the bar when he asked the question.

Homer's head spun around to find the two glasses right where Mr. Moorehead and Mr. Worthington had left them. "Ah, ah, they must have been left over from last night, I just hadn't washed them up yet." He could feel his face redden.

Both detectives knew there was more to those glasses than being left over from last night, but Rad held up his hand to Rabbit. "Why don't you go outside and line up the chink in the wall and the broken window. It might give us a good idea of where the bullet was fired. I'll stay here and talk to Homer while you are gone."

Rabbit nodded and headed for the door leading to the member's parking lot.

Speaking calmly at first, Rad's voice grew in intensity as he continued, "Homer, we both know there was someone with you in this room when the shot was fired. And, we both know someone was either trying to kill someone or give them a very positive message. You might not think it advisable to tell us now who was here at the bar, but you will probably change your position later. For now I'll let it go, but there must have been something else you saw or heard either before or after the shot. That I need to know now."

"Sir, before the shot I didn't see anything unusual. I do remember there weren't any golfers on the first tee; it's the one you can see from here. After the shot hit the wall, I'm pretty sure I heard a car speed away from the parking lot just outside this room. I didn't see anything cause I ducked down behind the bar right after I heard the shot. There were two customers, but they didn't want to be identified. I can't give out their names, unless you force me."

Rabbit came back into the room just as Homer ended his statement. He went to the bar and looked back at the broken windowpane. "Whoever was sitting right there," he pointed to the seat under the bullet mark in the wall, "was either very lucky the shot went high or the shooter was just trying to scare him. If you line up the broken window and the bullet impact, the shooter must have been right at the edge of the parking lot. It made for a pretty long shot, but not impossible. It also made for a quick getaway." Rad nodded in agreement. "I vote for someone wanting to send a message; how about you, Rad?"

"Homer here says he heard a car speed away right after the shot. The shooter probably only had time for one quick pop, and I agree with you, someone wanted to get someone's attention. There were two customers, but they want to remain anonymous at this time. I'm sure we will find out their identities when the time comes." Rad gave Homer a long look. "I think we've got all we need for now, let's speak to the club manager on the way out. It might be interesting to know who is on the board of governors for this prestigious establishment. I'm sure there will be a few pillars of the community on the list. Homer, we'll be back in touch, so don't run off too far."

"Oh, I'm not planning on going anywhere. I need this job and the life style it provides me, so the only place I plan to be is right here. Let me call the manager's office so he can meet you at the front door. That could save you a few minutes. He knew I was the one who called the police, so I'm sure he wants to see you."

The bank president's secretary seemed to waste very few words, "If you will take a seat, Captain Snyder, Mr. Moorehead will see you in a minute." She then turned quickly back to her typewriter, leaving no chance for further conversation.

Jordan took a seat in the small outer office and looked around for something to read. The few magazines available were outdated so he decided to kill the time by secretly trying to analyze the secretary. She was no spring chicken, but used what she had to its best advantage. She had to be in her late forties and probably an old maid since there were no rings on the fingers of her left hand. There was a single diamond pendant around her neck, which looked expensive. From what Jordan could tell, she must have been with the bank for a long period of time. The string of trusted employee plaques behind her desk attested to long and loyal service. Also there were several pictures of her with Mr. Moorehead at what appeared to be a picnic. The pictures were placed in a prominent place on the credenza behind her desk. There were two fresh long-stemmed red roses standing in a slender vase at the corner of her desk. Either someone brought her flowers every day or they were from her own flower garden.

A buzzer shattered the calm with an irritating sound, which brutally ended the analysis. She picked up the phone, listened a second and turned to Jordan. "Mr. Moorehead will see you now." The Mr. Moorehead sounded like the lord and master.

The bank president's office was enormous when compared to the outer one he had been waiting in. A large picture window behind an oversized mahogany desk made it difficult to see the bank president's face. It made him appear ghost-like. His words came out without seeing his lips move, "Captain, whatever your name is, I don't have time to see every police officer on the force. I've expressed my thoughts to your chief, and that's all I intend to do."

"Sir, your bank was robbed yesterday and we still need to talk to some of your people to determine exactly what happened. That is the reason for my visit; I just wanted to let you know what I was doing."

"Well, you can wait until I'm ready for you to talk to my people. I deal only with Captain Winston and I've also made that clear to your chief." He turned and hit the intercom, "Get me the chief of police on the phone."

"This isn't Captain Winston's case. It is my responsibility and I plan to carry it out," Jordan's voice boosted an octave.

The buzzer rang, "I have the chief on the line."

"Chief, one of your officers, a Captain Snyder, is in my office saying he plans to talk to my people. As you told me yesterday, you run your police department and I want you to know I run this bank. I don't intend to have my people browbeaten about something I think isn't any of the police's business. Now you tell this person to get out of my bank before I have him escorted out." The pause was only momentary before Moorehead handed the phone to Jordan with a smug smile on his face, "Here, he wants to talk to you."

Jordan listened for about a minute then said, "Yes sir." He laid the phone back on its cradle and turned to the bank president. "I'm sure we will be seeing each other again."

Passing through the outer office, Jordan leaned over to the secretary and whispered, "When was the last time he took you out

52

of town for an overnight trip?" Her eyes went wide and before she could speak he was out the door.

Jordan thought there had to be more to being denied access to the bank's personnel than meets the eye. He would talk to the chief tomorrow; maybe he will know something that isn't common knowledge.

Main Street was busy with shoppers but Rad and Rabbit easily found a parking space across the street from the pool hall. They were only in the next block from the bank, so the scene of yesterday's crime was within shouting distance. They proceeded to the corner before crossing and spoke to officer Stevens, a patrolman they had both known for many years. He had the beat for this section of downtown.

"First time I've seen you two out of uniform. Is that going to be the new detective outfit?"

"It is if the chief will buy Rad's idea of how we are supposed to dress. It does have its advantages." Rabbit winked at Stevens and quipped a few more pleasantries. "We're headed for the billiard parlor, see you later."

Nearing the six-pocket emporium they noticed a rather shabbily dressed individual standing in the doorway of a vacant store. As they came abreast he hailed them. "I say there you two, can you look over here for a minute?"

"You talking to us, mister?" Rabbit started towards the man.

"Yes, sir. You two look like you could use a good bargain and I'm just the man who can provide one of the best you've ever seen. Right around the corner I have some of the best corn liquor in this or any other county. And, I can let you have as many bottles as you want for only two dollars a bottle." He smiled a toothless grin.

"Is that so. Well now, why don't you show us what you have? We could be very interested, you can count on that." Rabbit was egging the man on as he motioned them to follow him into a small alleyway between the buildings.

As Rabbit and the seller disappeared, Rad ran to the corner and signaled for Patrolman Stevens to follow him. When Stevens caught up, Rad said, "I think we've got someone who wants to sell us some of the best corn liquor in this county. They are his words. If it's true, you can make a collar and he'll be more than surprised he was hawking two detectives."

"Suits me." Stevens drew his nightstick and followed Rad into the alleyway.

Sure enough, not more than fifty feet down the pathway were Rabbit and the bootlegger standing over at least 125 bottles of amber liquid. All were placed in neat rows and the blanket covering them had been thrown back so the stash could be viewed. The bootlegger was rubbing his hands together anticipating a big sale.

Rabbit looked the bootlegger straight in the eye, "I don't think my buddy and I are interested in what you have, but I think this fellow is."

Officer Stevens stepped forward.

"Oh, shucks. I'm afraid I know Officer Stevens." The bootlegger went pale.

"And I know you, don't I, Barney? Seems you've done this sort of thing before. I'm sure this will cost you a tad more money and jail time than before. It hasn't been three months since the last time you were busted. Seems you will never learn. Good thing these plain clothes policemen were your first potential customers." They both turned to look for the two detectives but they had disappeared as if in thin air.

"You mean there are policemen going around without uniforms on?" Stevens nodded as Barney continued, "Why, that's almost unconstitutional. How's a body going to make a living? Times is hard enough anyway."

Probably before Officer Stevens could get the cuffs on Barney, Rad was pushing open the swinging doors of the pool hall. "We should find at least a couple of our contacts hustling some unsuspecting pigeon this time of day."

Rad and Rabbit entered the long smoky den, which was filled with an extended series of green clothed tables illuminated by individual shaded lamps. The radiance of the fixture barely cut through the haze. There were high chairs lining each wall with racks for cue sticks spaced every few feet. The place was doing a good business for this time of day. The majority of the tables were active with anywhere from two to four players at each one.

After proceeding halfway down the hall Rabbit nudged Rad in the arm and nodded towards two men engaged in what appeared to be a friendly game. Then again, it was probably more than a friendly game since several greenbacks were on the edge of the table.

"There's Glen and Norris playing on that last table. Let's take a seat and let them come over to us."

"Sounds like a good approach, they only have four balls left to pocket to complete their game." Rad made sure they had been seen before he and Rabbit moved over and took seats in two of the high backed chairs against the wall.

Glen pocketed the last ball without scratching the cue ball and scooped up the money as he moved over towards the detectives. Norris stayed by the pool table. "To what do we owe the pleasure of your visit? Are you slumming or are you here on business?"

"We haven't seen you two for quite awhile, thought we'd drop in to check if you've been keeping your noses clean." Rad shook hands with Glen and Norris who had moved closer. Rabbit walked over to greet the two then moved to the pool table. He lagged the lone cue ball down the length of the table as if he was getting ready to set up for a new game.

"I almost didn't recognize you in civilian clothes. Are you on or off duty?"

"We are on duty, this is our new guise, and it seems to be working better than the last time we came in here. Last time when we arrived in uniform, we were almost run down by people thinking the place was being raided."

That brought a smile to Glen's face, "What can we do for you?"

"Undoubtedly you've heard about the bank robbery yesterday. There was also a man shot over in White Rock, he was a teller at the bank but wasn't working that morning. Heard anything concerning either incident?" Rad looked from one to the other as he was talking.

Norris seemed to get nervous as Rad's gaze penetrated the hazy air. Glen spoke first, "Yeah, we heard about the bank being hit. Heard

55

the robbers were captured within hours of the heist. Don't think they were from around here or we might have known them. But, about the teller being shot, that's news to us. Where in White Rock was he tagged and who was he?"

"His name was Clyde Bishop and he was in the home of a man named Will Sutter. Seems he was in some type of business with Sutter." Rad made his way over to the table to stand by Rabbit. "Apparently the person who shot him made his escape in a car that was parked behind the house. We should be able to find out the make of the car in a day or two."

"If you can give us a couple of days, we'll see what we can come up with. There ain't too many murders in this town so someone should know something. Norris here got a sister-in-law who works with a lady whose son works in the bank. Maybe there's some gossip around about Clyde Bishop." Glen looked pleased and Norris's nod attested to what Glen had just said.

"Make it faster than two days, time is critical." Rabbit gave the cue ball one last fling down the table making it hit the cushion hard enough to bounce it off the table. The crashing ball caused the players at the next table to look in their direction. They immediately diverted their gaze when they saw Rabbit's gun protruding from under his coat.

"We'll expect a call no later than tomorrow." With that the two detectives headed for the front door. It was amazing how agile the other players were at clearing a pathway for them. Word must spread fast when lawmen decide to frequent a pool hall.

As they approached the corner, Officer Stevens was signaling for them. "There's a call out for you two. Word is Councilman Brenner plans to hold a press conference at two o'clock this afternoon. Chief wants you to be there."

CHAPTER FOUR

The steps in front of City Hall were far from being overcrowded. What was to have been a full-blown press conference given by a prominent city councilman was expected to draw more than the few people who were in attendance. It had been hastily called, but with the forthcoming election one would have anticipated more interest by the media. When it was learned there was only one member from the local newspaper in attendance and no representative from the radio station, it was evident somebody had dropped the ball.

Councilman Brenner's temper hit a new level. When he finally came back to earth, he had an assistant tell the sparse crowd his statement would be postponed for a few minutes. They blamed the timing for his communiqué on a misunderstanding, which would be remedied momentarily.

Sure enough, two minutes hadn't gone by before a bright blue coupe with the top down came to a screeching halt by the curb that fronted City Hall. Two members of the local radio station popped out and retrieved their gear from the rumble seat. They had their recording equipment up and working in record time. It was also noted that another member of the newspaper had quietly joined the group. One had to suppose our local media moguls must have underestimated the power of politics.

The delay had worked well for Rad and Rabbit; otherwise they might have missed the first part of Councilman Brenner's declaration.

57

There were a few false starts and several throat clearings before Councilman Brenner began his statement to the public. "As you are well aware, the election for our city council will be forthcoming in a matter of days. I want to be on record with my supporters that I have always stood for justice and honor. As the head of the committee that oversees our police department, I have taken it upon myself to ensure our force serves the public in the most economical and efficient ways. I've not always been successful because of interference by our police chief. That will change when I'm again selected for office. I plan to insist on certain changes, which will ensure the police department is more attuned to the public's needs. I feel, for instance, the bank robbery earlier in the week could have been thwarted if our policemen spent more of their time guarding Main Street rather than riding around town on those dreadful sounding motorcycles waking up innocent and sleeping citizens."

"Think he's talking about us, Rad?" Several listeners in the back of the crowd looked around at the two detectives since Rabbit's statement was more than a whisper.

"A series of recent break-ins haven't been totally solved to my satisfaction. We could have a crime wave on our hands if the likes of these incidents aren't stopped. A specialty store was robbed of silk stockings two days ago, there were two cases of shoplifting in the five and dime only last week, plus a restaurant on Fifth Street was recently broken into and is missing a quantity of tobacco, chewing gum, and candy. A number of offenders have been rounded up, but there are still many remaining at large to cause trouble aplenty. The elimination of such events will be a top priority when I'm re-elected.

"Another important item is the money I have tried to save this city. When the police chief asked to purchase new uniforms for the force at a cost of $1500, I demanded his request be denied. I was afraid other departments like the Fire Department or the Sanitation Department would ask for increases and ruin the current budget. Unfortunately my veto was overturned by a unanimous vote from the other council members. But rest assured, when I'm in office again, frivolous expenditures and outlandish requests will not be allowed."

His droning voice continued on for another half hour. He really didn't have any new items; he just repeated his previous points in slightly different words. By that time most of the small audience had drifted away. The few remaining were almost outnumbered by the members of the press and the radio technicians who were locked in for the duration. The entire group had their eyes at half-mast. Finally, sensing his time was up Brenner said, "I will be talking to you again before the election; in the meantime, please tell your friends that a vote for Brenner is a vote for better city government."

A single handclap was heard and within seconds the steps of City Hall were completely empty of onlookers. Brenner and his aide were left standing alone at the top of the steps; even the radio and newspaper people had packed up and were gone. Rad and Rabbit had slipped away before his last words, unseen by the overbearing councilman.

The chief wasn't in when they went to his office to report on the Councilman Brenner's press conference. His absence certainly didn't make them unhappy, for they weren't anxious to relate the councilman's comments. When they told Rachel what had transpired, she said she didn't want to be anywhere around when the chief heard the news. They all agreed the chief would hit the ceiling when he learned how much the councilman had insulted both the police force in general and him in particular.

Even though they would have liked to spend more time talking to Rachel, especially Rad, they didn't linger for fear the chief would walk in and they would be forced to voice their findings in person. They had seen him near the top of the Fire and Brimstone Scale before and weren't about to stay around to personally witness a new high water mark.

Rad leaned over and whispered something to Rachel, which brought a smile. She was about to respond when she suddenly stopped and pulled a note from her desk drawer. "A Jay Stevens called for you, Rad. Said he had your radio problem all solved, whatever that means."

"Great, hear that, Rabbit? We can stop by on our way to the Sutter residence."

"I wonder what new and wonderful things he will show us today?" Rabbit's expression wasn't one of great anticipation.

"Rachel, don't mention the Jay Stevens call to the chief, just tell him we're headed back to White Rock and will be in touch."

"Yeah, please don't tell him we are wasting our time with some radical person who thinks he can provide us with a two-way radio." The irony in Rabbit's voice attested to his anticipation of success with Jay Stevens.

Glen and Norris were leaving Woody's Tavern after a hearty lunch when a Model A Ford came barreling into the parking lot. It must have been doing at least thirty miles per hour. They quickly stepped back on the walkway to avoid the speeding auto. They watched it slide into a parking space near the back of the building and observed two large men emerging from the vehicle. Glen and Norris started towards the individuals to register a complaint, but neither of the men glanced their way. Instead they headed straight into Woody's, unaware anyone had been ruffled by their speedy arrival.

"I've never seen those two before, wonder why they were in such a hurry? They certainly aren't from around these parts. Maybe we should go in and see just who they are?" Glen made a move towards the tavern, but Norris grabbed his arm.

"I think it's best we don't. No need to get those two biggies riled up." Norris continued towards their car.

"Did the detectives say what kind of car they were looking for? If it was a Model A Ford, there might be some connection," Glen took time to copy down the license number.

"I don't think they mentioned the make of car they were looking for, but we need to get back to them as soon as possible. We don't want them on our case anymore than necessary." Norris got behind the wheel of his car as he spoke. "We can give them a call and maybe that's all the information they need."

"I doubt that, those two detectives are always looking for more information than we have. But, at least we can give them what we have."

Jay's workshop wasn't any neater than it had been on their previous visit. However, the eager look in his eyes still gave the impression he knew the exact status of every project, where it was located, and when it would be completed.

"I'm ready to install the radio equipment which will provide two-way communications between your patrol car and a base station which I assume will be positioned at police headquarters. The little glitch I had with my gear was only a loose wire, which I found after a few minutes search. Hadn't soldered it properly," he shrugged his shoulders as if to say he had better be more careful next time, "but I assure you all the connections are solid now."

"Don't you think we ought to test it before we take it to headquarters?" Rabbit's voice had a large amount of skepticism in it.

"Certainly we're going to test it. Can you beat your overnight installation estimate, Jay?" Rad was anxious to get on with the project even though Rabbit had his doubts.

"Since we talked last, I've found a procedure that allows me to get the gear in your car in less than thirty minutes. We can do it now if you have the time."

"We're pretty tight on time. We should be in White Rock as we speak. We need to preserve some tire tracks, which could lead us to a murderer. We need to dig them up before they are washed out by today's predicted rain."

"I have just what you need." Jay moved towards a bench strewn with various bottles and cartons. One large carton contained a white powder. "Here is some plaster of paris. All you have to do is add water, pour the mixture on the tracks, and wait a few minutes for it to dry. When it's dry it will be hard enough to lift out leaving you with a perfect impression of the tracks."

"Wow, if you are correct about that method, it would be great. I've made a sketch of the tracks, but if we don't have to dig up the entire piece of ground, we would really save a lot of time and effort." Rabbit's growing interest could be seen as he moved to take the box offered by Jay.

"We'll go over and secure those tracks and return to let you install the radio gear. We should be able to give it a test before we demonstrate it to the chief. We'll get back before dark. You will be here later?" Rad's question was more in the form of a request than anything else.

"Certainly, I'll be here. I also want to show you some additional capabilities I have which should interest you. I wrote a letter to the police department six months ago explaining my crime prevention equipment, but I haven't received a reply as yet."

Rad and Rabbit were moving towards the door as Rad responded, "I'm sure we can use any and everything you have invented and somehow, someway I'll see that you get paid for it. We must be off but we'll be back in a couple of hours to set up the chief's car."

The jangle of the phone startled Rachel who was still in deep thought about the councilman's press conference earlier in the day. The chief, since his return, hadn't indicated he was aware of any comments, pro or con. Maybe this was someone calling to inform him; she hoped not.

"Chief of police's office. Can I help you?" Rachel's voice didn't indicate she was expecting anything dire, she was using her usual melodious tone. "I'm afraid you have the wrong number to contact Detective Childers, however, I can relay any message since he isn't in the headquarters at this time."

If it hadn't been for the long pause, punctuated by a high pitched, "Oh, I see," the chief probably wouldn't have become interested in Rachel's phone call.

After several "Yes, I know; As soon as I see them; I have your phone number," Rachel finished with, "I understand clearly, Homer; they will get your message."

The chief was at her desk almost before she hung up her phone. "Who was that on the phone?"

"It was the bartender from the country club; he wants Detective Childers or Tankers to contact him. Says he may know who fired the shot out there this morning. Said he would only tell the detectives, he's afraid someone may be after him."

"Don't you bother with the note, I will tell them about the call when they come back in. I still want to talk to them about that motorcycle accident and those civilian clothes they are wearing. Those two need to be throttled down a little. Wonder if they covered the councilman's press conference? Did they say anything to you about it?"

Rachel tried not to look directly at the chief; instead she kept her head down while transcribing the information from the bartender's call. Slowly she raised her head and handed the chief the slip of paper. "Here is all you need on the bartender's call and yes, they did come by after the press conference was over but you were out. They said to tell you they would talk to you later since they were on their way back to the crime scene in White Rock. They didn't say anything to me about the councilman's comments to the press."

"I sure would like to know what he said before I read about it in the paper. I would bet a half-month's pay it wasn't anything good. If they call in again, tell them I want to see them the first thing tomorrow morning."

"Yes sir, I'll make sure they get the message." Rachel's voice faded as the chief strolled back into his office and closed the door.

The officer guarding the crime scene was on his feet as soon as Rad and Rabbit pulled up to the curb in their patrol car. "Nothing been happening here. How much longer you gonna need this place guarded?"

"You can take off now, all we need is to get an impression of the tire track the shooter's car left in the back of the house. Then we'll be through here."

"What are you gonna use to get an impression? We've always had to dig up the entire area around anything we wanted to save before. And you know as well as me, lots of times the ground just crumbled away in our hands and we got nothing. You got some new and fancy way to save things now?"

"As a matter of fact, yes. Come on and help me get a pan and some water out of the kitchen. I'll show you some magic you won't believe." Rabbit was holding the box of white powder under his arm as he led the way into the house and down the hall to the kitchen. Rad could only smile, as Rabbit seemed to be taking charge of his latest tip from Jay Stevens. Maybe now he would be just as excited about a two-way radio system.

63

The tire imprint was still in place and hadn't been disturbed. Rabbit stirred his brew with the hands of an expert and with minimum effort was able to pour the plaster of paris concoction into the depression. "We'll let that set for a while until it hardens, then we'll have a permanent piece of evidence without a lot of dirty work involved." He looked up at the officer and grinned. "Just guessing, that tire print sure looks like it was made by a Model A Ford. I'll check it out with the tire store to make sure."

"Robert, if you will come tell us when this stuff hardens, we'll go back and take one final look at the crime scene. Then we can officially close down this place and be on our way. We'll give you a ride anyplace you want."

"That's OK detectives, I'm only a block from where I live. I'll watch this stuff and get you when it's hard."

As they were about to enter the back door, Captain Snyder came around the corner of the house. "You two about finished here?"

"Yes sir, we were just on the way to have one final look at the crime scene. Want to come along? We've just poured some plaster of paris on a tire print we think was left by the shooter. We have to wait for it to harden so we'll have some time to show you around." Rad was surprised to see the captain; it was one of the first times he had ever come out to check on them in the field.

The captain's nod was positive but his expression was confused. "What plaster of paris in what tire track?"

Rad and Rabbit turned back to where Robert was standing. "Well sir, we have a partial eye witness who says he saw a car parked back here in the rear of the house. He says he heard a shot go off inside the house but didn't stay around to investigate. When he came back a few minutes later, the car was gone. We are thinking the car might belong to the shooter."

"Sounds logical enough, but what's this plaster of paris and where did it come from?" The captain walked over and looked down at the cloudy liquid, which was already turning white in spots and beginning to harden.

Rad thought a moment and tried to pick his words carefully, "We got it from an individual by the name of Jay Stevens. We have been working with this young man on several ideas he has designed, which we believe are sure to help our overall ability and efficiency in solving crimes. This," pointing to the tire track, "is just a small one he put us on to today. The real reason in going to him in the first place was to get a two-way radio installed in the chief's patrol car. If it works, and I'm sure it will, we hope to get the money to install them in all our patrol cars. We were going to talk to you about our plan as soon as we had something concrete. Of course, money will be a major factor in what we will be able to do."

"Sounds promising, I would like to meet this Jay Stevens sometime in the near future."

"We can certainly arrange a meeting. He has more than a few ideas, which could revolutionize our work. He told me he had written a letter to the department several months ago explaining the capabilities of his crime prevention equipment, but hasn't gotten a reply as yet. I'm not sure who would have received his letter, but if I had to guess, Captain Winston would be on the top of my list. He hasn't been much help to Rabbit or myself. If he did receive the letter, I would've thought he might have forwarded it to one of us for comment, but nothing so far. I will start looking for it tomorrow."

"When you find it, let me see it and if it has any merit, we'll see if we can't incorporate Stevens efforts into the department. In the meantime, I'll get the funds to pay for the initial two-way radio installation in the chief's patrol car. Now let's see the crime scene."

As Rad and Rabbit led Captain Snyder into the office area where the body had been found, Robert called to Rabbit telling him the plaster of paris had hardened. "Rad, you go ahead and show the captain the crime scene and I'll make sure we get an unbroken tire impression. I'll meet you two in back when you finish."

Rad nodded to Rabbit, then turned to the captain and spent the next ten minutes outlining the facts, the suspicions, and the unknowns. Facts were: the victim had been a teller at the bank; he hadn't gone to work that day; he had come up to this house, according to his wife, to do business with its owner, Will Sutter, who was also his partner. The shooter had made his getaway in an automobile he had positioned at the rear entrance of the building. No witnesses had seen the shooter, only heard the shot. Suspicions were: the crime had to have some connection to yesterday's bank robbery, however, as of now there appears to be no tie-ins. Unknowns were: identity of the shooter, how or even if the crime tied in to the bank, and did the shooting at the country club have any connection to the bank robbery or the murder?

The captain listened intently only interrupting once to ask if Will Sutter, owner of the house, could have been the possible shooter. When assured Will was in Richmond at the time of the incident, he had nothing more to add.

"Well, that's about all we have as of now, Captain. We have our nets out and should start getting some feedback pretty soon. If our suspicions are founded, there's got to be a lot of people who know why a lone teller of a robbed bank got diced when he hadn't even been at work the day of the robbery."

"Keep me up to date. I need to get back to headquarters, so I'll get out of your hair. You can get on with your business without me being in the way. Where are you headed now?" Captain Snyder moved down the hallway as he spoke.

"We will be going over to Jay Stevens to let him install the prototype of the two-way radio in the chief's car. He claims he can complete the work in thirty minutes. I sure hope it works when we show it to the chief tomorrow morning."

"Remember I want to meet this young man."

"You'll see him at the demonstration tomorrow morning. He will have to set up the base station at headquarters; it is key to the entire operation."

"I'll look forward to it." The captain returned their salute, rounded the corner of the house, and headed for his car.

Just as Rad and Rabbit were getting ready to depart, Mr. Williams, the witness who had seen the car parked at the rear of the building, came around the corner of the house; he must have passed the captain on the way. He yelled out, "Detectives, have you got a minute?" He was breathing hard and his face appeared to be a bit ashen.

"What can we do for you, Mr. Williams? Catch your breath, we have a moment."

"I need to tell you something I should have told you yesterday; I think it may be important. Things got a little confusing for me when the boy suddenly came around the house saying you had a call from headquarters. Anyway, the thing I didn't tell you was that car parked out back had a driver. I'm not sure I can identify him, but I thought you would want to know there was someone waiting in the car."

Rabbit slammed his hat to the ground and stomped his feet. "You thought we would want to know? YOU THOUGHT WE WOULD WANT TO KNOW? You darn right we would want to know. We aren't mind readers, Mr. Williams. Why didn't you tell us this yesterday?" Rabbit started towards the man as if he meant to do him bodily harm.

Rad shook his head as if to clear cobwebs, which suddenly had lodged in his skull while at the same time holding his hand out to calm Rabbit. "Mr. Williams, please explain what you have just told us. You say there was someone waiting in the car you saw here," he pointed to the spot where the plaster of paris had been moments earlier, "before the shot was fired. You say he was in the driver's seat, but you can't identify the individual. Why in God's name didn't you tell us this yesterday? We have wasted almost twenty-four hours that we could have used trying to find this individual."

The man's face went from ashen to a ghostly white and for a moment the two detectives weren't sure he was going to remain standing. "As I said, when the boy came running around the corner of the building to tell you about the call on your radio, things became confused for me. You left before I had time to tell you everything I had seen. I'm sorry if I've messed up your investigation, but at least now I have told you everything I saw and heard."

"Sit down before you fall down," Rad held Williams by the arm as he eased himself to the ground. "Rest a minute and get some blood back into your head. When you feel normal, try and picture the driver and tell us what he looked like. Was he husky or thin? Did he wear a hat or was he bare headed? Was he a white man? Close your eyes and try to let your subconscious take over."

The detectives stood looking down at the pitiful sight of a man trying to keep from fainting while at the same time trying to make his mind replay a scene he didn't want to remember. He had closed his eyes and was leaning against the frame of the back door. He rocked slowly back and forth while he hummed some unrecognizable doleful tune.

After what seemed like ten minutes, Williams spoke, "As I told you before, I had been walking by this place and was almost to the street when the shot was fired. The car had been parked near the back of the house and I only recalled this when I looked back at it after I heard the shot. That's when I realized someone was in the car. He must have been a big man for I can't remember seeing the top of his head when I passed the car. He was white and was wearing a dark suit or coat. I don't remember seeing his face, I'm sure he didn't look in my direction when I passed by. He didn't get out of the car when I looked back and I kept walking towards my house. That's all I can remember."

Rabbit moved closer, "Did you notice a license plate number?"

"No, but for some reason I think it was a local plate. Don't know why, but that was the impression I had at the time."

"Mr. Williams, we are going to find that car and the people who were in it. When that happens, do you think you would know the car if you saw it again?" Rad was in his face as he got to his feet.

"Maybe, but you know a lot of those cars look alike." The blood was beginning to drain out of his face again.

Again Rad grabbed him by the arm, but this time it was to keep him upright, "Listen carefully, you keep trying to remember everything about that day and time that you can. If you come up with anything, however trivial, I will be expecting you to contact us immediately. Do you understand what I'm saying?"

"Yes sir, and again I'm sorry for not telling you yesterday."

"You go home and take it easy. If you don't contact us before we find the car, we will be in touch with you when we do." Rad and Rabbit left him standing by the back door as they headed for their car.

The shrill ring of the telephone shattered the quiet in the coach's small office located in the corner of the high school gymnasium. Coach Jimmie Webb scooped up the phone without taking his feet off his battered desk. He was a fixture in the city, having been the varsity basketball coach for the last twenty-five years. He personally knew every young man in town and most of their families. He was highly respected and his credibility had been established long ago. "Hello, Coach Webb speaking."

"Coach, Jordan Snyder here. I need to talk with you about something of grave importance to you and this city. Can we meet for lunch tomorrow?"

"Hope it doesn't have anything to do with me being in trouble with the police department. Just joking, but you do sound a wee bit serious. We've had lunch before and your invitations haven't been this grim."

"I don't mean to sound sinister, but I do have something of importance to discuss with you. How about noon tomorrow at the White House?"

"Fine with me, I'll see you there." The coach hung up the phone and stared at the wall. *Wonder what's so important in this city that Jordan Snyder would want to talk to me about it?*

Both detectives sat in silence as they motored down the hill from the White Rock murder scene. In fact, they were well on the way to Jay's workshop before either of them spoke. "Can you believe he forgot to tell us about someone being in the car?" Rabbit's words were hardly audible above the noise of the engine.

"Thank goodness he finally told us today. That gives us another body in the mix, the more the merrier. Our contacts will have an even better chance to scrape together something we can use with more people being involved. Someone is bound to let something slip, particularly if there is a tie-in between the murder and the bank."

"Hope you're right. Hey, there's Jay standing out in front of his place. Maybe we can get this patrol car rigged up and get home at some decent hour tonight. I still haven't gotten Bess over the see my sister Mary; maybe I will finally get to keep my word." Rabbit bounded out of the car as it came to a stop in front of the somewhat ramshackled workshop.

Jay was at the entrance of a lean-to big enough to hold the patrol car. Several assorted pieces of equipment ringed the sides and his toolbox was near at hand. "Pull the car over here under this shed, it looks like it might rain and we can't afford to get any of these components wet."

Rabbit guided Rad as he slipped the car into the tight quarters. "This good enough, Jay?"

"That'll be just fine. As soon as I get the transmitter and receiver installed in the car, we can test it. I have the base station located far enough away to give us a valid check. If one of you will hold this light for me, I'll get started."

"I'll help," Rabbit was quick to answer. "Boy, did that plaster of paris work like a charm, Jay. I wish we had known about it a long time ago. I look forward to seeing some more of your gadgets."

Rad had to smile to himself at Rabbit's turnabout concerning Jay's mysteries. *Only this morning he had been skeptical about anything Jay offered. The plaster of paris had really made a believer out of him.*

"Well, thanks, Rabbit, for your kind words. However, I would like to think of my inventions as a bit more than gadgets, maybe we could call them improved devices to fight crime. That would put them a step above thingumajigs." He chuckled at his own little joke. "Would you hold that light over this way a bit?" Jay was almost totally swallowed by the trunk of the car, all you could see was rear end and feet.

In less than an hour all of the components that had been surrounding the car had disappeared. Jay, with a wide grin on his face, slammed his toolbox shut and dusted his hands. The job was complete, now for the test.

"Rabbit, you drive the car a mile or so down the road. Turn on all the gear and wait until you get a green light on the box located under the dashboard. When the light is a steady green, use the mike clipped to the box to give us a call. Our call sign will be Base Control. If you come through loud and clear, we will return your call with instructions for you to follow. You will be Mobile One. If you don't hear anything, wait five minutes and drive back here." Jay stood with his fingers crossed as Rabbit drove away.

It had been a long day, but Rad was alert and eager as if the day had just dawned. He felt like he was about to be witness to Graham Bell's first telephone call. He was almost holding his breath for fear his breathing might interrupt the radio waves. Five minutes must have passed. Despair was beginning to set in when a crackle was heard over the receiver. Jay gently adjusted the main dial on the control box. Another crackle, then: "Base Control, Mobile One, how do you read? I repeat, Base Control, Mobile One, how do you read?"

"Mobile One, Base Control, we hear you, we hear you. Return to Base with emergency lights flashing. I repeat, return to Base with emergency lights flashing. Out."

Silence prevailed and Rad began to wonder if he had really heard Rabbit's voice. Then in the distance a dust cloud rose from the road leading to Jay's workshop, in front of the dust could be seen flashing lights normally associated with a police patrol car. Instructions complied with; the test was a success.

Rad was shaking Jay's hand as Rabbit screeched to a stop. "The transmission sounded a little tinny, but it was clear. I think we've got something that will even excite the chief." Rabbit's grin told the entire story of what he thought about Jay and his improved devices to fight crime.

"We'll see you in the morning in time to get the base station set up. I'm not sure when the chief will be available, but it will be sometime tomorrow morning. Do you have everything you need for the base station?"

"Yes, I have everything I need. I plan to position the antenna near the top of Memorial Stairs behind the Court House. That location should give us the coverage we need for the test, anyway it will be good for starters. When we get more installations in more cars, we may have to locate the antenna at some higher point."

"You know the reservoir near the high school should give us complete coverage of the city," Jay's eyes showed his excitement. "I'll start working on the needed permits as soon as we complete the test."

"Sounds good to me, see you in the morning." Jay was still smiling as they departed.

"Well, Mary, it is good to see you. I never thought my husband would bring me over to see you. He and that partner of his stay so busy they don't have time for anything else." Bess hugged her sister-in-law and placed her goodies on the kitchen table.

"We will just have to make him take time. Family should be more important than anyone or anything else. Please take the easy chair and tell me how the children are." Mary was pleased to see her brother's wife; they had always been close.

Their talking continued on for an hour, only disturbed by Rabbit's snoring, which they ignored.

It was dark in the back room of Woody's, but it was quiet. There wasn't much chance of being interrupted while making a telephone call. The large man in a dark coat waited until the operator came on the line, "Would you ring 581, please?" He could hear the operator make the connection and listened for the first ring. He was sure this was Rachel's home phone number. It had been sometime since he had had the occasion to call her.

CHAPTER FIVE

Rad was more than upset at having to be at headquarters at this early hour. Having to report to Captain Winston was even more agonizing. He was supposed to get to the chief the first thing this morning to demonstrate the two-way radio he and Rabbit had worked out with Jay Stevens. They weren't the only officers who could investigate every little incident happening in this town, although it appeared Captain Winston thought so. He walked into the captain's office, right on time.

"Captain, you do realize Detective Tankers and I have our plates full with the Main Street bank robbery and the White Rock murder. We really didn't have the time to look into these other robberies, particularly this latest one dealing with two brain trusts."

"Childers, I'm the assistant chief, and what I assign to you and your fumbling partner will be my choice, not yours. What did you two find out?"

"Well, it seems the local hardware dealer happened to look out the back window of his quarters above his store and saw two men leaving his property carrying two bathtubs. He immediately called headquarters to inform them of the ongoing crime. The patrolman on duty swiftly apprehended the two at the corner of Seventh and Church streets. They were carrying the bathtubs, although with some difficulty. When we contacted the hardware dealer, he claimed those tubs were worth fifty-six dollars apiece. When we talked to the perpetrators in the jail, they pleaded not guilty. Their

73

story, which was a whopper, claimed they weren't the ones whose idea it was to take the tubs. They alleged some man paid them to take the tubs, telling them the tubs were his property and had been paid for earlier. They led us to the man who hired them. He was a swindler we've had trouble with before. It wasn't the first time we had arrested him for a crime. We released the two men but not before giving them a good lecture about taking someone's property without knowing why. It took a day and a half just to straighten out a weird misunderstanding."

"It is good you did your job for a change. It is imperative we respond to our leading businessmen to let them know there's a competent police force in this town. As you well know, we had to capture those bank robbers for you. Next time, I'll expect you to get to the bottom of things in a more rapid manner."

"Where were you, Captain, when we were chasing those crooks through the woods into your waiting hands? I didn't see you with any dirt on your clothes, in fact you weren't even at the scene." Rad's voice was rising and the veins on his neck were beginning to throb to prove his blood pressure was about to reach new heights.

"That will be enough, detective. If I need you again, I will call. And next time, I will expect you to respond immediately. Not when it suits you. One of these days in the near future, maybe after the elections, there will be a new chief. When that happens, you might be back on a beat, that is if you are still on the force." Captain Winston spun his chair around leaving only the back of the chair for Rad's view.

The salute Rad rendered as he departed wasn't something that could be classified as formal.

The chief's outer office was just down the hall from Captain Winston's, so Rad was there in plenty of time to meet Rabbit and Jay. It was quiet this time of morning, Rachel hadn't even arrived at work and she was usually early. No sooner had he walked into the outer office than Rabbit and Jay came in. It seemed like the threesome were in a world all their own. Jay was excited and immediately started to explain where he had positioned the antenna for the base station and how he planned to demonstrate the two-way radio in the chief's patrol car. All seemed to be in readiness, but Rad was still concerned. He wanted to make sure everything was in order so he was turning to Jay to ask him to go over everything again when Captain Snyder walked in.

All three jumped to their feet and Rad quickly stepped forward, "Sir, this is Jay Stevens, the young man I told you about. I believe we are all set for the test on the chief's patrol car, at least as soon as he arrives. We expect him anytime now."

"I've heard a lot about you, Jay, and I'm looking forward to seeing some of your work first hand. What did this initial installation cost?" The captain went right to the meat of the subject as he waved them to take seats.

"Well sir, the equipment in the car cost me close to twenty-five dollars. The paraphernalia for the base station including the antenna setup runs about seventy-five. Of course, it is only a one time cost; we will be able to use all that equipment when we put the antenna in its permanent location."

"You mean additional cars will only cost us twenty-five dollars a car?" The captain almost smiled as he said the amount.

"Yes sir, that is if all the cars have radio receivers in them like the chief's. There could be a few unknowns, but I don't think it will drive the cost up very much from what I've quoted."

Rad raised his hand to get attention, "Captain, I think Jay has left out his labor for installation. His price is just for parts and such."

"Well, of course. We don't expect Jay to work for free. If I have my way, he'll be a part of the force. That should take care of his labor costs." Captain Snyder had hardly gotten the words out of his mouth when the chief walked in.

"What have we here, an overthrow?" The chief frowned as he walked over and sat down behind his desk.

"No sir, not yet," Rad's comment caused the furrows in the chief's brow to deepen. "Just kidding, Chief."

"Before you say another word, you received a call from the bartender at the country club. According to the message he left with Rachel, he thinks he knows who fired the shot into the bar yesterday. I want you to get in touch with him and find out who he suspects. I want it to be top priority with you and Tankers here. And on another note, when in the devil are you going to get that two-way radio installed in my patrol car?"

"Thought you would never ask, Chief. This is Jay Stevens, the young man I've been telling you about who will help remedy our two-way radio problem."

"That's all fine, but when can he do it?" The chief reached over his desktop to shake Jay's hand.

"We are here to demonstrate it right now. The installation is in your car and was completed last night. Jay, earlier this morning, temporarily positioned an antenna so we can give the radio a proper test. Of course, a permanent antenna will be centrally located when we get the go ahead to install transmitters in all of our patrol cars. That way we will have coverage over all parts of the city. But first, the test to show you what we have, we are ready when you are." Rad moved towards the office door with Rabbit, Jay, and Captain Snyder following.

"Don't let it be said I'm the one keeping you waiting. This is something I will have to see to believe. Or, I should say, hear to believe." The chief slapped his desktop as he rose from his seat.

As the group proceeded down the hall, Rabbit slowed Rad and whispered in his ear, "At least he didn't say anything about the motorcycle accident or the civilian clothes."

As they reached the stairs leading to the street, the chief turned and said, "Oh, and by the way, we'll talk about that motorcycle you ran through the fence the other day and those outfits you have on when this is over." Rabbit's eyes rolled skyward causing him to almost miss the top step. The handrail saved him from life in a wheelchair.

Rachel had just entered headquarters by the rear entrance when she caught a glimpse of the group moving down the hallway heading towards the front entrance. She wasn't sure what was going on, but she hoped the demo of the two-way radio was about to happen. She knew Rad had been working hard to show the chief something, which would calm him for the time being. She also wondered if the chief had mentioned the bartender's call. Knowing the chief, she was sure he had.

She had no sooner put her purse in her desk drawer than Captain Winston dashed into the office. "What's going on? Where is everyone headed? I saw the chief with that group, what are they up to?"

"Since I've just arrived, I'm not sure what everyone is up to. You are one of the assistant chiefs; I would think you would know what happens around here. Why don't you go find out?" Rachel's tone was anything but cordial.

"Regardless what the chief has going on with those two so-called detectives, I need to see him as soon as possible. If you will be so kind as to give me a call when he returns, I would appreciate it very much." Winston turned to go, but stopped for one last comment. "Did you hear about Sergeant Bailey's daughter, Mary Sue, who was to be married last weekend?"

"No, what happened now? I know they've had difficulty in several attempts." Rachel was acquainted with the sergeant's daughter.

"Her fiancé was killed when a car he was riding in turned over. The driver is being charged with running an automobile unlawfully and speeding. He claims the steering gear wasn't working properly. These rapid drivers will ruin this entire town before long. When I get to be chief, I'll do something about it." Captain Winston's smug look made Rachel look away for a moment.

However, in an effort to close the conversation she added, "That is really fate. I know the groom had told Mary Sue something would prevent their marriage. Their first attempt ended when the death of the bride's uncle postponed the wedding. On another occasion they drove over to the county seat and found the clerk's office closed. The third time failed when they couldn't procure a license. I guess he was correct; their wedding must have been doomed from the beginning. Too bad, she is a sweet girl. They should have run away like they first planned. I know that's what I'll do if and when the time comes." Rachel paused and busied herself at her desk.

"If you are in a hurry, I'll be glad to help you out. We could become good friends if you would only give me a chance. How about getting together some night?" Again the smug look, which was Winston's standard look nowadays.

Rachel's glare could have melted ice. "I'll tell the chief you want to see him when he returns." Her fingers hit the keys on her typewriter with a vengeance. The conversation was at an end and Winston knew it; he walked slowly out the door.

The chief's patrol car pulled to the curb in front of the police station with a smiling chief behind the wheel. "It's about time we showed some progress in this department. I couldn't believe it when Mr. Stevens responded with my exact message to him. There wasn't even any static on the line, better than the reception I get on my radio at home. It was like magic. Now, how long will it take to get this capability into all our cars?" He looked first at Rad in the front seat beside him and then at Rabbit and Captain Snyder sitting in back.

Rad and Rabbit sat closed mouth; Captain Snyder was first to respond. "First we'll need to get the money for the project, and then we need to hire this talented individual to be a part of our force. I'm told he has many other items which will enhance our work, let alone what he may come up with in the future."

"Christ, Snyder, you know we hardly have enough money to pay the police force we have now. What with the good Councilman Brenner brow beating me about new uniforms and motorcycle noise, we'll be hard pressed to squeeze any additional funds for another person or for things like radios." The chief shook his head as if in despair.

"Don't you have a special fund for things like this which are over and above the normal budget? I've never seen you use it, but you told me about it when I first made captain."

"Yes, Captain Winston maintains a watch on the account for me. I have him keep the bankbook in a safe place. I've never used much of the fund, but now this radio equipment seems a good place to put part of it to work. As to hiring additional people, I'll have to talk to the councilman. Maybe we can add it to our upcoming budget which is to be presented for approval right after the forthcoming election."

"Well, if the councilman is re-elected, I'm worried he won't be in favor of any increase in our budget, regardless of how much it would improve police protection in this city. What we need is a new councilman who would be more in tune with the future than the one we have now. I also have an idea on how that can come to pass. I'm meeting a prospect for lunch today. If I get the proper response, I'll let you know what I'm talking about." Captain Snyder appeared to be very guarded with this last statement.

Without further conversation, everyone got out of the chief's car just as Captain Winston came running down the front steps. The chief waved at him, "See me in my office as soon as you can."

"Rachel, this is Alvin." There was a long pause interrupted only by deep breathing. Apparently Alvin had been expecting an answer. "Do you remember me? I used to wait on you when you made your daily visits to the bank. I was the teller in the third window."

"Oh yes, Alvin. I didn't recognize your voice. I haven't seen you there recently. What can I do for you?"

"I need to talk to someone about the bank robbery before I leave town. I tried to call you last night, but you must have been out. That's why I'm calling you at work."

"Well, I'm not sure but I may be able to get one of our detectives to talk with you. Can you come into headquarters in the next few days?" Rachel still couldn't place a face with the name, but she felt it could be important for either Rad or Rabbit to talk with this man.

"No, no! I'm leaving town tonight. My train leaves from the Ninth Street station at 12:15, fifteen minutes after midnight. I can't wait any longer so it's imperative I talk to a detective before I depart. My life could depend on it."

"All right, Alvin. I remember you now. You are the nice looking man with the black mustache who was always so nice to me when I came into the bank. I'll get Rad Childers, one of our detectives, to meet you at the station before your train departs."

"How will I know him? Where will he be? I won't have much time to look around for anybody."

"OK, so you will know, I'll come with him. That way you can pick him out. We'll be in a black Ford in the parking lot, no later than 11:30. We'll stay in the car, so you should be able to find us there. Be watching for us."

"Great, I'll be on the lookout for you. Please don't be late, my time window is very small and if I don't make contact it could be the end for me." The phone went dead, Alvin must have been in a hurry, he didn't even say goodbye.

Rachel's first thought was if Rad would allow her to accompany him to see Alvin? Second, it was a little out of the ordinary for a secretary to be getting information from someone who needed to speak to a detective. Regardless of what Rad would think, what would the chief have to say about such abnormal behavior? Well, all she could do was present what she had been told when contacted and see what actions would be taken.

The barroom at the country club was empty except for Homer, the bartender. He appeared to be cleaning up the place rather than tending bar. It was a bit early for anyone to be drinking; there weren't too many places on this side of the ocean where the sun had passed the yardarm.

"Hello, detectives, good to see you again." Homer put down the bar rag and moved to meet Rad and Rabbit who were halfway across the room before he saw them.

"So you know who fired the shot in here the other day? From what the chief told us, you think the shot was fired by a club member?" Rad looked directly at Homer as he spoke.

"I didn't tell the chief anything, I didn't even talk to him. I talked to his secretary and told her I had a good idea who fired the shot. I told her I wanted to talk to you two detectives about it."

"Then how did the chief get involved in this?" Rad was beginning to show some impatience as he looked over at Rabbit and shook his head. Rabbit moved around behind Homer, almost looking over his shoulder.

"I don't know, for crying out loud. I'm trying to help you guys and you start giving me a rough time. All I know is, it must have been a club member. He knew where to park to make a quick getaway, and he must have been upset enough to fire a warning shot into the club. Those two hotshots had been cramming every motion in their favor through the club's board for the last year. No wonder someone's blood boiled over. I'm not surprised a shot was fired to get their attention."

"You told us you had a name. When you can come up with a name, then call us. We've got a murder on our hands along with a bank robbery. A random shooting at the country club doesn't have a top priority with us. We don't need you calling headquarters saying you think you know who fired the shot into the country club. We don't need the chief of police running us around because someone who doesn't know what he's talking about calls in on a whim. We don't have time to go through the club's roster, and even if we did, we wouldn't know whose name was who. Homer, I've a good mind to run you in for obstructing justice." Rad was positive this visit was another waste of their time.

"I was trying to help out, and I thought this bit of information would help you some. You said this might tie into the bank robbery and the murder. I thought you wanted all possible information pertaining to the case. Give me some credit for being one of the good guys." Homer was almost pleading.

"As far as you being one of the good guys, we will have to wait and see. The key for you is to give us a name. And, when you have it, call us." They departed shaking their heads, another wild goose chase.

There was only silence from the chief as he held the phone to his ear. His grip on the instrument tightened as he listened. Slowly the color of his fingers whitened as the monologue on the other end of the line continued. Finally, the chief broke into the conversation, "Wait until I see that two-timing scalawag. If he thinks he can talk about this police department that way, he has another think coming. He can berate me if he so desires, but when he starts in on this force, he's barking up the wrong tree. Thanks for filling me in on his so-called press conference. I sent two of my detectives to listen to his remarks, but they haven't had time to report to me yet."

The chief listened again making a couple of notes on his desk pad, "Don't worry, he won't know where I got the news. I owe you one, be talking to you later. Goodbye."

The White House wasn't as crowded as normal, so Captain Snyder and Coach Webb had their choice of tables. They made small talk until the waiter had departed with their order.

Captain Snyder didn't waste much time. "Coach, you are going to be retiring next month and you will have plenty of time on your hands. This town needs you in a greater capacity and I along with many others think it is time you paid your dues."

"Paid my dues to what? I've spent these many years coaching at the high school. I've coached nearly every boy in this town. I've gotten to know most of the families and their children whether they played for me or not; I think that's dues enough. The wife and I plan to take it easy for a while, maybe do a little traveling." The coach shifted in his seat and took a sip from the water glass next to his plate.

"I will admit, you've done a lot for us, but we need you to do more. There are several important people in this town, as well as myself, who want you to run for the upcoming city council position. We didn't realize you would be available until you recently announced your retirement. When you did, we knew you were the man to beat Brenner. He needs to be ousted after the miserable record he has compiled during his tenure in office. The next election is just around the corner and time is short. But, I'm sure you could win, hands down."

"You mean you want me to run against Councilman Brenner? Why, he's been on that council ever since I can remember. He's a fixture and probably has all the backing he needs."

Their food arrived, which gave Captain Snyder a moment to let the coach think about the proposal. After his first bite he said, "Coach, if I can show you the support you would have, which is considerable and enough to win, would you run?"

"Well, I don't know. I would have to talk with the wife to see how she feels about such a thing. Goodness knows, I've never thought much about going into politics. I also haven't had any great confidence in Councilman Brenner or what he's done with his time on the council." Coach looked away as he pondered his last statement. "He seems to be more against progress than for furthering the goals of this city."

"I'll gather some of the people I've been talking about and let them tell you in person how much you can do to help this town. Time is our enemy with the election only days away, but I'm sure we can get our message across before Election Day." Captain Snyder smiled.

"I don't mind talking to whoever you have in mind. You've hit me out of the blue so I need some time to think and talk to the wife, like I said earlier. Then I'll let you know." The coach had his game face on.

"OK, Coach, you've got a deal. Just let us know as soon as possible." Captain Snyder's eyes gleamed, Coach hadn't said no.

Captain Winston tapped on the chief's office door, "Rachel called and said you were free. I've needed to see you and apparently you wanted to see me. You asked me to stop by when I saw you out front."

"Yes, you should have been with us this morning. For the first time in my life, we've got two-way communication between the field and headquarters. Detectives Childers and Tankers found a young man by the name of Jay Stevens who is a wiz at electronics. He was able to install a two-way radio in my patrol car."

"What are you talking about, Chief?" Captain Winston's puzzled look reflected every indication the chief had surprised him. "I've heard the name of Jay Stevens before, but I'm not sure where it was."

"Well, you need to remember it now. This young man has been able to rig up a base station, which can be in contact with our patrol cars. When he installs transmitters in all the cars, we will have a capability unlike any we've seen or heard of before."

"That's ridiculous, there isn't any such capability anywhere in the country. You must have been tricked. Any demonstration must have been rigged to make you think you were getting two-way communication." Captain Winston paused and squeezed his eyes shut as if visioning something far away. He snapped his fingers and opened his eyes, "Now I remember where I've heard the name Jay Stevens. He sent us a letter some weeks ago trying to explain about all these fantastic things he had invented. I was sure he was some kind of crackpot and tossed his letter into the trash. You haven't been taken in by this charlatan, have you?"

"Winston, I'm beginning to think you don't know what you are talking about. What I saw and heard this morning wasn't any trick or rigged demonstration; it was real. And, I don't care what the rest of the country can or can't do; we are going to be the ones who set the standard. What I wanted to see you about is the money we will need to buy the equipment to outfit our patrol cars. Please bring me the bankbook you have been keeping on that special fund I have for extemporary expenditures."

"There may be some complications in getting those funds. It isn't easy to get at that money, it may take me a day or two. But, I will try to expedite a withdrawal." Captain Winston shifted nervously in his chair. "How much do you want to withdraw?"

"I'm not sure what the costs will be. Just bring me the bankbook and I will handle the withdrawal." The chief was starting to get impatient. "You do have the book, don't you?"

"Certainly I have the book. I keep it at the bank in a safe deposit box and it isn't something I can put my hands on immediately. Mr. Moorehead gave me a special safety deposit box and hasn't charged us anything for its use."

"Why on earth would you keep a bank book in a safe deposit box? And, why would you have Mr. Moorehead involved with how we keep track of our special funds? Those funds are for things that I decide they are to be used for, and two-way radios seem to be special. The only reason I've had you keep track of the account is to give you some responsibility and to be a witness to how the funds are allocated. You have that book on my desk no later than tomorrow morning. If I didn't know better, I would think something funny is going on." The furrows on the chief's brow appeared even deeper now.

"I assure you, Chief, nothing funny is going on. I'll have the book in your hands by tomorrow morning. Is there anything else you need me for?" Captain Winston was on his feet and ready to leave.

"That's all I have, just be sure that book gets to me by tomorrow morning, first thing." The chief paused and looked questioningly at Captain Winston, "Wasn't there some reason you wanted to see me?"

"Oh, it wasn't anything important. I forget what it was now." Winston stuttered through his words. He was out the door before the chief could say another word.

After his departure, the chief made a note, which he underlined with a dark mark. It said, "Why a safe deposit box?"

Rabbit was grinning like the cat that had just eaten the proverbial canary as Rad walked into their joint office. "What has you looking so pleased? At least it must be good news, which is a step in the right direction." Rad sat down behind his desk and looked at Rabbit in anticipation of some momentous bulletin.

"Jay just called and has confirmed the car Williams saw behind the Sutter home was in fact a Ford." Rabbit's grin widened as he spoke.

"Well, that is good news. It narrows things down a bit. Why don't you take our tire sample over to the Ford dealer and see if he can tell us how many Ford cars in this town have that type of tire. Hopefully there won't be too many since we believe those tires aren't standard on Fords. If we can find out who owns these cars, maybe we can find our killer, or at least who drove him away from the murder scene. I would go with you but Captain Winston wants to talk to me again about those stolen bathtubs. I think that man is trying to divert us from our real problem. If I didn't know better, I would suppose he doesn't want us to solve these major crimes."

"You could be right, he sure hasn't done anything to help us." Rabbit was putting on his hat as he spoke. "I'll check back with you before we cut out for the day."

"Yeah, be sure you make contact because we need to get some concrete evidence that the bank robbery and the murder are tied together. Unless we do, we could be back to the drawing board."

"Well, what we know so far sure seems to point that way. A dead man who was a bank teller from the bank that was robbed the day he was shot. Seems to be more than coincidence." Rabbit tipped his hat and was out the door.

Councilman Brenner was pacing back and forth in Rachel's office when the chief returned to his desk. The scowl on his face made it clear he wasn't very happy to see the councilman. "You here to have

85

another press conference? From what I hear of the one you held yesterday, you don't think much of what the police force or I have been able to accomplish during your term of office. What do you want now?"

Not bothering to take a chair, Councilman Brenner said, "Don't get yourself in a tizzy, Chief. We've had our differences, but yesterday's comments were just to let the people know I am on top of things."

"Well, you certainly have a funny way of telling it as far as I'm concerned. Plus, your past actions haven't been what I would call support for this department."

With a wave of the hand the councilman seemed to brush the subject away, "I'm not here to discuss yesterday's press conference. I'm a busy man and I need this department to give me support in the upcoming city council election. As you know, I'm running again and while I don't anticipate any problems I would like your endorsement. It wouldn't look good if the police department, for which I'm responsible, wasn't behind me 100 percent."

"Well, I don't know about an endorsement, Mr. Councilman. Why should we support you when you continually go out of your way to berate the department? For instance, when I asked for the much-needed new uniforms, you didn't support me. In fact, you did everything in your power to see that my request would be disapproved. If it hadn't been for the complete support of the rest of the council, our patrolmen would be walking around the streets of this fair city in the threads we had been wearing." The chief cleared his throat, and continued in an octave higher, "That's not the only thing in my craw, you seem ready to criticize almost everything we do. From my standpoint, you have been more of a stumbling block for this department than an aid. With any kind of support, we could be one of the most outstanding police departments on the east coast, but you have made sure we didn't get it. I guess my short answer to you is, No Way."

"You'll regret this, Stoddard. When I'm re-elected you can pack your bags. I won't have an insolent individual like you running this police force. When I have people like Captain Winston waiting in the wings who know where their respect should lie, I don't need the likes of you. Maybe he should take over now."

"Well, you aren't re-elected yet and until that day comes, Captain Winston won't be running this department. Now get out of my office before I throw you out." The chief rose from behind his desk and pounded his fist into his open hand.

The councilman was halfway down the hall by the time the chief got to the door. Rachel looked up with a smile, "Nothing like a positive understanding between those in positions of authority."

The chief grunted and disappeared back into his office.

The chief teller had been over his figures for a third time. He was sure he couldn't be mistaken, but he wanted to make sure they were correct before he ventured into the bank president's office with his findings. He was about to fold his account sheet when he decided to spend another hour for one more check.

Three million was more than just a slight error in the books. This was a major deficit, one that could cause the bank considerable problems if the patrons were to hear about it. There could be a run on the bank if monies weren't available to back the accounts. At this point, there was no way to tell how this loss came about. The only thing possible was someone must have absconded with the money. Who could the culprit be? He'd better let the president know immediately.

The secretary, all prim and proper, looked up from her work rather begrudgingly. With her most sanctimonious tone, she said, "Yes, Mr. Skinner, what can I do for you?"

"It is imperative I see Mr. Moorehead. I have a matter of grave importance I need to discuss with him."

"I'm sorry, but Mr. Moorehead isn't in. You can tell me your problem and I will relay it to him. He plans to call in before closing today."

"I can only discuss this with Mr. Moorehead. When do you expect him to return?" Skinner became somewhat flustered, he had been certain the bank president was in. From the vantage point of his desk he normally would see him depart. Today he was sure Moorehead hadn't slipped out without him noticing. *It is possible the secretary wasn't going to let anyone in to see him. She had been called the Palace Guard more times than one. Maybe I should just go to his door to make certain.* It was during this thought process that the phone on the secretary's desk rang.

"Mr. Moorehead's office. How can I help you?" This time her voice was all honey and cream, a tone she very seldom used with the employees. "Yes, Mr. Moorehead. No, Mr. Moorehead, only Mr. Skinner was in to see you. He said he had something urgent to discuss with you but he wouldn't leave a message with me." She paused and listened, then, "Yes sir, I'll tell him and I will see you tomorrow. Have a good evening, sir."

"That was Mr. Moorehead on the phone, he won't be back today. He said to tell you he would see you the first thing tomorrow morning."

"You didn't tell him I was standing right here. You made it sound like I wasn't even in the office. Had I been able to talk with him, he very well may have returned tonight."

"Mr. Skinner, if I let everyone who enters my office use my phone, there wouldn't be any need for me. Mr. Moorehead said he would see you the first thing tomorrow morning. I'm sure that will be soon enough for your business."

"You could be very, very wrong my dear." With that, Skinner spun around and walked out of the office. Moments later at his desk, he rummaged through his papers for the listing of the state bank examiner's phone number. In a matter of seconds that line was ringing.

The chief was getting ready to leave his office when Rachel poked her head around the door. "Mr. Worthington is on the phone for you. Do you want me to tell him you've already departed?"

"No, I'll take the call." He went back to his desk and picked up his phone, "Hello, Worthington, what can I do for you?"

"I told you I would be calling back, Chief. How about stopping by the club on your way home and have a drink with me. I have something I would like to run by you. Aren't you about ready to leave?"

"As a matter of fact I am. And, a drink sounds good. See you there."

It was a few minutes before eleven thirty when they arrived. The lighting in the parking lot was dim at best. Rad and Rachel parked under a light stanchion closest to the station, which gave them a vantage point covering most of the waiting ramp. The mail trundles were already in position for the anticipated arrival of the 12:05, ensuring quick loading when the train pulled in. However, there wasn't anyone in sight.

"He said he would be here by eleven thirty, and I told him we would be in the parking lot. He should be here any minute now." Rachel's hand brushed Rad's arm as she turned to talk to him.

"Maybe we would be a little less conspicuous if we sat closer together. Why don't you lean back against my shoulder? That way we'll look more like lovers rather than a stakeout." Rad didn't have to ask Rachel twice. He had to admit her hair smelled good and her head pressing on his chest did present a pleasant feeling, which surged through his body. It certainly made the time pass rapidly.

"My goodness, it's almost twelve and Alvin hasn't showed up yet. Do you think we should get out and look for him?" Rachel's voice was a whisper.

"If he is here, we've sure made it easy for him to find us. I think we ought to remain in the car." He shifted his position to make it easier for Rachel to move a tiny bit closer. "Outside it would be obvious to anyone we are police, and we don't want to trigger anything which could cause Alvin trouble. He did tell you his life could depend on talking with us."

The sudden roar of the steam engine filled the confines of the station area as it blasted into view and came to a rumbling stop just as the large clock on the platform showed 12:05. It also brought Rachel and Rad to an upright position in the front seat of their car.

They watched as the baggage loaders went to work emptying the wagons, which had been burdened with mail minutes before. However, there wasn't a soul in sight who appeared to be boarding any of the passenger cars.

"We'd better get out and look for Alvin, if in fact he's even in the station." Rad was halfway out his door as he spoke. "You go down the line of cars while I take a look in the station. If he's here, one of us should spot him."

The conductor's whistle sent a shiver along Rad's spine. For a moment the air was still, but then, as if by design, the chug, chug, chug of the laboring engine filled the vacuum. The train began to slowly move away from the station like it had some enormous fire-breathing monster at its head. Before a full minute had passed it had crept from its berth and slowly vanished from view. Only two small red lanterns disappearing in the distance could attest to the fact that it had really been here. It was only then that the previous solemn and quiet slowly settled back on the scene.

Rachel was approaching Rad from the south when she yelled out, "What's that on the other side of the tracks? It looks like a body."

The yell caught the attention of the station manager along with several of the loaders. They started towards the location of a prone figure. It was face down in some deep grass across the main tracks, opposite the loading ramp. Rad and Rachel arrived first. "It looks like it may be Alvin," Rachel whispered.

Rad eased the shoulder back so part of his face showed. Rachel gasped in recognition. "Appears somebody got to him before he could reach us. I wonder what he had on his mind? For sure we'll never know now."

Rachel turned away from the corpse. "Maybe we should have looked for him instead of waiting for him to contact us."

"He's been dead longer than before eleven-thirty. He's been stabbed, and even if we had been early, we wouldn't have heard anything. I'll go call headquarters, this is all we need now, another murder."

CHAPTER SIX

The sun had barely risen above the horizon when Rabbit arrived at the Ford dealership. He was waiting at the service entrance when the manager arrived. "You said you had some information about that tire imprint I left with you, hope you don't mind me coming by before you've opened."

"Not at all. I have the imprint in my office, just follow me and I'll get it for you."

Rabbit followed the manager through the cavernous maintenance shop, which now stood inactive with several automobile carcasses in various stages of repair. The office was at the far end of the shop and their steps made unreal sounds, which echoed off the silent walls. Rabbit entered the office behind the manager and watched intently as he picked up the plaster imprint taken at the White Rock crime scene. The manager's tone of voice left no doubt about his facts as he pointed to the tread marks, "I know for sure there aren't more than twenty sets of tires like this in the entire town. The extra grade tires were part of a special sales promotion we made on the first cars we sold for that month. We didn't carry that promotion for very long since we didn't get the response we had expected."

"Do you have a list of the customers who bought those cars equipped with the extra grade tires?" Rabbit's voice was more hopeful than questioning.

91

"I'm sure we do, although it was several months ago when we ran that particular promotion. It may take me a little while to find it, but if it will do you any good I'll go look it up."

"You bet it will do us some good. If we can determine whose car was at the murder scene, we will be close to finding the man who fired the fatal shot."

The manager pulled open a side drawer of his desk and rummaged through a makeshift filing system. Not finding what he wanted, he did the same drill on the opposite side of the desk. "It may take longer than I expected to find that list, can you come back this afternoon?"

"Certainly I can come back, but the sooner we have that information, the sooner we can start closing in on the murderer. Would it be possible for you to give me a call at headquarters as soon as you find it? Here's my number." Rabbit had scratched out his phone number before the manager could close his drawer. "In fact, I've got to insist you find that list as soon as possible."

"Let me get my mechanics started on today's problems, you can see we have one or two cars left over from yesterday and I need to get them back to their owners before close of business today. As soon as they get to work, I'll do nothing but look for that list. I'll call you when I find it." The manager picked up the slip of paper with Rabbit's number, "It shouldn't take me long, it's around here someplace."

"Let's hope so. It has been several days since the shooting and we haven't progressed very far along in solving the case. As I said earlier, when we find out who owns that car, it should give us a good leg up on catching the culprit." With that parting shot, Rabbit was out of the office and headed for his car.

Moorehead's secretary hadn't softened her demeanor overnight; her greeting to Mr. Skinner had all the softness of a hungry tiger gnawing on an old bone. "I've told Mr. Moorehead I would send you in as soon as you arrived. He's been in for fifteen minutes, you could have come sooner."

Skinner hardly looked in her direction as he passed her desk, he had had enough of her haughtiness to last him a lifetime. He strode forcibly toward the office door and silently turned the doorknob to the bank president's office. He was careful to ceremoniously close the door behind him, making sure the secretary heard the click of the latch going into its slot.

"Well, what's so all fired important that you had to see me the first thing this morning? I've got other important business, so make it fast." Moorehead was drumming his pencil on a scratch pad as he spoke.

"I want you to remember I tried to contact you last night, but you weren't in and your secretary failed to tell you I was in the office when you called."

"All right, you've made your point. What is it you have that I need to know?"

"I've discovered what I believe to be a three million dollar deficit in our books."

The expression on Moorehead's face was that of shock, "You've what? That's impossible. There is no way our books could be off three million dollars, I've personally reviewed those ledgers, just last week." The bank president dropped the pencil he had been tapping on the pad.

"The discrepancy didn't occur all at once. It took me some time to find how someone had attempted to cover up the fact that the money wasn't still in our vault. I've checked my figures, not once but several times and I'm sure they are correct. Since I couldn't contact you last night, I took it on myself to notify the state bank examiners." Moorehead's face suddenly went stark white and the sound exiting from his throat was something near a gagging cough. The reaction didn't slow Skinner, he didn't miss a beat, "As you well know, if they aren't made aware of such a major discrepancy immediately, they could close the bank and order a federal audit. Something of that magnitude could cause a run on the bank which wouldn't be good if our customers thought we didn't have the funds to cover their accounts."

Moorehead's usual flushed color didn't return and he was having difficulty breathing. Finally, after several more coughs, he said in a screaming voice that could be heard out on the street, "Skinner, if I had a gun in this desk you would be a dead man." Then in a somewhat quieter tone, actually more of a loud whisper, "Who do you think you are calling the bank examiners? Those books are in perfect balance and I don't need some thick glass, bifocal state snoops prying around in my bank."

It was only moments after the outburst when the office door burst open. The secretary almost sprang into the room, being closely followed by a security guard. Several other bank employees were gathering in the outer office, wondering about the cause of the scream. The look of despair on the secretary's face was enough to make Skinner smile. At least her smug expression had been erased. She pleaded, "Do you need help, Mr. Moorehead?"

"I want this nincompoop thrown out of this office. In fact, Skinner, you are fired. Get out of my sight, I never want to see you again."

As the security guard started towards Skinner, he put his hand out to stop him. "Hold on there McCaulty, I'll leave on my own accord, but I don't think you had better fire me, Mr. Moorehead. Since I'm the one who called the bank examiners, I'm the one they will want to interrogate as well as you. I'm positive there is something wrong with our books and I plan to make sure I find out where the discrepancies lie and who made off with the missing money." With that, he was out the door before any of the group could put a hand on him. He did pause in front of the secretary long enough to offer her his handkerchief, he was sure she was going to need it from the way she was beginning to wail.

As Skinner proceeded through the foyer of the bank to his desk, stares of disbelief from his fellow employees greeted him. Several near his area tried to ask him what in the world was happening. He only looked at them with knowing eyes and busily went about gathering his papers. He certainly wasn't going to leave his findings and have them altered before the examiners arrived. It only took him minutes to complete his task. Here he was, going home for the day and the bank hadn't even opened for business yet.

The piercing ring of the telephone sounded twice before it was snatched from its cradle, "Rad Childers speaking, what can I do for you?"

"Detective, this is Glen, from the pool hall. I think we have something you might be interested in. I don't want to say anything over the phone. Where can we meet?"

"Are you at the pool hall now?"

"Yes sir, we are at the pool hall."

"In that case stay right there and either Detective Tankers or I will stop by within the hour. Maybe it will be both of us, but regardless stay put until one of us arrives. I'm hoping you really have something for us. Don't be calling us down there on something you've made up."

"No sir, we have something worthwhile or I wouldn't be calling you. We'll hang around for sure until you arrive. See you then."

Rad put the phone back on its cradle and looked at Rabbit. "Seems our informants might have something we can use. You heard me tell them one of us would be there within the hour."

"If it works out, why don't we both go? Those two seem to talk a lot better when both of us confront them. I'm hoping the Ford manager calls before long, then we can go by the Ford dealership on the way to Main Street." Rabbit's confident look attested to the fact he was satisfied with his plan. "In fact, I'll give him a call now and see what he has."

The voice of the Ford manager sounded confident as he said, "I was just about to call you, Detective, I've located that list for you. I thought there were twenty buyers on the list but there were only eighteen. I must have over estimated our sales program." A grunt followed the statement. "No wonder we canceled the promotion after only a few weeks."

"Great, we will be by in a matter of minutes to pick it up." Rabbit paused before hanging up, and then added, "Are all eighteen buyers residents of the city? If you could break down the list for us, it may help us in the long run. We are on our way."

Rabbit turned to Rad as he picked up his coat, "Our timing is good. Now we can get the list of people who put those expensive tires on their car and get on down to the pool hall before noon."

Rachel was busy at her typewriter when Captain Winston stuck his head around the edge of the door into her office. She had her back to the door, but sensed someone behind her and stopped typing immediately. Slowly she turned her chair and almost went nose to nose with Winston who had closed the distance to the desk and was leaning part way over its width. Her recoil was more from instinct rather than fright, but she was firm in her movement to open the space between them.

"I've just popped in to see if you've given any thought to my suggestion we spend more time together? We didn't have a chance to really discuss it yesterday. I'm free tonight if you are? When should I pick you up?" Captain Winston had leaned back from her desk, but he was still closer than she liked.

"For one thing, I'm not free tonight or any other night. I've tried to make it clear I have no interest in spending any time together with you. I recognize you as one of the senior officers in this police force, and I honor that. I will do everything required to support you in that position, but I don't intend to have any association with you that isn't strictly business." Rachel crossed her arms as if to present an additional barrier to back up her desk.

"Well young lady, you may regret that viewpoint one of these days. For your information, it's very possible I will be coming into a considerable amount of money in the near future. I could take you away from this drab town and let you see a bit of the high-life. Besides that, if the city councilman election goes as planned, I could be the chief and then you might see things differently." He was slowly moving towards the door as he spoke and stopped to rest his shoulder against the doorjamb before issuing his last comment about being chief.

"So you will know exactly how I feel, I like this drab town as you so put it, and I expect to stay here and raise a family. The part about you becoming chief, if that comes to pass, then you will have some extra duty. You will need to find someone else to take this secretary's spot. I wouldn't work for you if it was the last job in this town." She spun her chair around to face the typewriter, ending the conversation as far as she was concerned.

But, Captain Winston wasn't about to depart without getting in the last word. Looking back over his shoulder he said, "And just who do you think will help you raise a family, not that half brained detective who can't think his way through a simple murder. You would be smart to set your sights a little higher."

The dish holding her eraser hit the door jam just inches from where the captain's head had been. Considering it had been thrown from a backwards-sitting position, her marksmanship wasn't bad.

Luckily, the captain had made a rapid exit into the hall. He might be sarcastic, but he was smart enough not to linger any longer after his parting remark.

The patrol car was making good time after leaving the Ford agency as the detectives headed downtown towards the pool hall. As Rad paid attention to his driving, Rabbit was poring through the list of Ford buyers. "There are several names on here that I recognize. However, none of them seem to jump out as possible suspects. The pastor of the Methodist church, Reverend Stokes, is on it; Doctor Williams, who delivers most of the babies in this town is on it; the lawyer, Broadburn, with the office just down the street from headquarters is on it. There are several names I don't recognize but according to the Ford manager, none of them are out-of-towners. Here's Charles Worthington's name along with Jason Russell's, they are the last two names on the list. I think Worthington is one of the senior partners at the shoe factory, and Russell is president of the foundry. Really high muck-de-mucks."

Rad nodded, "Sounds like you have a who's who of this town on that list. Let's study it for the time being, then maybe someone we aren't familiar with will ring a bell. For sure, one of those people on that list owned the car that was at the scene in White Rock. Maybe they weren't there in person, but I'll bet they know who was. It's just going to take us longer than we would like to determine which one." Rad paused as he moved through traffic on Main Street. "Hey, there's an open spot right in front of the pool hall; we are in luck."

The Chief's ring finger and little finger supported the speaking tube portion of the phone while he cradled the hearing portion between his thumb and forefinger. This permitted him to move away from his desk at least as far as the phone cord would allow. One of these days he knew someone would build a phone where the talking and hearing parts were in one single instrument, but he guessed it would be a few years away. However, since this call was from Councilman Brenner, he moved back to his desk to make some notes. He always made notes when Councilman Brenner called; he might have to refer to them at a later date.

"I've heard a rumor about the bank I need to discuss with you. I'll be over this afternoon, I'll expect you to be there." The councilman's tone was more dictatorial than informative, a feature which was particularly antagonizing to the chief.

The chief shouted into his speaker, "I'll try to be available." Unfortunately, his parting comment went on deaf ears as the councilman had already hung up. One of these days he would get in the last word if it killed him.

The atmosphere hadn't changed any from their last visit to the pool hall. The smoke was heavier if anything, and the light fixtures were still barely cutting through the haze. It reminded them of being in a long, low misty tunnel where the light at the other end could barely be seen. As before, the two informers were all the way in the back, which in a way was good. It would make for a more private conversation; unfriendly ears wouldn't be able to listen in.

Glen and Norris moved forward to meet the two detectives, large smiles on their faces. This time was different from the last; they knew why they were being visited. Arrest wasn't a possibility, at least they hoped not.

"OK, what do you have for us? What's so confidential you couldn't say it over the phone?" Rad wasn't wasting any time in getting to the point.

"Well, one of our city's high-and-mighty was seen the other night on Fourth Street consorting with more than the ladies. He was observed in the company of two undesirables who have been involved in various shady deals in this town, as well as around the state. We understand they have hired out more than once for things well above your average misdemeanor." Glen seemed pleased with his answer.

"Who is this pillar of the community you are talking about?" Rad leaned close to Glen to make sure he heard every word.

"He's a big wig at the shoe factory, his name is Worthington. We've seen him up there before, but only with the ladies. Never seen him meeting with the likes of the two he was with. He didn't look comfortable talking with them."

"And, who were these two stalwarts, anybody we might know?" Rad eyed the two while pulling Norris closer even though Glen had been doing the talking. He wanted to make it clear he expected answers from both of them.

Rabbit moved in behind Norris when he heard the name Worthington. "Are you sure the man's name was Worthington, not someone who looked like him?"

Norris turned and said, "I'm sure it was him, we've seen him on several occasions when we were working part time at the shoe factory. That's been a few years ago now, but it was him for sure. I'll never forget his debonair personality. He sure had a way with the ladies."

"How long did he stay with the two undesirables? Did any of them have a car? If so, what kind was it? Did you see any of them leave? How many days ago was this meeting?" Both Rad and Rabbit were pressing with the questions now.

"Well first off, I think they had several drinks together. They must have been together for at least a couple of hours. Don't you think so, Norris?" Norris nodded in agreement. "Didn't get to see any cars, but Worthington owns a black Ford. Come to think of it, I recollect those two characters leaving in a black Ford. Isn't that what you saw, Norris?" Norris's head bobbed slightly. "It could have been Worthington's car, but I'm not sure." Glen was beginning to hedge a little on his answers, where at the outset he had sounded more positive.

"Look here my friends, we need firm answers from the two of you. You just might have to testify in court, and half answers won't get it done." Rabbit looked intently at both men before continuing. "At the beginning you were sure it was Worthington, now you are starting to be less positive with what you did and didn't see. Let's get this straight, was it Worthington, did you see the two associates leave in a black Ford, and did that car belong to Worthington?" Rad was holding Glen by the lapels of his coat, while Rabbit had Norris by the arm.

"Yes, to everything. It was Worthington for sure and the other two left in his black Ford." Glen pulled away from Rad before saying, "We have to live in this town and if word gets around we have ratted on people, our life span could be in jeopardy. If we have to appear in court, our worth to you will have ended." Glen's eyes were at their soulful best.

"Don't worry, I don't think you will have to testify in court, but your information better be right or I'll put your lives in jeopardy." Rad made his point by tapping his finger against Glen's chest.

"You don't have to worry about us, what we've told you is the truth." Glen was quick to say as he slowly tried to back away from the two detectives.

"You still haven't come up with any rumors flying around town about the murder in White Rock or the bank robbery. Now there has been another killing last night at the train station. Guy's name was Alvin, and he used to work at the bank. Some way, some how, there has to be news on the grapevine and we expect you to pass on to us what you hear. Otherwise some of your past misdeeds might come back to haunt you in the future." Rad and Rabbit started to leave but stopped when Norris stepped forward.

"Don't think we don't appreciate what you two detectives have done for us. You can count on us to get the latest gossip to you, especially about any killings. As we told you the last time you were here, the bank robbery is still a mystery to us. Those two out-of-towners who did the job are in your jail. And, as far as what's being said, it was a hired deal with no local talent involved."

"OK, we'll expect to hear from you soon. Remember, that was a local person who got knifed at the station, somebody should know something." They exchanged handshakes and started for the front of the room. Again, the other occupants made it a point to get out of their way. The two detectives departed the poolroom thankful to breathe in some fresh air.

The meeting wasn't an overly large gathering, but most everyone who had turned out could have a major impact on the forthcoming city council election. If a count had been made, the attendance wouldn't have numbered more than fifty. Captain Snyder sat at a table in front of the gathering flanked by three men. On his left was the foundry president, Jason Russell, and Charles Worthington from the shoe factory; to his right in the seat of honor was Coach Webb. In the audience were several pastors from various denominations, three ladies who represented the major women's clubs, the fire chief, the president of the allied merchants association, the chairman of the PTA, and others who were responsible for organizations that went to make up the voting public of Hill City. The managers or their representative of all three hospitals were also in the room. It was a well-rounded group who played a big part during city elections.

"I appreciate you coming to this meeting even though I know it has cut into your morning routines. Because of that I will be brief. I'm here to introduce Coach Webb. Now I know all of you know Coach Webb and what he has meant to the athletic program in our high school. You also know what a positive influence he has made on the youth of this city, and some of those youths include you who have grown-up during Coach's long and outstanding tenure. Well, now is the time to show what he has meant to this town, and how he can continue to be of benefit to this community. Coach has consented to run for the city councilman position presently being held by Councilman Brenner. In his modest way, he wasn't sure he would have the support to enter such a race. I assured him he would have and that's why you are here this morning to prove it to him."

One of the pastors in the back rose to his feet and said, "Coach, we need an honest upright person to help run the government in this city. We all feel you are the person for the job. If you will accept the nomination, we will do everything in our power to get you elected."

An attractive lady who was president of the Hill City Garden Club stood and said, "Coach, after my husband's untimely death, your influence on my two sons personally taught them the basic fundamentals which guided them into manhood. They are outstanding members of their communities today and I give you much of the credit for their success. We think you are the person to replace Councilman Brenner; please accept our support."

Almost everyone in the meeting had a short say pledging overall support for him if he would run for the office. Finally Captain Snyder stood and held up his hand to silence the group. "Maybe we should hear from Coach himself, otherwise we could be here for the rest of the day." His statement was met with a standing ovation with shouts of, "Coach, Coach, Coach."

Slowly the coach stood with his head slightly bent in an effort to shield his eyes, which had become misty from the warmth and emotion being showered on him. "The confidence and trust you have always placed in me has been the main reason my wife and I have decided to remain in Hill City for the rest of our years. You took us in those many decades ago and we became a part of you. It has been our pleasure to get to know the majority of you personally and to be able to count you as close friends. I have treasured my association with your children and their families. During my tenure as coach, we had some good years and a few bad ones, but we never had any when something wasn't gained by trying.

"What you are asking me to take on is far from what I think I'm capable of. But, if you want me on your city council, I will do everything in my power to give you an honest and faithful term. I will try to bring honor to the position; that's all I can promise."

The room exploded into a frenzy of noise. There were some catcalls and whistles, while others just applauded. Some came up and patted Coach on the back while others tried to shake his hand. Every person in the room wanted to let him know how much he was needed and wanted.

It took Captain Snyder several minutes to get some type of normalcy back into the room. Still holding up his hands for quiet, he said, "Now that we have our answer, we need to get down to business if we expect to get the word out by election time. I have already spoken to some of you who have volunteered to serve as committee chairmen. We will have some flyers by tomorrow and we can get those out immediately. The rest of our campaign strategy will be completed by tonight."

Worthington stood and motioned to Captain Snyder, "If you can get those flyers to Russell and me the first thing in the morning, we can get them out to our employees. Between us we have the largest work force in town. They can make a meaningful difference in getting support for the coach."

"Fine idea. Now before we leave here, does anyone have an idea for a slogan?"

A couple of voices made suggestions, but nothing anyone seemed to think was catchy enough to be worthy. Then the coach got up and said, "Why don't we just say, 'Isn't It Great to be Alive in Hill City, Today." There was no more discussion on that subject. The campaign was off and running.

The lunch menu at the White House Restaurant was mostly the same every day, with only slight variations, which were handled with a small insert marked, Specials. Actually, there was only one special today, a Hot Turkey Sandwich w/drink.

"I told the chief I would be meeting you for lunch, and he said he needed to see you and Rabbit this afternoon." Rachel moved closer to Rad since he held the only menu, or at least that was her excuse.

"I'm planning on stopping by anyway, although Rabbit may be tied up. The chief needs to be advised on what we know about the killing last night. Also, we may have a connection with the murder in White Rock. I think we have established who may own the car that departed the crime scene right after the shot was heard." Rad didn't mind the encroachment; he still remembered the warmth of her body from last night. It was something he could get used to. "By the way, does the chief know you were with me last night?"

The waiter arrived before she could answer and Rad quickly said, "We will both have the special with iced tea."

She waited for the waiter to leave and said, "Yes, he knew we were to be on the stakeout together. He just wanted to make sure I wasn't putting myself in harm's way, which is thoughtful of him. He did say he hadn't gotten the full story about the motorcycle accident and your reasons for wearing civilian clothes. I hope you can explain everything to him, you know how fussy he gets about the little things."

"Not to worry, I think I can convince him we are in the correct attire for the job we do. Also, that motorcycle accident was just that, an accident. The department has to accept an occasional bending of the equipment if we are to be effective in attempting to apprehend people who break the law."

Their food arrived which ended their conversation for the moment. As Rad finished the last of his iced tea, he said, "I will make sure you aren't put in harm's way again. It was stupid of me to have you down there at the station. It could have become dangerous and I certainly don't want anything to happen to you."

"You needed me because you didn't know what Alvin looked like. However, I enjoyed being a part of your work, we should do more of it." She slid closer to him and he met her halfway.

"Don't worry, we will have more time together, but it won't be on a stakeout. One of those new 'Talkies' is scheduled to be at the Academy this coming weekend, maybe you would like to see it?"

"That sounds good, I'll look forward to going with you."

As the two were walking out of the restaurant, they stopped to speak to Gus at the register. He was a friend from way back and it was nice to not only eat in his establishment, but to find out how things were going in his life. Their conversation was short, but to the point. They said their goodbyes and went out the door to the street.

They didn't linger long in front of the restaurant for Rachel was due back at work. Rad said he had to make a stop before he saw the chief and he also needed to get with Rabbit and see what he was up to.

Rachel gave him a brush on the cheek as she turned to leave. He watched her as she moved down the sidewalk, always a pleasant sight to see. She waved as she went around the corner towards Church Street.

Rabbit was extremely intent as he watched Jay Stevens make the two-wire connection on the bottom side of the telephone instrument. He then ran an additional wire to a small recording device and secured it to a receiving post. Pointing to the telephone and then the recorder, he said, "When a call comes in or goes out, the recording device will start when the hearing cone is taken off its hook. Of course, the recorder could be much further away from the telephone. It could be hidden someplace where the small recorder would be out of sight. That way, the person whose phone we are recording wouldn't know his conversations were being saved. One of these days it will take some legal action to do this sort of thing, but right now, there haven't been any complaints, probably because such a device has yet to be used extensively in criminal investigative work."

"We know a couple of prominent people own automobiles like the one involved in the White Rock murder. One belongs to a Mr. Charles Worthington; he is senior partner at the shoe factory. The other belongs to a Mr. Jason Russell who is the president of the foundry. To what extent either of these gentlemen is involved, we don't know. A device such as this recorder might be what we need to find out whether either one has any involvement at all. If we get you the opportunity, do you think you could attach a recorder to each of their phones?" Rabbit pointed to the set up in front of them.

"That might be difficult if you mean going inside their homes, which it would require. That's against the law even for you. Maybe I can find a way to hook up a recorder on the outside of the house. I've never attempted such a thing, always on the phone instrument only. But, if we could get to the telephone jacks outside the house, it should be pretty easy to make a connection and then run a wire to a recorder close by. Let me work on it for a day and I'll give you a call when I have something. I'm sure it will work; it's just that I've never tried it before. There is one slight problem; I currently have only one recording instrument. You need to pick which place we plan to bug first."

"You look at each location and pick the house you feel would be the easiest. After a couple of days if we don't get what we are looking for, we can set up on the other house. We need to find out as quickly as possible if one of these guys is in any way connected with the crime in White Rock. So, anything you can do will help our cause. I'll give you a call this evening. Do you think you will have something by then?" Rabbit was getting ready to depart as he spoke.

"Shouldn't be a problem if I can find my climbing irons. Used to work with them when I was with the phone company, always thought they would come in handy one of these days. Hope I haven't forgotten how to use them. I don't want to come sliding down a pole on my stomach."

105

"I'm sure you still have the ability to shimmy up a telephone pole without getting yourself hurt."

"I know they've got to be in here someplace." Jay was still fumbling in an old chest when Rabbit went out the door.

The chief was leaning back in his chair, feet up on the corner of his desk when Rad walked into his office. He waved a hand towards a chair in front of the desk and continued to rock slowly. "Well, I must admit you look nice in your suit and tie. Much neater than when you came out of the woods a few days back. Now tell me again why being attired in these clothes is to our advantage."

"Chief, there are several advantages these clothes give us. I'm not sure which reason is the more important, but for one, it gives us a chance to get close to people before they are aware we are cops. When we have to, we show our badges and attach them to our coats so people know we are the police. But for instance, we were approached by a man selling illegal whiskey the other day and were able to apprehend him before he could sell his evil brew to some unsuspecting people. Shortly after that episode we went to the pool hall to meet with our informants. We entered without alarming the locals, who previously would run out the door before we could make contact. And last, but not least, all the major detective squads in the big cities are in civilian clothes. It is the way of the future, just like two-way radios in our patrol cars."

"I must admit the two-way radios will give us something I've wanted for a long time. You finding a method for us to move forward with two-way communication is certainly a way of the future. So, I'll give you the benefit of the doubt and let you continue to do your job in civilian dress. You and Tankers will even get the allowance for clothing you normally get for your uniforms. Now, what about the motorcycle?"

"It was an accident, plain and simple. However, if we hadn't chased those bank robbers with the motorcycle, they would have gotten away scot-free. We would have apprehended them before they got into the woods if it wasn't for the accident. Rabbit and I were lucky we didn't get injured when the bike went sideways and through the fence. It was something beyond our control."

"OK, but don't do it again. I'll sign off on the accident, but our good councilman will put his two cents in and it won't be pretty. I will say I wish I could have seen his face when you went by his house so early in the morning and in civilian clothes. He didn't know what to think when he called me. I wish at the time I knew it was you two. Well, do you have anything else, and where is Tankers?"

"He has a meeting with Jay Stevens on a new device we want to try. I'll fill you in when we have it." Rad paused and adjusted himself in his seat; "I'll also have more about the stabbed man last night at the train station. I think it and the White Rock murder are tied together in some way. We now have a lead on the car that was seen leaving the murder scene after the shot was heard. Don't know if there is any involvement, but both Charles Worthington and Jason Russell own that kind of car. We have the tire imprints to prove it."

The chief's face showed surprise, "I know them both. They are pretty big men in this community so be careful on how you go about getting them involved in these crimes. As a matter of fact, Charles Worthington invited me for a drink at the club last night. He wanted to be sure we knew he supported our efforts. It was the first time he had ever voiced his opinion to me, but he sounded very sincere." The chief stood up as he finished. "Take care, Childers, we could be playing with some tough customers when all this comes together."

Rising and moving towards the door, Rad replied, "We'll be careful." He was ready to depart, but the chief had one last comment.

"By the way, how is your bathtub case going?" The Chief slapped his thigh, his laugh ringing from the walls. "Don't worry, I'll keep Winston off your back from now on," but he didn't stop laughing.

The call had been put through without using his secretary. Moorehead cupped his hand over the speaking tube and said, "This is Jack, we could be in some trouble if we don't act soon. I have bank examiners coming to look at my books. You know what that could mean?"

The individual at the other end of the line only grunted. After a pause he then added, "You had better take care of this or the entire scheme could go down the drain. It is more than just you and me involved, we have a third partner as you well know."

"I'm well aware of that. Do you want to give him a call, or do you want me to contact him?"

"Just hold off until we know more. No sense in getting him worried when we may not have a major problem. It was you who said there wasn't to be any problem with the money." A moment of silence again as before, "Now, you had better make that come true."

"All I'm saying is, we had better speed up our plans before the entire thing comes unglued. I'll do my part, I'm just warning you so you will know where we are. It was our plan to wait until after the city council election, now I'm not sure we can do that."

"Have you heard about Coach Webb entering the council race at the last minute?"

"No. When did that occur?" You could hear the surprise in Moorehead's voice.

"Just happened. Seems a large majority of the leaders in this town have asked him to run and he accepted. They have virtually every civic organization in town behind them. It includes ladies groups, churches, police and fire departments, and every school-going-child's parents through the PTA. He could be a formidable opponent even on such short notice. They have gotten their campaign in full swing in less than a day. You should hear about it before the day ends. It will certainly be in the evening newspaper for sure."

"OK, I'll see what I can do about holding off the examiners, a week could give us the time we need. I still have a few friends in Richmond who owe me a favor. Talk to you tomorrow." A click was heard and the phone went dead.

Rabbit was in the office when Rad returned from meeting the chief. "Where were you when I needed you? I had to take the chief on all by myself. However, I'm happy to report he is on our side. You won't have to pay for the motorcycle and we can wear our civilian clothing and be paid for it."

"That is good news. Now I have some for you. Jay will have the two-way radio setup ready this afternoon. He is also working on a device, which will record telephone conversations. He thinks it can be done without going inside where the phone is located. He's to let

108

us know something when we go over to have the radio installed." The ring of the phone stopped Rabbit in mid conversation.

Rad grabbed the instrument, "Rad Childers speaking."

A faint whisper answered, "This is Homer, I need to meet you at the Overlook Bar on the Heights as soon as possible." The line went dead.

Rad replaced the hearing cone to the base instrument and looked at Rabbit with a puzzling frown. "That was a very strange call."

"Who was it?" Rabbit queried.

"It was Homer, the bartender from the country club. I was barely able to hear him. He wants us to meet him on the Heights at some place called the Overlook Bar. Know it?"

"Yeah, I know the place. It's a small dive overlooking the river. Never did get the clientele they had hoped for. Seems only the usual riffraff frequent the place. Do you think he really has something for us?"

"He better have. I don't want to be going out on some wild goose chase this time of day. That two-way radio installation has priority for us this afternoon." Rad rose to leave.

"My sentiments exactly." Rabbit grabbed his jacket as they headed for the door.

CHAPTER SEVEN

The telephone rang before the two detectives could get to their office door. They both paused, "Guess we had better answer it, could be something from Jay, he may be ready for us." Rabbit was closer to the door so Rad reluctantly returned to the clanging instrument.

"Rad Childers speaking," after which he listened for the best part of thirty seconds. Finally he spoke, "Yes sir, we will wait here for you." Rad's tone was with a bit of reluctance as he beckoned Rabbit back into the room.

"Who was it?" Rabbit was still at the door, hesitant to return.

"It was the chief and he is on his way to see us. Said something important has come up. It may require one of us taking a short trip."

It was less than three minutes before the chief arrived. He was breathing hard and immediately sat in one of the chairs facing the detective's desks. "Here, Chief, have some water." Rabbit handed the chief a small glass filled to the brim.

After two sips the chief spoke, "Just got a call from the Star City Police Chief. He said they had picked up a drunk early this morning wandering around their train yards. The drunk wasn't a vagrant because he had a large sum of money in his wallet. He was mumbling about some incident, which sounded like it had occurred in our town, maybe last night. During further interrogation they claimed the drunk kept muttering something about, 'the guy should have gotten out of Hill City while he could. When he didn't, he

111

had it coming, he had it coming'." The chief added, "There is a statewide warrant out on this man for a felony he was involved in someplace in the Tidewater area. Since sobering up this morning, he has refused to say anything else. If what he claims has any truth, I thought we might want to talk to him before they called Norfolk."

"If he was picked up in their train yard, he probably arrived earlier this morning by train. If that is so, he might have departed our fair city on the 12:05. That was the last train out of this town headed their way. Don't know what drove him to get so walleyed drunk, maybe it was something he saw or was involved in. Wonder if he might know something about the stabbing?" Rad made a few notes as he spoke.

"It is always a possibility, Rad. We can pick him up if you think he might shed some light on our problem." The chief looked from one detective to the other waiting for a response. "They said they would release him to us and we could contact Norfolk after we finished with him."

"Chief, we were on the way to meet the bartender from the country club. He called us saying he had some information we could use. He might be ready to tell us who fired that shot into their barroom. If it's OK, Rabbit could go up to Star City and pick this guy up while I go over and meet with Homer." Rad looked at Rabbit to see whether he agreed with the plan.

"Suits me, Chief. I could get out of here on the 2:15; it will only take an hour to get there." Rabbit reached into his desk looking for a train schedule. "Then if I can catch the Pocahontas which departs Star City," he ran his finger down the page, "at 4:55. I could be back before six. Of course, I would have to make all the right connections."

"Get on your way. Take one of the patrol cars and leave it at the station so you will have transportation when you return. I'll call the Star City chief and have everything greased so you won't be held up when you pick up this guy. Maybe you can get a few words out of him during your trip back."

"I'm sure he will have a little something to say." Rabbit waved as he left the room.

The telephone in the Webb home rang softly several times before the instrument was lifted from its cradle, "Hello, this is Mrs. Webb."

"Mrs. Webb, this is Captain Snyder, could I please speak to Coach?"

"Certainly, just a minute." She handed the instrument to her husband saying Captain Snyder was on the line.

"Hello, Captain, what can I do for you?"

"Coach, I wanted you to know all our campaign actions have been put into motion. However, there is a town meeting set for tomorrow night. We've just learned we can get you on the agenda along with Brenner. There will be a few other candidates there who will be running for other city offices. The main thing for us is the councilman position and Brenner thought he would be the only speaker for this seat. Now we will have a chance to take him head-on." Captain Snyder was almost breathless with excitement. "This is a chance we didn't think we would be able to get and with the election only three days off we've got to strike fast."

"What do you want me to say? We really haven't worked out what politicians might call a platform." The coach sounded as if he wasn't sure he was ready for a full-fledged political showdown.

"I'm sure you can tell it like it is, just like you did at the meeting this morning. There will be questions, which will give you the opening to tell the people why we need the change. We all know Brenner has been ineffective and pompous. He claims to have done so much to improve the police force of our city, plus other city needs. To the contrary, he has done everything possible not to improve necessities required by a growing town. There will be enough people in the audience to make him eat his words. Those people who were there this morning will be in attendance to back up any position you take. You know why you were willing to run against a man who hasn't used his position to improve our town, then all you have to do is tell the voters your reasons. It should be enough to give you a large majority."

"Well, I said I would run, so I think I should be ready to handle this. Where will the town meeting be held and what will be the time?"

"In the Armory at seven o'clock. Several of us will meet you there at six-thirty. Coach, getting to participate in this meeting will give us more exposure than anything we had hoped for when we asked you to run for office."

"I'll see you there." Then in a very philosophical tone before he hung up the phone, he said, "I think I'll make myself a few notes between now and then."

The Overlook Bar's only redeeming feature was its view of the James River. The panoramic scene of the water glistening as it cascaded over the dam would have been spectacular. Unfortunately, it was barely visible through streaked windows, which appeared not to have been washed for weeks.

As Rad entered the low ceiling room, it looked like the place was empty. But, after peering into the gloom for a few seconds he was finally able to focus on two people near the end of the bar. One individual beckoned Rad over; it was Homer.

"Glad to see you, Detective. This is my friend Patty; she runs this place for the owner when he's away, and he's away most of the time. Would you like a drink?" Homer's lethargic grin attested to the fact he had had more than one. There was a half-filled bottle of beer and an empty shot glass in front of him.

The place had been so dark that Rad hadn't noticed the other person was a female until Homer introduced her. Not that it would have mattered because Patty wasn't as young as she would have liked to appear. It was evident she had been around the course a few times, and put away wet more than once. She was very well endowed in the upper body, no doubt her most redeeming feature. "No thanks, I came here to talk. What have you got for me?"

Homer slid off his bar stool and walked towards the windows; Rad followed. After they were out of ear shot of the bar, Homer turned, "No need to bring Patty into this, she doesn't know why I asked you to meet me here. I'm ready to tell you all I know about the shot being fired into the country club barroom the other day."

"And I'm ready to hear it." Rad was getting impatient and ready to get on with the business at hand. "I haven't got all day," he beckoned for Homer to continue.

"It was Mr. Moorehead, and Mr. Worthington sitting at the bar when the shot was fired. They tipped me to say they weren't there and made it clear to the club manager not to breathe a word either. However, something was funny about that entire scene. If anyone had really been trying to kill someone, they could have shot the person or persons without any trouble. I think the whole thing was staged to create a situation so someone could use the incident as an alibi."

"An alibi for what? And who else could be involved? Let's hear some reasoning or I may think you had something to do with the whole thing." Rad was becoming more impatient as the time went by.

"No sir, I'm not just making this up. For instance, Moorehead, the bank guy; Worthington, from the shoe factory; Russell, the foundry president; and your man Winston always met in the bar at least once a week. There were one or two others who would join them from time to time, but I'm not sure I know their names. They would all sit off in a corner with their heads together as if they were plotting something or the other. I can't prove anything, but I think the shot was fired only to throw someone off in case their plans were discovered."

"That's pretty far-fetched, Homer, even for a bartender. Who were these other two people you saw meeting with Moorehead and his crew?"

"Let me think and maybe I can come up with some names. Anyway, I think both Moorehead and Worthington knew the shot was coming. I recollect after going over and over it in my mind, that both men had ducked for some reason a fraction of a second or so before the shot hit the wall. I thought at first one of them had dropped something on the floor, but actually they knew to get down just in case." Homer was signaling for Patty to bring him another beer.

"Well, you certainly have placed a different slant on what happened than any I've heard before. However, it might be a good question to ask Moorehead and Worthington. I think I'll do just that the next time I see them."

"Gee, Detective, I wasn't expecting for you to go tell those two what I've been telling you. This was to be in the strictest confidence. I could lose my job if those two get upset with me." Homer's hands began to shake as he thought about the possible consequences.

"Don't worry, it isn't every day I get to see those two and as far as I'm concerned, your theory is pretty remote. It doesn't track even for them." Rad started for the door, then paused, "Did you ever know an Alvin who used to work at the bank?"

"No sir, that name doesn't ring a bell with me." Homer turned to take the beer from Patty who had come around the bar to place the glass of suds in Homer's shaking hand.

"Well, in case it does, give me a call. Somebody in this town has got to know him." Rad waved and started for the door of the bar. He was about to depart when Homer snapped his fingers.

"Now I remember. Those other two gentlemen are also members of the board of governors. One owns a beer distributorship down on Commerce Street. I think his name is Coleman or something like that. They call him Brad. The other one I believe is a lawyer. At least they call him Shyster for some reason. Don't rightly know his last name but I could find out at the club."

"You do that and let me know. It will give me a good idea of who Moorehead's buddies are. That could come in handy later on." With that, Rad turned and was out the door.

Councilman Brenner didn't wait for an invitation to sit, he just barged over and plopped into a chair in front of the chief's desk. "Are you aware there are rumors about money missing from the bank?"

"I'm aware there was money stolen from the bank a few days ago, but that money was recovered and returned to the bank. I personally placed it in the bank president's hands."

"You say you returned it, did anyone see you hand the money to the bank president?"

"What are you trying to say, Councilman? The stolen money was given back to the bank and we have the robbers in jail to prove it."

"I've come onto some very disturbing information a short while ago that leads me to believe either that money never got back into the bank, or there could be an additional amount of money missing from the bank. These are damaging statements about a bank president who has given his life to his institution. I want you to investigate and to inform me of what is going on. I want this man's name cleared of any wrongdoing or I will be going to the newspaper to give them what I believe to be the true story. It has been my contention all along that this police force doesn't know what is going on under its own nose."

The chief was almost out of his chair when he said through clinched teeth, "And I don't suppose you would be willing to share your disturbing information. You never have before, although you make a pretty front about your undying support for the police so they can provide the needed protection and safety for this town."

"Chief, it won't be long before you will be replaced. There are only three days left before I will be elected again. When that happens, you will be out of a job and Captain Winston will be taking your place. In the meantime, I expect you to follow my instructions and they are to find out who started these rumors about the bank and report your findings to me. Is that understood?"

"Mr. Councilman, I will meet the requirements of this office with or without your threats. In the meantime, I would suggest you leave this office while you are still able to walk. Otherwise, I can't be responsible for your safety."

"Let me tell you something, Chief," Brenner came to his feet. "There are some powerful people in this town who are ready to see you leave this office. Moorehead, Worthington, Russell, as well as myself, just to name a few. Your slap dash handling of this police force has been the laugh of the state."

The chief had both hands curled into fists and had risen from his chair. He cocked his head with a quizzical look in his eyes. "Your list of names is a bit odd to me. Captain Snyder only an hour ago told me both Worthington and Russell were at the meeting to support Coach Webb for your position on the city council."

"What?" Brenner seemed to fumble for his words.

"Yes, maybe you don't have the support you think you have."

"I don't believe you. Regardless, I won't tolerate any longer the insubordination you have exhibited." The councilman didn't wait for the chief to reply. His last comment was made as he passed through the office door and moved down the hallway towards the front door.

The Stevens place didn't look any neater when Rad entered through the raised door, "Jay, I had to come alone. Detective Tankers was sent on special duty to Star City to pick up a suspect to a stabbing we had the other evening. We don't know if he is the man we want, but he arrived up there under some very suspicious circumstances." Rad handed the keys of the patrol car to Jay. "How long will the installation take?"

"We should have it done in about thirty minutes. Can you wait?"

"Guess I will have to, unless I want to walk all the way back to headquarters. Maybe if I could help, we can finish sooner."

"Great, you can help me and we can get this job done in almost half the time. Anyway, if you have the time I've got something I want to show you. It could come in handy if the guy Detective Tankers is bringing back seems not to have his facts straight. Also, I hope he told you about the recording device."

"Yes, he did. We can certainly use something of that capability."

"Well, you can tell him I've worked out the problem of making a recording without entering the house. It can be set up in minutes so whenever you are ready, just let me know." All the while he was talking he was making the installation for the two-way radio. In fact, with Rad's help in holding the supports while Jay made them tight, he was through with the patrol car in less than twenty minutes.

"I went ahead and positioned the antenna on the water tower near the high school, like we talked about. That way this radio will work when you get the car back to headquarters. I also made sure the dispatcher had the rules on how everything operates at the base station. I have lined up equipment for at least two more cars, but we will need some money. The little you gave me has run out."

"Good, I'll get with Captain Snyder and get more money. He's supposed to be obtaining it from a special fund the chief has. I'll have it by tomorrow."

118

"If you still have the time, let me show you this machine I've been working on." Jay went to a table strewn with straps and wires. They were connected to a rather large box, which looked something like a typewriter. Instead of having a keyboard, there were three long thin pens, which inscribed ink onto a long paper roll.

"This is some weird looking machine, Jay. What does it do?" Rad walked slowly around the table as he spoke.

"Here, sit down and let me put these straps around your chest and arm. You can sit in this chair next to the machine." Jay made the connections while Rad looked somewhat perplexed.

"Are you sure you know what you are doing. This thing looks like a small electric chair." Jay only smiled at the detective.

"I'm going to ask you some questions, I want you to answer all the questions with a yes answer regardless if it is true or not. Ready?" Rad nodded.

"Is your name Rad Childers?"

"Yes," Rad watched as the thin pens made little marks on the roller page.

"Is your partner's name Tankers?"

"Yes," and again the pens only made little marks as the paper rolled on.

"Are you the chief of police?"

"Yes," Rad's eyes widened as the thin pens went into a frenzied dance making big marks on the sheet of paper.

"Did you rob the bank a few days ago?"

"Yes," and again the pens danced their wild dance.

"Do you have strong feelings for the chief's secretary?"

Rad was quick with a "No." The pens hesitated then went into a flurry of large swings.

Jay couldn't hide the smile that spread across his face. "Appears as if someone is trying to beat the system, Detective. I think the machine may know more about your feelings for the chief's secretary than you do."

"Get me out of this contraption before I find out more about myself than I want to know." Rad's smile was more quizzical than Jay's for a lot different reason.

"If the man Detective Tankers is bringing back will agree to answering some questions, you may want to try him out on this machine. I believe it can tell if a person is telling the truth. I'm planning to call it, a lie detector. I think the overall results have about a 90 percent probability of being correct, although I haven't really completed my testing yet. The more people I can get to test, the better my percentage of correctness will be."

"Jay, you are amazing. What will you come up with next?"

"I may have a few more projects which could be of benefit to your work, but I think the ones I have shown you will have to suffice for now. I need to perfect what I have, then I'll branch out on additional experiments."

"As soon as Detective Tankers returns, I will tell him about this machine you have which can tell if a person is telling the truth or not. Of course, I won't admit it is always correct, let's say maybe 99 percent of the time." Rad's smile attested to the fact he had a sense of humor.

"I will wait for your call about when and where you want someone's phone tapped. And, as soon as you get the additional money for me, I will purchase the equipment we need for two more patrol cars. Installation won't be a problem, you saw how easy this one went."

Rad waved to Jay and moved out to the patrol car. He started the car and let the engine warm up until the green light on the radio control panel became steady. He flipped the switches and picked up the mike. "Base, this is Det 1. How do you read?"

Only static came over the receiver in the patrol car. "Base, this is Det 1. How do you read?" Again, no clear reply was received.

Rad put the brake on and motioned for Jay to come over to the car. "All I get is static. Have I pushed the wrong button?"

Jay bent down so he could get a good look at the receiver box. "Call the Base again." Rad made the call and when the static started, Jay made a slight adjustment to the back of the box.

"Roger, Det 1, I read you. How do you read me?"

"Loud and clear now. Please inform the Chief my ETA to headquarters is twenty minutes."

"Roger, Det 1. We have a message from the Chief saying he wants to see you as soon as you return to Base."

"Roger, tell him I'm on my way. Det 1 out."

Jay stood by the window of the patrol car and looked in at Rad. "I'll make a note to ensure I won't make that mistake again. The receiver frequency was set off a notch. Should be OK now. See you later."

There was hardly any activity at the train station when Rabbit and his prisoner departed the train. Little notice was taken of a man in handcuffs, particularly since the sleeves of his coat covered most of the hardware. The short walk to the patrol car didn't raise anyone's curiosity even though Rabbit was forcibly guiding the man by his arm. Rabbit was glad to get Allen Jenkins, the suspect, secluded in the vehicle without any trouble.

"You didn't have much to say during our train ride back to Hill City. Maybe now that we are alone in the car, you have something you want to tell me." Rabbit turned to look directly at the prisoner before he started the car.

"I don't know why you have me in handcuffs? I haven't done anything to be locked up for. I was a little drunk in the Star City when the police found me in the train yard. I had been sleeping there and they thought I had just come in by train. Why would you want to bring me back to this little one-horse town?"

"Well it seems someone saw you here in the train station last night. The money you had in your possession wasn't what a bum might have on him when he elected to sleep in a train yard. The thinking is you might have had something to do with a stabbing we had here and that you had been paid to silence a man named Alvin. Got anything to say about that?"

"I don't know what you are talking about and I refuse to say anything about anything until I've talked to a lawyer." Allen turned his head and looked out the window of the car, refusing to look in Rabbit's direction.

Rabbit put the car in gear and pulled out of the station parking lot without another word. He was well up Ninth Street before speaking, "Suits me my friend. Just sit still and enjoy the ride. We are on our way to this one-horse town's jail. It has needed some renovation for years but we are having trouble getting any money from the city council. Maybe after you spend a little time down there, you can give us some suggestions. Seems the rats have almost taken over the place, but don't worry about them, most are friendly. After you see the accommodations you might want to give talking to us a second thought."

Allen didn't comment, but he did turn to give Rabbit a long questioning look.

Rad had barely parked the patrol car and was in the process of opening his side door when Rachel jumped into the front seat. She was almost breathless but blurted out, "Before you see the chief, you have to listen to me."

"What are you talking about? I got a call on the two-way radio just before I left Jay's place that the chief wanted to see me as soon as I got here. Has something happened between then and now?"

"Not that I know of, but you need to know what transpired between the chief and Councilman Brenner before you talk to the chief."

"And pray tell, what did happen between the chief and the councilman? Did they get into a fistfight or something? I wouldn't be surprised the way those two get along."

"Well, the chief might have throttled him, but the councilman was at least smart enough to leave the office before the chief got around his desk to get a hand on him. I was afraid I was going to have to call the duty sergeant to break up a mauling."

"What in the world would cause such a ruckus?" Rad settled back in his seat since he was sure the story wasn't going to be short.

"The councilman came over and almost accused the chief of not returning the stolen money to the bank. He said there was money missing from the bank and he wanted to know why. If the chief didn't find the problem he would be turning his suspicions over to the newspapers. He also added that the chief was lacking in his position and that he wouldn't have a job when the election was over. That's when the chief literally chased him out of the office."

"Maybe that is why the chief wants to see me. I'd better get in there and see what's going on. For sure, there is never a dull moment, at least not until the election is over. Do you know if Rabbit has returned from the Star City? He should have returned by now."

"Yes, he brought in a prisoner not more than fifteen minutes ago. He is probably in the interrogation room with him right now."

Rad casually put his hand on Rachel's knee and turned towards her, "Are we still on for the talkie this Saturday?" Rachel nodded as Rad continued without a pause, "I'm looking forward to it, and I hope you are?"

"I am. Now we better get inside before someone thinks we are doing more than talking out here in the parking area." She had placed her hand on top of his and wasn't in any hurry to move regardless of her words to the contrary.

The long moment was broken when Rad reluctantly turned abruptly and opened his door. He hadn't noticed Rachel starting to lean her head in his direction with her eyes closed.

Rabbit had just pulled his chair back on the opposite side of the table from Allen when Rad came through the door. "Well, I see your trip was successful. Gotten any good words out of him yet?"

"Not yet. He seems to think we have been mistaken by bringing him here from Star City. Says he doesn't have any idea why we want to talk to him. But when he finally understands that he can be tried for murder and put away for life, he may be willing to come clean. However, there may be an out for him." Rabbit leaned back in the chair as he spoke.

Rad rested his shoulder against the door jam and looked directly at Allen saying, "Yeah, all he has to do is remember who gave him all that money he had on him when they found him and the purpose behind it. He could maybe get off scot-free."

Allen stared unblinkingly at Rad without a response.

"Can you stay for a while or are you just passing through?"

"Can't stay. I was just looking in on my way to see the chief. Seems he and the councilman had a bit of a run-in and he wants to tell me about it. All I can say to you is, unless he starts talking soon, why don't you just lock him up and forget where you put the key.

No one except the people from Star City know he's here and they aren't real interested in his whereabouts now that they signed him over to you. He'll enjoy those cool cells we have, and since they are in the basement, he won't be bothered, except by the rats. I'm told they have taken over that area now since we don't put very many prisoners down there anymore. They will be good company for each other."

"I told him about the rats; it didn't seem to bother him none." Rabbit's smile was more than sinister. All the while this conversation was going on, Allen's head was going back and forth from one to the other. It looked like he was watching a tennis match. However, when the word rats came up, his eyes brightened and he raised his hand.

"You have something you want to say?" Rabbit turned to look directly at the prisoner.

"You can't put me down with no rats, and what's this about getting off scot-free?" Sweat was beginning to pop out on Allen's brow and his hands shook when he tried to lace his fingers together.

"I'd better get in to see the chief and leave you two to hash out what really happened the other night in the train station. Let me know what your friend here has to say. I'm sure it will be interesting." With that Rad was out the door while Rabbit busied himself with some papers on the table. He let Allen stew in the silence of the moment.

Only the ticking of the large clock on the wall broke the silence in the room. After what seemed like five minutes to Allen, Rabbit lifted his eyes and said, "You know you don't really want to be the only one who takes the entire weight on your shoulders for what happened the other evening. If you make a clean breast of it, we will help you all we can. To us, you are as much of a victim as the man left on the ground when the train pulled out of the station. I'm going to let you think about this entire situation overnight and then Detective Childers and I will be back in the morning to see how you feel about cooperating. A night in our lock-up may do wonders for you."

"Now wait a minute. If I talk to you, I'm going to need protection. These people play for keeps." Allen lowered his head into his hands and slowly rocked back and forth.

Rabbit opened the interrogation room door and yelled out, "Jailer, put this low life away for the night. We'll be talking to him in the morning."

"You can't put me down in that cell…" Rabbit didn't hear the last of it as he closed the door on Allen's ranting. He smiled and nodded to the jailer as he went into the room.

The chief was busy at his desk when Rad entered his office. He hadn't stopped at Rachel's desk; he only nodded in her direction as he passed her position. She hardly looked up at him other than to wave her hand towards the chief's door. To a bystander it was a very cool exchange between the two; what they wouldn't have noticed was the wink Rad gave her as he entered the outer office.

"Well, from the message I received from the dispatcher, we now have two-way communication between at least two patrol cars and headquarters." A slight smile crossed the chief's face as he nodded his head in the affirmative.

"Yes sir, and as soon as we have the money, we can add two more. Jay is ready to purchase the equipment he needs and I don't want him to feel we can't keep him busy. Do you think the money will be available soon?"

"I've told Captain Snyder to get the money from Captain Winston, it should be in his hands by tomorrow. However, that isn't the reason I wanted to see you. Councilman Brenner came over here today and almost accused me of not returning the stolen bank money we recovered from those two bank robbers. He said he believed there was money missing from the bank and that the police department better find out what was going on. I don't know anything about other money the bank may have lost, but I do know I personally gave the robbery money back to Moorehead. Also, his secretary was a witness. I want you and Tankers to sniff around and see if the bank has a problem we don't know about."

"Sure, Chief. You are aware we now have two murders we are trying to deal with. I'm sure we can take on missing money without much of a problem."

The chief seemed to brush Rad's comment off with a wave of his hand. "Did Tankers get back from Star City yet?"

125

"Yes sir, he has the prisoner in the interrogation room as we speak, and was beginning to question him. I don't think he got much out of him on the train trip back, but we mentioned something about putting him in one of the basement cells, which piqued his attention."

"OK, you keep me informed. I'll contact you when I get the money from Snyder so you can pass it on to Jay. In the meantime, you can use my patrol car with the two-way radio. That way I will be able to keep in touch with you. The second one we can have on patrol."

Rad started to the door but stopped and said, "I did see a very intriguing piece of equipment at Jay's when I went to pick up our second patrol car. It can tell whether a man is telling the truth or not. It's something that could come in very handy in our business. Maybe when you have the time I can get Jay to give you a demonstration."

"Sounds promising, but it probably won't ever replace the rubber hose. Ha!"

"Good night, Chief. It's after hours so I will be taking your secretary with me." Rad didn't wait for an answer as he all but scooped Rachel up as they hurried out of the office.

CHAPTER EIGHT

It was the very beginning of the business day when Captain Winston and Jack Moorehead sauntered into Rachel's office as if they were on a casual visit. They were smiling and chatting to themselves, seemingly without a care in the world.

Rachel's surprise showed on her face as she quickly looked at her calendar, "I didn't have either of you on my calendar to see the chief; did I miss something?"

"No my dear, not at all." Captain Winston was attempting to use all his charm, but he really wasn't getting any place with it. "I know the chief won't be in until later and the bank president and I would like to use his office for a few minutes. Would that be all right with you?"

"It's unusual, but fine with me. Just give me a minute to get some papers off his desk so they won't be in your way. Can I get you gentlemen anything? Coffee maybe?"

"No, no we'll be fine. We just need a little more privacy than my office offers. We shouldn't be long." They both stood in the office doorway as Rachel gathered up the loose papers and straightened up the area. While doing so, she deftly flipped the intercom key on the Chief's desk to its 'On' position.

"All ready, gentlemen." Rachel gave them a small smile and started for the door.

127

However, true to his nature, Captain Winston made it difficult for her to get out of the room. By using more than his half of the doorway, he put the squeeze on her as she exited the room.

She had to turn sideways which caused her to almost brush her breast across Winston's chest. He smiled, or was it a leer, as he looked down. She closed the door firmly without looking back.

She immediately went to her desk and adjusted the volume on her intercom box. Low voices could be heard, but for the moment they were too far away to be clearly understood. Finally she heard Moorehead's voice say, "My chief clerk thinks he found an error in the bank's books amounting to approximately three million dollars, either missing or unaccounted for. He took it upon himself to notify the bank examiners before contacting me. Now, they will be here the first part of next week. I tried to stop them but didn't have any luck with my contacts in Richmond."

"Oh boy. How many people know about this?" Winston's voice was almost a whisper as if he didn't even want Moorehead to hear him.

"Virtually most of the bank people and, of course, my secretary. This time she protected me too well. This idiot had come into my office the night before he called the examiners to tell me of the supposed error he had found. But she wouldn't put him on the line when I called in so he proceeded on his own." The despair in his voice suggested a hangdog look.

"We need to pass this on to our friend. We can't keep it to ourselves." From his tone, Captain Winston's mind was going at double time.

"You are the first one I have told, other than those I mentioned. But I agree, we had better pass the information before too much time passes. Maybe we need a new timetable on moving out of this place before news gets out to everyone. The money is safe for now, but after the examiners get here, all hell could break loose. The situation is getting too hot for me. I'm not sure how much of this I can take."

"Come on Moorehead, don't get squeamish on us now. We've spent too much time working this out. I agree; we might need to alter our timetable and move on earlier than planned. I had hoped we could wait until after the election, you never know, I could be the new chief of police if Brenner wins again. Then we would be home free." Captain Winston's tone was getting more resolved as he spoke. "Speaking of money, you know the money from the chief's special fund I used to help plan our departure? Well, I need it back immediately. Seems the chief wants to spend it on radios or some far-fetched idea and I can't stall him any longer. Can you make sure I have the proper amount on his bank book before noon today?"

"I'll handle that, don't worry, you'll have the money in his account by this afternoon. But, I'm concerned about the councilman winning the election over the coach. If it were to happen it would remedy a lot of things for us. But Brenner isn't a shoo-in as far as I'm concerned. The coach will be a formidable opponent. Also, did you know our partner was one of the prominent individuals at the kickoff meeting to support the coach's election?"

"No, I certainly didn't. Who told you that?"

"The chief himself, right here in this office. What do you think is going on?" Moorehead sounded confused.

"There must be a logical answer to that. I'll make contact and find out. In the meantime let's do this; the bank examiners won't be here until just after the election. If we hang on until then, we may have a chance to see this thing through. We could then depart as we originally planned." The volume was getting weaker by the minute. Rachel had her volume wide open and her ear close to the box, but the last thing she heard before the machine went dead was, "You contact…"

Rachel wasn't sure what had caused the malfunction. Maybe they saw the open switch and turned down the volume or clicked the machine off. Maybe they realized someone, mainly her, could have been overhearing their conversation. Maybe the machine went dead on its own, it had never worked very well from the day it was installed. However, she wasn't taking a chance on the latter; she didn't want to be at her desk when they came out of the chief's office. She immediately departed for the ladies room, but not before closing the switch on her desk.

Rad and Rabbit were already in the interrogation room when the jailer brought Allen in from his basement cell. They looked in amazement for they hardly recognized him as the defiant man they had seen the day before. He was cringing by the side of the jailer, haggard, and white as a sheet.

"Sit here, Allen; you look like you've seen a ghost." Rabbit pulled the chair out for him and helped him ease into the seat.

Grabbing the jailer by the arm before he could leave the room, Rad whispered, "What on earth happened to him since we saw him last?"

"I don't think he liked the accommodations. He yelled and screamed all night. Luckily we didn't have any other prisoners down there with him or we could have had a problem. I'm out of here and glad to have him off my hands for a while."

They let Allen sit quietly for a few minutes before asking him if he wanted coffee. He only shook his head from side to side in the negative and stared at the corner of the room. A full five minutes must have gone by before he suddenly looked up, "I can't stand another night in that basement. Rats were all over my cell and if I hadn't been able to climb up on the top bunk, they would have been all over me. I didn't get a minute of sleep; I wasn't about to close my eyes with those vermin all over the place. I'm not going back down there again; I had rather die first. Please help me, please."

"We need some cooperation out of you, Allen. We want to know what happened the other night at the train station and if you had anything to do with it. If it wasn't your total doing, who else had a hand in it? If you answer some questions, we may be able to make things go easier for you. That's what we told you last night and we will standby it now."

"I don't know what happened at the train station. I wasn't there when the man was stabbed."

"If you weren't there, then how did you know a man was stabbed?"

"Ah, that's what they told me in Star City, I think. Listen, I will cooperate in anyway I can if you won't put me back down in that basement. I'm innocent. I was just passing through this lousy town."

"OK my friend, if you want to cooperate, how would you like to take a lie detector test?"

"What kind of test is that?"

"It's a device we have which will check out the answers you give us. There are a few wires we attach to your body, nothing to hurt you in any way. You might get a kick out of it plus it will only take thirty minutes or so. If you are innocent as you say, this machine will confirm it beyond a shadow of a doubt."

Allen looked at both officers for a long moment before he nodded his head. "I'll take your test if I don't have to go back to one of those basement cells."

"You've got your wish. We will see you as soon as we can setup the machine. And, you won't be in the basement any longer. In the meantime, think seriously about the answers you plan to give. If we catch you lying, not only will you be back in the basement, but you can be sure you will be there for a long time. We think you know more than you were just passing through town. So make sure you want that to be your answer. Remember, this machine can catch you in a lie." Rad and Rabbit smiled as they called the jailer and told him to put Allen in one of the upper cells.

One couldn't be sure whose look showed the most relief, the jailer or Allen. For sure, the jailer wouldn't have to put up with Allen's ranting and raving; maybe he was the happier one.

Captain Snyder was waiting in the outer office when the chief returned. He hadn't minded the wait since his conversation with Rachel had been very pleasant. Even though he was married with three kids, she was still a pleasing person to talk with.

"Chief, have you gotten the additional money for the new radios? I was told by Childers that Jay was ready to go to work on the additional cars when we could get the money to him."

"Winston is supposed to be getting it for me as we speak. There was something about the bankbook for the fund being in a safe-deposit box. Don't know what he was talking about, but I told him to get it to me today. If it isn't here, I may need to get you more involved."

"Fine with me. I'll check back later today."

Captain Winston looked at the instrument in his hand as if it were going to bite him. Finally he placed it to his ear again and continued. "What I've just told you is sad but true. However, I don't think we have to panic, but we may need to alter our plans if things go completely haywire. Another thing, Moorehead is getting nervous and his color doesn't look good to me."

"You aren't a doctor, are you? So what does Moorehead's condition have to do with anything?"

"For one thing, he was told by the chief that you were at the kickoff meeting for the coach. What is that all about?"

"Don't worry about my actions. It could be a good thing to be in the enemy's camp. That way we will have first hand information Brenner may be able to use."

"OK, but all I'm saying is, with the screws being tightened down, Moorehead could go and lose it all. And he has the money put away some place and we don't know where that place is." Winston didn't raise his voice but he was talking distinctly to make his point.

"Don't worry about it, I will take charge of the money. I will get it from Moorehead for safekeeping. What with the bank examiners coming, it will be better located so we can get our hands on it quickly."

"Do you think the three of us should get together to alter our plans?"

The voice on the other end of the line grunted in what sounded like a loud cough. "No, by no means should we be seen as a group anytime soon. That fiasco at the club the other day was bad enough. We'll stay calm and see what happens with the election and the bank examiners. When the time comes to move out, I will give the go sign."

The phone had been dead in Winston's hand for a few seconds before he realized the conversation had ended. He sadly shook his head and slowly placed his hearing piece back on its cradle. He walked out of his office, head down, and brow furrowed.

There weren't many times when the chief closed his office door to have a private phone conversation, but this time it didn't really matter because the chief's voice was in high pitch. The phone instrument he held in his hand could have been discarded. He could have stuck his head out the window and gotten his message to the jail.

"What do you mean they are being released? Who is he to be dropping charges?" The chief's face was beet red as the veins in his neck almost stretched to the bursting point.

"Mr. Moorehead claims he is the one who had them put here because they were supposed to have robbed his bank. He is now claiming he can release them since he isn't sure of their guilt. So he says he is dropping charges." The jailer's voice was literally pleading since he was virtually stuck between his boss and an irate bank president who was pounding on his desk as he and the chief spoke. "Also, Councilman Brenner is here supporting Mr. Moorehead's point. He claims he is within his rights. The councilman said we work for him and if I expected to have a job next week, I had better open the cell. I don't think I had any other choice."

"Put Moorehead on the line." The pause gave the chief a moment to sit down which helped his blood pressure drop back to a reasonable level. The sound of Moorehead's voice brought him back to his feet, "What do you think you are doing by going over to my jail and demanding the release of my prisoners?"

"The councilman says I am within my rights. He says if a citizen can make a public arrest, he should be able to make a public release. Captain Winston told me earlier he's not sure these were the men who came out of the woods with the money. Therefore, I feel they have been falsely accused and I demand their release."

"The councilman or Winston don't have any idea what they are talking about. Winston wasn't even at the scene when we arrested those two. I'm getting in touch with the district attorney so you had better wait for me there at the jail." The chief's veins were back at full stretch.

"You're too late, Stoddard. These two men are walking out of this building as we speak. Plus, there is a car waiting for them at the curb. Your call to the DA is too late."

"Well, I will tell you something, Moorehead; if I can't find those two when I want them, I will be putting you and the councilman in jail in their place. You may run that bank of yours, but you certainly don't run this police department and neither does your sidekick

133

Brenner, regardless of what he may think. As for Winston, I will tell him who releases prisoners in this police department. Put the jailer on the phone." There was a pause as the phone changed hands.

"Smitty speaking, sir." The jailer's voice wasn't all that steady.

"What the devil is going on, Smith? These men shouldn't have been released; we caught them red-handed with the money. Who signed the release?"

"The councilman and Captain Winston. I had no choice but to let them go."

"Where are they now? Is Winston still there?" The chief's voice was rising again.

"No sir, he left with the councilman. Only Mr. Moorehead stayed around to talk to you, and he is going out the door right now.

Rad was on the phone when Rabbit come back from lunch. Rad held up his hand and motioned for Rabbit to pick up the adjacent instrument. "What I'm telling you detective is that the man stabbed at the train station had a brother who used to be a bodyguard for Worthington. You know, the shoe factory guy. I'm told both of the brothers had been seen driving around town in a late model Ford."

"Do you know who owns that car? Could it perhaps have belonged to Worthington? According to the Ford dealer, he had purchased one from them not too long ago."

"Not sure, but I'm told the ex-bodyguard had the use of the car whenever he had some business. He worked a lot of different jobs, not all of which were legit."

"OK Glen, try to find out who that car belongs to and get back to Detective Tankers or me as soon as you can. The information you've given us is good so far, keep it up and things may turn out better for you and Norris. Hope to hear from you soon."

"We'll do the best we can." And Rad heard the phone click off.

Rad turned to Rabbit who had just laid a parcel on the desk, "Looks like we are finally getting something from those two deadbeats from the pool hall. What have you got there?"

"This is the lie-detector equipment I picked up from Jay. Let's get the jailer to bring Allen over. Then maybe we can tell fact from fiction when we talk to him."

"Did Jay tell you how to setup this rig? We don't want to get it all screwed up and not get any valid information."

Rabbit stroked his chin and then rubbed his hands together. He pulled the main box from the package and started to attach the needles into their slots. He gave Rad one of those long stares, which was meant to show complete control over all things. Then he smiled his friendly grin and produced a sheet of paper. "You don't think I would have come away without the directions, do you? Let's get Allen and see if this thing works."

"Fine with me, but we have to put Allen on hold. Rachel called just before you came in and said the chief needs to see us immediately."

Rad and Rabbit were waiting by Rachel's desk when the chief called out, "Detectives, please step in here a minute before things get too heated out there in the outer office. Please bring Rachel with you."

The chief waved for them to take a seat and said, "Rachel overheard some startling information earlier today. Rachel, tell them what you heard."

Rachel repeated almost verbatim the conversation she had heard between Captain Winston and Moorehead. In finishing she said, "If the darn box hadn't gone dead on me, I may have been able to hear who they wanted to call."

"It sounds like you took a big chance in your clandestine role. You could have been caught and gotten in a lot of trouble." Rad's voice was more sympathetic than it was scolding.

"That's what I told her." The chief slapped his hand on his desk and continued, "But it is important information. It certainly answers the question about money missing from the bank. And, it also tells us someone has a plan to abscond with it, mainly Captain Winston, Mr. Moorehead, and at least one unknown third party. We need to keep a close watch on the two knowns until we can find out who the mystery person is. Keep in mind, there is a possibility it could be more than one."

Rad jumped in, "It could be a handful of people who have been close with Moorehead. Or, it could be just one. I personally think it is either Worthington or Russell. They are too squeaky clean for me."

"Well, we have Jay ready to put a recording device on someone's phone. The problem is; he only has one device so it may take a bit of time to ensure the identity of our third party." Rabbit looked for a suggestion from the chief.

"I don't have either one of them as a suspect. Snyder told me they both were at the rally for the coach. Someone is playing it cool. Pick one and we will see what we come up with." The chief then looked directly at Rad. "Do either of you," he nodded towards Rabbit, "plan on attending the debate tonight?"

"Which debate is that, Chief?"

"The political one, which will feature Brenner and Coach Webb. It's to be held at the Armory tonight at seven. We need to have a good representation there to support the coach. I'm hoping he cuts that phony politician to ribbons."

"I didn't know about it but I will be there for sure. I had other plans but they can be altered." Rad glanced over in Rachel's direction as he finished his statement.

Rabbit tried not to look at the chief.

Rachel's phone rang which broke the moment. She departed the office to answer it. Her expression was one of disappointment.

The chief came around his desk and confronted the two detectives, "Are you two getting any closer to solving these murders? I would like to wrap something up before too long."

"Yes sir, things are beginning to come together. We are about to put this guy Rabbit picked up in the Star City on that lie detector machine I've been telling you about. Should provide some insight to what went down at the train station the other night."

"We also plan to use Jay's recorder on one of our suspect's phone line. Should help us determine who is playing both ends of the game," Rabbit chimed in.

"OK, get on with it and I'll plan on seeing you two at the Armory tonight."

Rad closed the door to the chief's office as they departed; he needed a few private words with Rachel without the chief listening in. She accompanied him into the hallway after they passed through her office. Rabbit went on ahead.

After Rabbit passed out of earshot, Rachel's voice was matter-of-fact; "I was hoping we could have dinner at the White House tonight. But, when I heard the chief tell you he wanted you at the Armory, I knew that was out." She was smart enough to know police business took priority.

"Why don't you go with me to the Armory? We could catch a hotdog at the Texas Tavern and still make the debate. Afterwards we wouldn't be pressed for time and could have the rest of the evening together."

"Fine with me. I'll meet you at the Texas Tavern about six-thirty."

"Great, I've got to catch up with Rabbit so we can get on with our interrogation. He may have trouble with that newfangled machine."

"Oh, that was the other thing. The call I just received was from the jailer. He said you would have to wait until the first thing tomorrow morning to interrogate the prisoner. Seems he had to take him to see a doctor this afternoon. Something about a near nervous breakdown."

"I guess those rats last night must have almost driven him over the edge. Both he and the jailer didn't look too well when we saw them earlier. Let's hope he improves by morning or he will have more than a nervous breakdown. This is another setback on getting the information we need to solve these cases." He grabbed her hand and gave it a gentle squeeze. As he started towards his office he said, "See you at the Tavern around six-thirty."

Rabbit was sitting at the table with several of the connections to the lie detector attached to his body. The needles on the machine were still and the paper didn't have any marks on it.

"What are you trying to do? I don't think you can use this contraption on yourself even if you were to tell the truth."

"I was just trying to see if I could make the proper connections. Here, help me out of these wires." Rabbit had crossed a couple of wires but nothing that would harm the machine.

137

"Too bad we couldn't get Allen hooked up this afternoon. As soon as we find out the truth from him the further along we will be." Rad finished putting the connections for the machine back in their proper places.

"He had better be here in the morning, first thing. Under the conditions, maybe it is to our benefit to let him calm down. That way we should get better answers."

After they had setup the machine so it would be ready the first thing in the morning, Rad turned to Rabbit, "Are you going to make the debate tonight at the Armory? Coach Webb is going to need all the support he can get against Councilman Brenner. If Brenner gets re-elected we are in for some difficult times and it might even mean the chief's job."

"Gosh, Rad, I didn't say anything when the chief asked us if we would be there. But, I promised the wife I would be home early and I can't go back on my word. Think the chief will notice my absence?"

"No problem, go ahead and take off. I'll cover for you and see you here first thing tomorrow morning."

"Thanks, Rad. I'll do the same for you one of these days."

"If the chief asks where you are, I'll just tell him I don't know." Rad couldn't help from smiling as Rabbit started to turn back into the office, a look of despair on his face. "Don't worry, I was just kidding."

When Moorehead heard the voice on the other end of the line his heart rate went up several beats. "I think it best that I take care of the money. I can put it in a safe place where it can be gathered up quickly. Any problems with that?"

"No! When do you plan to pick it up? It will be ready tomorrow. I'll feel better to have it out of the bank, even though it's in a secure place."

The voice continued, "Another thing, get that assistant police chief and be at the debate tonight. We want Brenner to have as much support as possible. From what I hear, the coach won't know what to say when Brenner takes him on. If he does well against that amateur politician we could be home free. Otherwise, we could be in for a rough ride."

"Do you plan to attend?"

"I'll be there supporting all candidates, but don't even look at me. We've been seen together too many times already, no need to push our luck."

"OK, but it could seem odd to people when we don't even speak to each other. We've been friends for a long time." Moorehead's voice sounded a bit hurt.

"If it seems appropriate, speak but don't make like we are together. I'll talk to you tomorrow when I pick up the money. Goodbye!" The phone clicked dead in Moorehead's ear.

The Armory always seemed to have an empty and serene look to it, but tonight it was rippling with the anticipation of a knockdown, drag-out fight. A small stage had been located at the far end of the open arena. Chairs to accommodate several hundred people had been placed halfway down the vast expanse of the hardwood floor. The chairs were filling rapidly, and only standing room was going to be left. Luckily Rad and Rachel had gotten their hotdogs to go and had found two seats on the next to last row. It was going to be a sell-out crowd for sure.

There were a lot of separate conversations going on around the armory while the crowd waited for the activities to begin. Some were political in nature while others were just friends greeting friends they hadn't seen for a while. Also small groups in support of various candidates seem to be polarizing in sections of the seating area. These were mostly huddled together in what must be last minute strategy sessions.

Exactly at seven, Judge Sweeney, who would oversee the debates, came to the podium. Silence fell on the gathering. "Ladies and Gentlemen, tonight's debates will go in the order you see listed here on the stage. There will be a five-minute break between the various events so those of you who are interested can take care of any important business or calling. Our first group will be Councilman Brenner and Coach Webb who are both vying for one of the city council seats coming open at the end of this term. Each candidate will give opening remarks, which will then be followed by a question and answer period. Are there any questions?" The crowd remained silent. "All right then, Councilman Brenner, the podium is yours."

Brenner swaggered forward to the podium and pulled a small sheath of papers from his inside coat pocket. He took a moment to arrange them on the podium and then raised his head and said, "Fellow citizens of Hill City, I was shocked to learn that my position on the city council would be challenged after my outstanding tenure, but it has. While my opponent is a prominent member of this community, his background doesn't support the depth of knowledge needed in this demanding office. It has taken me the entire three years of my current term to establish the awareness required to meet the day-to-day duties. I'm sure you would be remiss to throw this experience away. Without my diligence, our fair city wouldn't be safe enough for women and children to walk the streets. And there is much more that needs to be done.

"I regret to say, by the hands of other people, money has been spent on frivolous items, which did not help the safety of this community. One, which I was vehemently opposed to dealt with a uniform issue for our police force. However, again, other members of the council overturned my disapproval. I am sure this time you will be voting the proper people into office with me. This will greatly aid me in keeping our budget in line during the next term.

"Part of these frivolous expenditures has involved motor vehicles." Brenner paused and shuffled the papers in front of him as if he had lost his place. "Uh, there also has been money spent on unauthorized communications without my approval. Some individuals belonging to the force run around this town on loud contraptions, seemingly on personal business, with no restrictions being applied by those in authority. These practices will be stopped.

"I am sure you are aware that in the past few weeks there have been two murders in our fair city. I'm appalled that our police department hasn't been able to solve either. This will end, I promise you, or we won't be safe in our own homes. I will institute a complete reorganization of this vital group from top to bottom.

"I will see to it that our city employees place the proper emphasis on support for our leading citizens. We recently had one of our major banks robbed in broad daylight on our very own Main Street. While it was rumored that the culprits were captured and the money was recovered, there is still some doubt about the facts of this case. I plan to get to the bottom of this and get the facts before further crimes impact our population.

"When I'm re-elected, I plan to have a more hands-on approach with our police department. I will move my office into police headquarters and provide day-to-day and hour-to-hour management suggestions to our law enforcement personnel." Several groans went up from the audience on this last statement. However, Brenner didn't falter in his delivery. "This should enable me to cut part of the overhead and provide for more responsive action on the part of our uniformed officers.

"So I say to you good people of Hill City, a vote for me is a vote for better protection at a cheaper price." Brenner stepped back from the podium and placed that insidious smile of his on his face as he looked out over the seated crowd. The applause was scattered at best. He quickly stepped back to the microphone and said, "If there are any questions I would be glad to take them now."

Judge Sweeney came forward as Brenner was about to call on a man who had raised his hand. "We will take questions after the next candidate speaks. Mr. Brenner, if you will take a seat, I will now call on Coach Webb to come forward." Immediately applause and cheering erupted from the crowd.

Coach Webb moved forward to the podium as if he were stalking an official who had just fouled out his star player. "Seems to me Mr. Brenner has just given you the definition of macro-management. To put it into more simple terms I can relate to, if the superintendent of schools Walt McNeil, or the principal of the high school Don Butler, had told me they would be putting out the line-up for each game I coached, it wouldn't have been acceptable to me. Even though they are both outstanding academicians, I don't feel we would have won three state championships and twelve district championships during my tenure as coach. Instead, they left that responsibility to me, a professional, a job I was paid to do. That is micro-management and it is what I intend to do if elected to the city council.

"There isn't any way I would like to leave the safety of our city in the hands of a non-professional. I'm positive Councilman Brenner means well, but I don't believe he is qualified to perform the functions he outlined earlier.

"If elected, I will provide the necessary support for the agencies under my authority and let the professionals do their jobs." Again cheers and clapping caused Coach to pause and hold up his hand for silence. "Bear with me for a few more seconds for what I have to say won't take long. All of our municipal agencies need renovating and only the police force has tried to move forward despite the interference encountered from Mr. Brenner. We need to modernize our fire trucks and street sweepers. We need to have two-way radios in all our patrol cars, not just one or two. We need better pay for our city employees who have been near the poverty line with their present wages. If Hill City is to take a prominent place in this state, then we had better have progressive government in place to get the job done. And I think I can help provide the direction needed."

The people were on their feet and it was difficult to say anything to the person in the next seat because of the reverberating noise in the armory. The outburst went on for a full three minutes before Judge Sweeney came to the podium and raised his hands for quiet. Even then, it took another minute or two to get the crowd under control. "Please, please, let me have your attention." He paused, looking out at the spots of continued clapping and slowly the audience responded to his wishes.

"We will now call the two candidates to the podium to field any questions." Judge Sweeney turned and watched as both Brenner and the Coach Webb moved forward. "I will point to the person desiring to ask a question, so don't blurt out before I indicate for you to speak. Also, when asking your question, speak loud and clear so the people in the arena can hear what you are saying. After the candidate has responded to the question, the other candidate, if desired, will have an opportunity for rebuttal." Looking at the crowd he pointed to a man in the second row.

"My question is for Councilman Brenner." The man smiled at Mr. Moorehead as he rose. He was an obvious plant from the bank. "Councilman, it would seem to me that what Coach Webb is advocating would cost this city more than we have in our coffers. What do you think?" As he sat back in his seat, the man threw another knowing glance at Mr. Moorehead.

Brenner smiled, knowing he was prepared for this question. "Well, I think you are exactly right. What the coach is recommending will cost this city more money than we have. Taxes will have to be raised and I think it will be the ruination of this town. My plan will put this town on a conservative program and you will see cost cutting that can only come from direct hands-on management. He talks about letting professionals do the job, why, he would be the most non-professional in the house."

"Your turn for a rebuttal, Coach."

"There is already money in our city government, which, if properly programmed, would more than pay for any improvements we plan in the future. I'm not talking about spending money head over heels. We need to formulate a positive plan with some solid direction to set the course for renovation. We haven't had such a blueprint in the past and if we don't put the proper people in charge, we won't have one in the future. I think a good question to ask would be. Where has the previous money already allocated for our city been used? It certainly hasn't been towards furthering the goals of this town. If I'm not mistaken, the chief of police has a special fund allocated for him to use when an unforeseen need or opportunity comes along. I'm told that in the past the chief has had great difficulty getting to that money." The low murmur in the audience sounded almost like the buzz of a swarm of bees.

Before Judge Sweeney could call for another question, Councilman Brenner jumped up to the podium. "If the coach is accusing me of having anything to do with money being withheld from authorized expenditures, he is greatly in error. I won't take these accusations without some retaliation." Brenner lunged for the coach. Judge Sweeney interceded.

"Hold it, hold it." The judge grabbed the councilman by both arms and physically moved him away from the coach. "Councilman Brenner, this isn't the time or place for this type of behavior." He then turned back to the audience.

"Ladies and gentlemen, this portion of the debate has ended. We will take a five-minute break, and continue with the other candidates." The judge slowly led Brenner to the corner of the stage where Captain Winston met him with a questioning look.

Winston led Brenner over to a corner of the arena, away from the main portion of the audience. When they were out of earshot, Winston first words were, "You must be out of your mind. This contest won't be decided on fisticuffs, you need to keep your composure. And to be perfectly frank, you wouldn't have lasted one round with the coach."

As Rad led Rachel out the door of the Armory, he commented, "Well, so much for public debates. Probably the best thing that ever happened for the councilman was that he didn't get to the coach. I'm afraid we would have had a very bent-up individual because Coach is no man to push around. I've seen him work out in the gym and he doesn't pull many punches."

"Yes, I'm sure the coach can hold his own, especially with someone like Brenner." Rachel held on to Rad as they moved through the doorway.

"Also, I thought it odd that Worthington; the senior partner at the shoe factory and Jason Russell, the foundry president weren't sitting together. Seemed to me Russell was avoiding Worthington on purpose, and I've heard they were supposed to be such great friends." Rad pointed in their direction as he spoke.

"Even Winston wasn't sitting with his country club crowd, but he was there to grab Brenner when he came down from the platform," Rachel chuckled.

"You are right, but what was really a surprise to me was when Worthington started over to where Russell was seated. Russell almost ran out the door before Worthington could get to him." Rad steered Rachel to avoid part of the departing crowd, "Who knows, maybe they are both on different agendas?"

Moorehead's phone was ringing as the night bank guard let him into his office. He reluctantly picked up the instrument knowing full well who was calling. "Hello!"

144

The voice on the other end was calm and calculating, "Well, with the performance we've just witnessed, we had better prepare other means if we expect Brenner to be elected. I've seen dumb acts before, but what the councilman did tonight takes the cake. The contingency plan we discussed earlier had better be put into effect. We can't take any chances."

"Don't worry, I've already talked to the people who need to know and they are ready to perform." Moorehead slowly sat back in his chair, feeling a void in the pit of his stomach that wasn't due to the lack of food.

"OK, make sure it happens," and the phone went dead.

CHAPTER NINE

It was only a few minutes past seven o'clock when Rad and Rabbit approached the interrogation room. The jailer, who looked like he had had a good night's sleep, was waiting with Allen outside the room.

"How is our prisoner's nervous condition today?" The question didn't seem to spark any particular interest from the jailer or Allen. "It's only going to take us a few minutes to have this lie detector ready to go, then we will start with the questioning."

The jailer removed the handcuffs from Allen's wrists and made sure he had him seated in the proper chair before he answered. "The doctor has given him a clean bill of health. However, I think the real reason for him being back to normal is that he didn't have to spend another night in that basement cell."

"You are probably right, but that is the promise we made and as long as Allen continues to cooperate, he won't have to go back down there." Rad turned and looked directly at Allen, "Are you ready to give us some truthful answers?"

Allen only nodded his head and continued to watch closely as Rabbit hooked up the lie detector leads to his body. It wasn't very noticeable, but there was a slight tremor in his body each time Rabbit attached a wire.

"Now, Allen, as we told you yesterday you won't feel any shock or sensation while the machine is running. You will only see the needles move on the paper scroll as it unwinds after each question.

147

As long as you are honest with your answers, the needles will move only slightly; it is when you don't tell the truth that you will see them dance all over the place."

There was a faint knock at the door. Rabbit went to it and was pleased to see Jay Stevens standing there. As he entered the room, he turned to Rad and said, "I thought it would be a good idea to have Jay here for our first run on this machine. He said he could make it when I went to pick up all the paraphernalia."

Rad nodded his approval and said, "Take a look, Jay, and see if we have this thing hooked up properly. If so, we are ready to go."

Jay quickly ran his fingers over the connections before he answered, "Everything looks good to me."

Rad seated himself opposite Allen so he could look directly at his face. He then pulled a pad of paper from his briefcase and said, "Now, Allen, I'm going to ask you some questions which I know to be true about you. It is information we have gathered from your arrest sheet and the record you've established during your association with other law enforcement agencies in this state. The questions are ones you will know to be true or false. I only want you to answer each question with a Yes or a No. Nothing else need be said, if you have further information you want to pass on, we will do it after we finish here. Understand?"

"Yes!" Allen's voice sounded a bit strained.

"Is your name, Allen Jenkins?"

"Yes." The needles only fluttered on the scroll of paper as it moved slightly.

"Were you born in Atlanta, Georgia?"

"Yes." Only faint movement again.

"Have you ever been arrested before?"

"Yes." Only faint movement.

"Have you ever served time before in prison?"

"Yes." Only faint movement.

"Have you ever been in Hill City before you were brought here the other day by Detective Tankers?"

"No." The needles on the paper danced wildly and their movement brought a startled look to Allen's eyes.

148

"I told you, Allen, if you don't answer me truthfully, we will see it immediately. Did you see how those needles shook when you answered No? That wasn't a truthful answer." Allen lowered his head but didn't choose to comment.

"Then you have been to Hill City before?"

There was a noticeable pause before Allen said "Yes." The needles only fluttered.

"See what happens when you tell us the truth?" Although calm in appearance, Rad was getting impatient with this slow process.

"Isn't it true you were in Hill City the night before you were brought back by Detective Tankers?" There was no answer from Allen.

"Were you at the train station that night?" No answer.

"Didn't you stab a man in the station before you departed for Star City?" No answer. Rad repeated the questions twice more before he slapped the table. "I want an answer, now."

"Yes, maybe, uh, I don't know, there were extenuating circumstances." Allen was screaming and lurching from side to side. "Get these things off me. I can't talk with all these wires hooked to me. Can't you just ask me questions without this machine?"

Jay went over to Rad and whispered in his ear, "You aren't going to get anywhere with these questions when he is frightened of the machine. You might as well unhook him and do some preliminary questioning in another room. Then tomorrow we can ease him back into this harness. The second time he should feel more comfortable being wired. If we take our time I'm sure we can catch him lying and he won't know he did."

Rad took a deep breath and leaned back. He nodded at Jay. "You're right. OK Rabbit, unhook him. We'll go into another room and continue this the old fashioned way. I'll be able to tell if he is lying to me by just looking into his eyes."

Jay motioned for Rad to stay behind as Rabbit led Allen out of the room. "Just a suggestion, but I believe it would be to our advantage to put the recording device behind the person being interrogated. That way if he tries to get away with a lie, he won't be aware we know better. We can then vary the questions to find out if he will tell us anything truthful. If we leave it in his line of sight, we really don't have any advantage over him. What do you think?"

"Sounds logical to me. Tomorrow we will relocate the recorder. I guess we have a lot to learn with these new devices. Of course, I could go back to our old devices like a rubber hose and thumb screws," Rad chuckled, then continued, "but we will continue to go with progress, thanks to you."

"If it wasn't for you and Detective Tankers, I wouldn't be able to get any of my ideas tested. Thanks to you, I can see if my theories have any real merit and whether or not they render a service which may further police work for the entire country."

"Well, you certainly are doing that, and we have more to accomplish with what you have in your bag of tricks. We will check with you before the day is over."

The phone rang on Captain Winston's desk as he was walking out of his office to see the chief, who had called only minutes before. "Winston, you can give the chief his bankbook now. The money is there to back the account. I had to juggle some other monies, but at least we have you covered for now."

"Good, because I just got off the phone with him. He wants me to come to his office and I'm sure the subject is money. It sounds like you are doing more than juggling with the money. I hope this doesn't blow up on us before we can get out of here."

"You let me worry about the banking business, and you spend your time worrying about police business. That way we both will know what we are doing. By the way, I'm not so sure the chief's secretary isn't aware of some of our plans. Someone, maybe her, has been checking with our travel agency about any future trips I may have planned. I can't be sure, but maybe she heard something when we used the chief's office the other day." Moorehead's voice was cutting and sinister to say the least.

"Don't worry about Miss 'Know-it-all' Rachel, I'll check on her. As to your handling of the banking business, it hasn't gone so well recently or the bank examiners wouldn't be on their way. You did say they wouldn't be here until after the election, didn't you?"

"That's correct, our partner has asked the same question more than once."

"When we get out of here, you and I might have to have a little sit-down. In the meantime, let's try to work together so things don't fall apart on us. I'll let you know what happens after I have a few words with the chief's secretary." Winston hung up the phone without further conversation.

The man sticking his face into the detective's office door looked familiar, but it didn't ring a bell with Rad or Rabbit at first. "What can we do for you, sir?" Rabbit was first to respond to the intruder.

"You might not remember me, but my car was used in the bank robbery the other day. The robbers kidnapped me when they drove out Rivermont Avenue. Do you remember?"

"Oh sure, it has been few days since we saw you and a lot has gone on since then. What did you say your name is?" Rabbit took out a pad to put down his name.

"My name is Jerry Holden, and my wife and I still have the store between Main and Church on Eighth."

"Sure, Mister Holden, what can we do for you?" Rad motioned for him to take a seat.

"Well, you two seemed to be the only ones who believed me when I said I had nothing to do with those robbers. Now those same two, who are now out of jail, and I don't know how that happened, have contacted me and demanded money. They claim they didn't get any for doing the robbery. Said they were promised money for the job but didn't get it, now they want it from my wife and me. Said they would kill the wife if we didn't come up with $20,000. I figured I'd better come to you two because first off, we don't have that kind of money and second, you might want to get them fellows back in jail where they belong."

"You mean these two are trying to shake you down for money? How did they contact you?" Rad was asking the questions and Rabbit was taking notes.

"I got a phone call late last night. They said I had until tonight to get $20,000 or something bad would happen to my wife. They said they wanted the money in a small satchel that could be inspected

151

quickly to make sure it was all there. Said they would call again by three o'clock this afternoon and give me delivery instructions. I was really surprised to know they were out of jail. How could that have happened?" Jerry Holden held his hands out in despair with his last statement.

"It seems the president of the bank didn't want to press charges. Said it couldn't be proved in a court of law that they took the money. Councilman Brenner and our esteemed Captain Winston went along with him and let them go before the chief could stop it. Odd and completely peculiar, I grant you. But, right now that isn't our problem. We need to catch those two red-handed and you have come to the right place to get it done." Rad turned to Rabbit and whispered in his ear. He drew a small sketch on Rabbit's pad and then looked to him for confirmation.

Rabbit erased one small item and then said, "It should work without any problem. I sure would like to get those two behind bars again and tonight will be as good a time as any."

Rad looked at the pad again and nodded to Rabbit. He tore off a new page and wrote a short paragraph and showed it to Rabbit. Rabbit nodded his agreement. He then turned to Mr. Holden, "Sir, when you are called again this afternoon, one of us will be there to see what the delivery instructions will be. If possible, tell them you want to meet them anyplace except where they dictate. Tell them you need the place to be closer to your store or from where you will get the money. They may buy it, but most probably they will want to pick the spot. Haggle with them, it is important." He handed Jerry the piece of paper. "We would like to use this address. It is close to the store, but away from seeing eyes, which might possibly be acceptable to them. Regardless of where, insist on meeting them at eight o'clock. Tell them you need that much time to get the money. If we are to trap these two, timing will be critical."

"But I don't have that kind of money. Are you sure this will work and what about my wife?"

"All you have to do is have a satchel in your hands when you leave your business for the rendezvous. Cut up some newspapers to put inside so it will give the bag the approximate weight in case you have to hand it directly to them. If you are being observed, they will think you have what they want. You should be safe until you reach whatever location they pick. As for your wife, we will have a patrolman watching out for her after you leave. Any questions?"

"I don't have any questions but I sure hope this works out. These people should be in jail and if this will put them there, I'm more than willing to do it." Holden seemed relieved comparing his state of nervousness to when he first walked in.

Rad and Rabbit led him to the door. "See you around three o'clock. We will be there when they call. Now stay calm, go home and rest. Everything is going to work out just fine. By tonight, we'll have these two back in jail where they belong."

They watched him as he made his way towards the front door. They waited until he had exited the building and then looked at each other. In almost the same breath Rad said, "I sure hope he doesn't get cold feet on us. It could be the pivotal opportunity we need to help us unravel this entire ball of wax."

The chief was at his desk when Captain Snyder walked into his office. Sitting in a chair opposite the chief was Captain Winston who seemed surprised at Snyder's appearance.

"Have a seat, Jordan, we need to discuss exactly how we will use the special fund money. Winston has finally found our bankbook."

"It wasn't lost, it was in a safety deposit box all along. I told you Mr. Moorehead said it was the safest place to keep it." Winston sounded defensive, and rightly so.

"That really doesn't make sense to me, but regardless, I will maintain this account and keep the book from now on. I don't need Mr. Moorehead telling me how to keep my funds safe. I may even put the money in another bank, from what I hear, there may be some problem with Moorehead's bank anyhow."

"There's no problem with the bank as far as I know. Moorehead has been very forthright with me in the past and I'm sure he would have said something if any such problem existed." Winston squirmed in his seat as he spoke.

"Whatever the situation at the bank, we aren't here to discuss their problems. We finally have our hands on our special fund money. Now, I need to find out how much money is required to

153

equip another three patrol cars with two-way radios. Can you tell me?" He looked directly at Captain Snyder.

"Yes, sir. The estimated cost per car is twenty-five dollars. As you may remember, we also need to cover the expenditure for the permanent base station, which was seventy-five dollars. So, the total for the base station plus three more cars will be $150. I'm sure that is all we need at this point."

"Good, get Jay Stevens going on the next cars, I want to modernize this force as quickly as possible." The chief was writing a check for $150 as he spoke. "Here, get this cashed while Moorehead's bank is still solvent."

"I must object to this expenditure," Winston was rising out of his chair as he spoke. "Councilman Brenner has told me more than once how he plans to operate the budget for this unit. I think he will be very upset when he learns of this."

"I'm sure he will learn of it as soon as you can get to a phone. Well, when you get in touch with him be sure to tell him I'm still running this police force and will be until relieved by proper authority. And, tell him he isn't the proper authority. He would need a majority vote from the entire committee to have the authority. Another thing, the next time you assist anyone in releasing prisoners from our jail, you will be the person looking for another place to work." The chief's temples were beginning to throb as he pointed the way to the door for Captain Winston.

The lunch menu at the White House hadn't changed in the past two weeks. Only their special changed which gave the diners some variety. Today it was corn beef and cabbage. A good dish when it was on the menu but not a normal item for a Greek restaurant.

Rachel was in the back booth facing towards the front. She spotted Rad the minute he entered and waved for him to join her. "Thanks for coming on such short notice. I had to talk to you before the day ended about a call I received only an hour ago."

"What kind of call did you get?" Rad settled in beside Rachel, leaving the other side of the booth empty. He picked up one of the ice teas, which had been delivered to the table.

"Before getting to the call, I meant to tell you about going by the travel agency on Seventh Street yesterday; I know the girl who works there. I asked her if she was aware of any travel plans by anyone we might know. She couldn't give me any positive information, but did tell me Mr. Moorehead had been in to ask her about various vacation destinations. Since there wasn't anything specific, I didn't think any more of it until I got the call this morning. I'm not sure who was calling, but the voice made it clear I had better stop interfering into other people's business. I'm pretty sure the voice was male, and it said, 'Or else'. I could have sworn it was Captain Winston's voice, but the caller had something covering the mouthpiece. It muffled the voice so I was unable to positively recognize it."

Rad put down the ice tea he was sipping and turned to look directly into Rachel's face. "The threatening phone call puts a whole new light on things. It worries me that you could be in danger. I'm believing murder, bank robbery, missing money, and conspiracy are all tied together, and I don't want you caught in the middle. I'll have some surveillance put on your apartment. Maybe I should stay over with you. You do have a couch in the living room?"

"You know I do. It would be nice to have you close by, although I don't believe I'm in any danger. If it was Captain Winston, I would like to give him a strong right anyway." Rachel balled her fists as if to strike out at some unseen object.

"There is something Rabbit and I have to do later tonight, but when I'm finished I'll be by your place. In the meantime, keep your door locked and don't let anyone in until I arrive. I should be there no later than nine-thirty."

Rad finished the sandwich he had ordered and was pulling money out to pay the check. He hadn't opted for the corn beef and cabbage, not at noon anyway. If he ate a meal that heavy in the middle of the day, he would have trouble staying awake for the rest of the afternoon.

"Will you be in time for supper? I could make us a good meal and you wouldn't have to worry about getting anything to eat before you do what you and Tankers have planned." Rachel rested her hand on his arm as she spoke.

"Don't worry about fixing anything. Rabbit and I will pick up something along the way. I don't want to put you to any trouble and I could be later than planned. Remember what I've said; keep your door locked until I get there. See you tonight." Rad rose to leave but she caught him by the arm.

"In case you are very late, here is an extra key. You can let yourself in." Rad gave her a peck on the cheek and left the restaurant.

The ring was shrill and piercing, almost foreboding in the quiet store. "Let it ring four times, then pick it up," Rad was standing close to Jerry so he would be able to hear the conversation.

Exactly on the fourth ring, Jerry picked up the phone and said, "Hello."

Rad could hear enough to make out a raspy and somewhat muffled voice, it was saying, "Do you have the money?"

"I will by eight o'clock tonight."

"That's too late, you need to meet us with the money on the corner of Twelfth and Church no later than seven."

"But I won't have the money by then." Rad patted Jerry on the back, he was doing well in not giving in to their demands.

The voice was faint and hard to understand, the caller must have put a handkerchief over his speaking tube. "We aren't playing any games with you Holden, you had better be at Twelfth and Church at seven or else."

"I hear you, but it isn't possible. I can't get the money until seven-thirty. I'm getting the money from a friend and he's on Commerce Street, near Seventh." Jerry paused; making sure the caller heard him catch his breath. "I could meet you just after seven-thirty, maybe at the corner of Commerce and Eighth, there is a vacant lot there. It would take me a good fifteen minutes to walk up to Twelfth and Church, and it's up hill all the way." Rad really patted Jerry on the back when he came up with those words.

There was a pause and it sounded like the person on the phone was conferring with someone nearby. After about thirty seconds the voice said, "All right, you be at the corner of Commerce and Eighth at seven-thirty with the money in a satchel. If you aren't there, you know what will happen to your old lady." The phone went dead.

"That was well done, Jerry. You handled it just like a professional. Now all you have to do is get the satchel and put the paper in it." Rad shook his hand and was pleased with the look he saw in Jerry's eyes. They had the look of determination, which was good. "There is one last word of caution. If they are in a car; and I think they will be, don't go over to them. Make them come to you and take the satchel from you. Regardless of what they say or threaten, don't take them the money. Set the satchel down on the sidewalk and move away from them and the car. If they threaten to shoot, run. They wouldn't fire at you because they certainly don't want to bring any attention to what they are doing; Main Street isn't that far away. Plus, we will be covering you. See you tonight."

'I'll do my best, but I can tell you for sure, I'm scared to death. I didn't do anything to deserve this. All I was doing was minding my own business when these thugs walked in and threatened my wife and me. Why, we hadn't even opened the store that morning. Don't know how they picked me."

"Sorry, Jerry, I can't explain it. But, we do need you to follow through. It will be over before long, I promise."

The room didn't offer much in the way of amenities, but the house phone was directly outside the door. "At least we didn't have to go halfway down the hall to make our calls. And, I believe we have that pantywaist so scared, he's going to get us that money after all. I didn't think he would go for the bluff. Did you line up a car?"

"Yes, and we have the use of it until tomorrow noon."

"By then, we'll be on our way to North Carolina and out of this flea-bitten town." Both individuals were smiling as they headed out the door.

It was after five when Rad drove the patrol car around to pick up Rabbit. They had planned to meet early so they could set up surveillance on Jerry Holden's store. If it worked out as planned, they could observe Jerry as he left the store and still get to the rendezvous location before his arrival. Rad looked at Rabbit as he settled into the front seat of the patrol car. "We have some time before we have to be in position at Holden's store, so let's drop by Jay's and get him to start on that recording device. I've selected two sites for him. He can pick the easiest one for the first set up. What do you think?"

"Yes, he told me he was ready. The great thing, since he worked it out, is we won't have to break into the house so he can install the device." Rabbit looked at the two names. "How come you picked these two?

"Well, we are pretty sure there is a silent partner someplace in this quagmire. By listening to some phone calls we may be able to eliminate one or the other. Or maybe they both could be involved. Either way, listening in could reduce our scope and also be the key in solving the murder in White Rock as well as the one at the train station."

"Then you don't think Brenner is part of the problem?"

"I'll admit he is part of our problem, but not to the extent he murdered anyone or had anyone murdered. I think he is being used and thereby causing lots of problems for the chief, as well as us."

"And I guess you've left Winston and Moorehead's name off because we know they are already involved in something shady?" Rabbit nodded to Rad's comment as Rad continued, "Although we might be able to find out the extent of their involvement."

"Maybe," Rabbit paused for a moment, and studied the names again. "It's hard for me to believe either one of these could be mixed up in murder. They are members of the country club and mingle with the best class of people in this town. You would think they had too much civic pride to get involved in anything shady."

"Maybe I'm wrong, but I've seen some of the most innocent appearing people get in over their heads before. This one name has come up before," Rad pointed to the top name, "we've got to give him more than a glance. If we don't get anything from listening to a few phone calls, we will at least eliminate a couple of people. However, I will bet you a coffee at Old T's that at least one of them has some involvement."

"No bet!"

Jay assured them he would have the first wiretap, which was to be the new name for the recording device, hooked up by noon tomorrow. From the looks of his workshop, he would be lucky to find the device by noon tomorrow. However, he hadn't let them down so far, and Rad and Rabbit didn't think he would start now. As they headed away from Jay's, Rad said, "Jay has a lot on his plate. Did you hear him say he had received the money from Captain Snyder for three more patrol cars? I'm sure the chief will be pleased when we can get four radio cars on patrol. That will give the force some rapid reaction never seen before in many of the police departments on the East Coast."

"Yes, I heard him. That money also included making the base station permanent. As I recall, it will be on the water tower next to the high school. That should give us all the transmission coverage we need." Rabbit sat back as they approached the alley across from Holden's store. It was dark now so they were almost invisible in the shadows.

"Holden should be heading out before long. Doesn't look like anyone is casing the place. There is Officer Patrick on the corner. Maybe you should tell him we will be moving on in a minute or two?

Rabbit was out the door and back before Rad could say scat. No wonder he was nicknamed Rabbit. "Patrick says he's got everything covered. He said he hasn't seen anything suspicious since he arrived around six o'clock. He will stay on post and make sure the wife is safe after Holden departs. He also has one other officer covering the back of the place, just in case. I think he is being overly cautious, but better to be safe than sorry. I don't really think those two will be worrying about the wife. They are after money. Let's move out so we can be in place on Commerce."

The vacant lot on the corner of Commerce and Eighth had been the site of a local moving company until the building was destroyed by fire two years ago. It had taken over a year before the burned-out shell had been partially cleared away. Rumors were that a beer distributor was to relocate to the site, but there hadn't been any activity to justify the stories going around.

Rad stopped the patrol car on the corner to let Rabbit out. "You find us a good spot so we can get to these guys quickly when they try to get the satchel from Jerry. I will hide the car in those shadows down the street so it won't tip off our presence. I'll be back in a minute."

Rabbit moved quickly. He used his flashlight to keep from falling over any rubble lying in the shadows. The lone street lamp, on the opposite side of the street, didn't provide much illumination for this vacant lot. Rabbit shielded the beam with his hand to keep the glare to a minimum. Moving rapidly, he selected a shadowy nook between two piles of bricks. It wasn't far from the corner and it offered a good vantage point to spot anything moving on Commerce or coming down Eighth. In fact, when Rad approached the lot, he had to whisper out, "Where are you?"

Rabbit blinked his flashlight and Rad moved towards him. "What time do you have?" Rabbit held his light on Rad's hand as he checked his pocket watch.

"It's quarter past seven. We should see Jerry coming down the street in just a few minutes. I'm going to cross over to the other side of Eighth Street and move up towards Main. I'll stay in the shadows and be ready to come in from their blind side. We will work them like a pincer." Rad trotted across the street and immediately disappeared in the shadows on the far side.

Sure enough, it wasn't more than a minute later when Rad spotted Jerry marching down Eighth with the satchel clasped securely under his left arm. He crossed Main and was looking straight ahead as if he were leading a parade. At the pace he was moving it wouldn't be more than two minutes before he reached Commerce.

Rad stayed in the shadows, hugging the building on the south side of the street, as he paralleled Jerry's path on the north side. They were almost to Commerce when Rad heard the low throbbing sound of a car engine not far away. He looked and saw a black sedan turn the corner from Main onto Eighth, it was moving slowly. Luckily its headlights didn't disturb the shadows that hid Rad.

Jerry Holden's movements appeared robot like. He arrived at the corner and immediately sat the satchel down on the sidewalk. He stepped back a couple of paces and lowered himself to a squat position. It was similar to the way the Chinese men sat on their backsides when on break behind the laundry on lower Canal Street. Jerry's head turned slightly, he had heard the car engine also.

Rabbit changed position so he could be closer to Jerry. He had the car in sight as it slid down the grade of Eighth Street. He couldn't see Rad across from him, but he was certain he was there. They had their trap set.

The car stopped close to the curb, "Jerry, bring the bag over to me." A darkened face spoke as it appeared through the window of the car.

"If you want it, then you come and get it." Jerry was still in his crouch. He didn't even turn to look in the direction of the car.

"Listen to me, you knuckle head. I'd just as soon shoot you as look at you. Now, bring that bag over to me or the next sound you hear will be the bullet coming out of my gun." The face turned back into the car as if he was answering someone close by.

"If you fire at me, you might bring the police patrol on Main Street down here in a flash. I'm sure you don't want that to happen." Jerry paused and came to an upright position. "I've done everything you've asked to get you this money, now you want me to hand it to you, too. Well, I say No! Definitely, No! I've had enough. You took both me and my car. You've threatened my wife. And now you want me to bring this money to you. If you want it, you'll have to come and get it. I'm out of here." At that, Jerry spun on his heels and started running north up Commerce Street.

A loud curse came from inside the car, followed by the door on the passenger's side bursting open. A figure dressed in a black sweater and dark pants emerged and started for the satchel. Before he could get halfway to its position, Rabbit stood between him and the bag with his gun aimed directly between his eyes.

"Take one step closer and it will be your last. Get on your knees, now!" The person believed him and fell to his knees with his hands raised.

At the same time, Rad had leaped to the open door of the car and had his pistol trained on the driver. "Put your hands where I can see them and then climb very slowly out of the car."

In only a matter of seconds, both men were face down on the ground with their hands shackled behind them.

Jerry had stopped his departure and had turned to watch the swift action of the two detectives. "Jerry, take your satchel and go home.

We'll handle the rest of this." Rad gave Jerry a salute for a job well done. Jerry whistled as he moved up Eighth Street, sounding like the weight of the world had been taken off his shoulders.

The chief was walking into the interrogation room as Rad and Rabbit were concluding the questioning of the two would-be embezzlers. "Sorry to call you out at this hour, Chief, but thought you would want to hear what these two have to say."

"You bet I do. These two should never have been let out of jail in the first place. Good work in catching them red-handed again. Have they said anything yet?"

"They have been very cooperative which may go well for them if they continue to speak up. Seems these two have been the victims of a little flimflam themselves. Sort of makes it even for the one they tried to pull on the storekeeper. According to them, they were to be paid $20,000 for robbing the bank of three million. Actually, they didn't know until after they were captured how much money was in the bank bags, which were waiting for them when they entered the bank. They had been told they would probably be captured, but not to worry. They would be released from jail and paid the agreed amount for their trouble. The person told them they would have police protection from the highest level. The best part is they claim they never saw the person who made them the promise; they only talked to him over the phone. To me that is faith at the highest level. Who said there is no trust between crooks? However, they got a little worried after they had been in jail a couple of days. But, when the bank president, a city councilman, and a police captain showed up and got them released, they felt better. They would have departed town, but they were due the money that had been promised. So, they waited to hear when they would receive what was owed them, but after two days nobody called. That's when they came up with the scheme to try and get the money from the owner of the get away car. They also thought he might know the name of their mysterious caller."

The chief smiled at the part about being paid $20,000 for robbing the bank of three million. But the smile faded rapidly when Rad talked about their release. His face became questioning over thinking

162

they could get money from the storeowner they had kidnapped. He slowly shook his head and said, "It would lead you to believe that some of our close friends know more about this crime than they have been willing to share. Also the fact that the moneybags were ready for them when they came into the bank stinks of someone in the bank being a part of the overall caper. I think my first piece of business tomorrow morning will be to talk to our high and mighty bank president. Mr. Moorehead has a few questions to answer for me. I'll give him a call tonight and tell him to be in my office first thing tomorrow morning. He can either come in voluntarily or we'll send someone to escort him."

"You know, it did seem odd to me at the time, although I didn't put it together until now," Rad scratched his head as if trying to remember the incident more clearly, "but that bank alarm went off way before these two ever came out of the bank. Rabbit and I were almost up to Church Street when the alarm went off. I had time to get back down to Main Street and was halfway to the bank when they came out. It was like someone triggered the alarm before they ever grabbed the loot."

"And while we are mentioning people who were involved, let's not forget our esteemed captain and the councilman. Both of them were part of the release of these two as well as Moorehead." Rabbit didn't want to overlook anyone if they were going to be pointing the finger of suspicion.

"Well, you two have done a good day's work. Get these two locked up and then call it a day. If Moorehead doesn't come in first thing tomorrow morning, I'll have you two help him find his way."

"OK with us, Chief. We're going to spend a little more time with these two before we lock them up for the night. We still haven't heard who in the bank had the bags ready for them. We'll let you know what we find out."

"Fine with me. See you first thing tomorrow." With that the chief was out the door.

The patrolman who had been staked out in front of Rachel's apartment was slumped against a tall maple when Rad walked up. He yawned and slowly stood erect. He said everything had been normal and quiet. He also let Rad know he had missed his supper. Rad gave him a brief rundown about the collar of the two bank robbers and then told him he would take over. He watched as the officer walked towards downtown, glad now to be the sole individual responsible for Rachel's safety.

When Rad entered Rachel's front room there was only a small table lamp left illuminated. He had intended arriving at her place much earlier, good thing he had told her not to fix supper. He approached the couch, which had already been made into a bed. Before he barely slipped into the sheets he heard a sound coming from the direction of Rachel's bedroom. It was followed by a subdued and sleepy voice wishing him a good night. Rad reluctantly cut out the light and laid there in the dark trying to get to sleep. It wasn't easy knowing what was in the next room.

CHAPTER TEN

The expression on the chief's face was one of disbelief. "Doctor, are you sure you are talking about Moorehead, the bank president? I was on the phone with him late last night and he didn't indicate he was in any pain or had a problem. I had told him to be in my office the first thing this morning, and he acknowledged he would be."

"Well, that may be all well and good, but Mr. Moorehead is in our intensive care center and he isn't in the best of condition. He is stable for now, but I'm not sure how long that status will endure. He asked me to call you and Councilman Brenner. You were my first call. He only wanted you notified; he wants to see Brenner as soon as possible. I'm not sure it is a good idea to let anyone in to see him. His condition is precarious and any additional distress could cause his death."

"It is imperative that I see him. I need to ask him what he knows about a very sensitive situation." The chief was busy making a note to Captain Snyder as he talked. When he paused, he put his hand over the mouthpiece of the phone, and yelled for Rachel to come into his office. Unfortunately, Rachel wasn't at her desk.

"Certainly not, no visitors of any kind," the doctor was emphatic. "The only exception would be his close family, and according to him he doesn't have any. As I said earlier, he is insisting on seeing Brenner, and that is against my objections. For certain, I won't have him interrogated. Something caused his heart to fail, and any more stress could put him over the hill. I'll let you know how his condition

165

progresses." The phone went dead; apparently the doctor was in a hurry.

The chief slowly replaced the phone and looked up to see the desk sergeant standing there. "You called for someone, Chief? Miss Rachel hasn't come in yet."

"Yes, would you believe Moorehead had a heart attack early this morning? Maybe things have come to such a turning point, the stress finally got to him." He picked up the note and said to thin air, "Rather than sending this to Snyder, I'll call him and ask him to stop by."

"He didn't look all that well when he passed my desk the other morning. Isn't Captain Winston pretty close with him? I can inform him if you like." The desk sergeant paused anticipating the chief's answer.

"Yes, he is. If he's come in, ask him to stop by my office. I would like to see the reaction on his face when he hears the news. I would also like to see the councilman's face when he learns the news, but I will have to miss that. Even though I won't be able to talk with Moorehead, things seem to be coming to a head. Which is good." The chief leaned back in his chair as the desk sergeant left to notify the proper parties. He passed Rachel coming into her office.

"Sorry I was late, Chief. But I had a problem getting ready this morning. What's going on?"

"Seems Mr. Moorehead has had a heart attack. I've got Snyder and Winston coming in, but I think we need to contact those two detectives of ours and let them know what is going on. I believe Childers has the use of one of the patrol cars with a radio. They used it last night when they captured those two bank robbers again. Ask the dispatcher to inform him to see me as soon as possible. They may be able to shed some light on Moorehead's condition."

Rad waited at the curb as Rabbit came out of his house. He had said he would pick him up since he still had the patrol car. He hadn't driven it back to the garage since it was very late when they finished with the arrest. He had dropped Rabbit off at his home on the way to Rachel's apartment.

166

Rabbit was taking his own sweet time walking to the car when Rad hit the siren. Rabbit looked up in alarm to see Rad beckoning for him to hurry. Rad was pointing to a car, which had just passed their position.

Rabbit leaped into the car, "What's going on? You about scared me to death when you hit the siren."

"See that car, the one at the corner? Well, I believe it looks like the Ford reported to have been at the house in White Rock. Let's pull him over and see." In a matter of seconds Rad had the patrol car going full out and was able to overtake the Ford in less than two blocks.

Rad pulled the patrol car diagonally in front of the black Ford, pinning it to the curb. The two detectives approached the Ford from both sides, leaving no chance for the driver or passenger to make a fast exit and get away. Both occupants looked surprised.

"Can I see your driver's license?" Rad leaned down as he talked to the driver who had lowered his window.

"What's going on officer? We weren't speeding."

"Is this your car?" Rabbit was back a few paces from the passenger's side while Rad questioned the driver. Rabbit had his hand on his revolver.

"It belongs to my boss, Mr. Worthington. I drive for him when he needs me."

"I see your name is Mathew Clement. That name sounds familiar to me." Rad held up the license and looked over at Rabbit, "The name Clement ring a bell with you?"

"Wasn't that the name of the man stabbed at the train station? It was something close to it if it wasn't Clement," Rabbit nodded knowingly. "Shucks, I'm sure it was Clement, and I think he had a brother."

"Are you Alvin Clement's brother?" The driver looked away from Rad in an attempt to hide his face. "Why don't you and your friend get out of the car and put your hands on the hood. I think you need to go down to the station with us. We have a few questions for you to answer."

"What have you got on us to take us in? We haven't done anything. You don't have anything to book us on. I want to see a lawyer." Mathew Clement was yelling as he was physically ushered into the backseat of the patrol car.

"How about suspicion of murder and robbery for starters. You will get one phone call, you can contact anyone you wish." Rabbit almost snarled as he pushed his man into the seat next to Mathew.

Just as the detectives finished securing the two suspects in the rear seat of the patrol car, the radio went off. "Patrol One, patrol one, contact the chief as soon as possible. I repeat; you are to contact the chief as soon as possible. Acknowledge."

Rabbit grabbed the microphone and said, "Roger control. We are on our way to headquarters with two suspects. Should arrive within a half hour. Tell the chief we have two people who might be able to shed some light on both murders. Out."

"If you will drive the Ford, Rabbit, I'll take these two around back to the jail when we get there. We can question them after we see the chief. I'll get the desk sergeant to book them and keep them on ice for us. They should be comfy until we can get back and have a nice heart to heart talk."

"Sounds good to me. See you there." Rabbit was in the Ford, had backed free from the patrol car and was on his way before Rad pulled away from the curb.

The line to the polling booth at the fire station on the corner of Fifth and Church was long. It appeared the election for city council was getting a bigger turnout than normal. One thing, which stood out as irregular, was Councilman Brenner standing next to the entrance to the voting booth. He was engaging each voter as they entered the booth, not only in violation of the voting laws of Hill City, but also slowing the line. One volunteer election official was attempting to get the councilman to move back to the authorized distance, but he wasn't having much success.

"Councilman Brenner, you must move back away from these voting booths. You know very well you are in violation of our local voting laws."

"I make the laws and I will stand anywhere I please. Now get out of my way before I do something you will be sorry for." Brenner pushed the official almost knocking him to the ground. That's when one of the other officials went to contact the police.

"Yes," the answering officer sounded frustrated, "we've already received one or two other reports on the councilman. He seems to be using the same tactic of badgering voters at all of the polling places he has visited. Officers are on their way to keep order and we've passed the complaint on to city hall. Word has it turnout is heavy citywide, which is affecting our response."

The group in the chief's office included Captains Winston and Snyder, detectives Childers and Tankers, and Rachel. She was there to take notes since the chief wanted a permanent record of this meeting.

"I understand you've brought in a man who may be the brother of the man killed at the train station the other night. If so, when do you think you will be able to make a positive connection?" The chief looked straight at Rad and Rabbit when he spoke.

"Well sir, we want to finish our interrogation of the felon from Star City first. We are almost sure he killed the man at the station, whose name by the way was Alvin Clement. We are using the new lie detector device and believe we can extract the truth from him. We think he will provide us with some important information, mainly the reason why he killed the man. Then we want to get back to the two bank robbers who we have back in jail where they belong."

"I can help on those bank robbers, Chief." Captain Winston leaned forward towards the chief's desk as he spoke. "I'll be glad to see what they know."

"I'm sure you would, Winston. You are one of the people who let them go. You stay away from those two. The main reason you are here is for me to notify you that your friend, Moorehead, is in the hospital with a heart attack."

"That's impossible. I saw him just yesterday and talked to him last night. I'd better go over and see how he is getting along." Winston rose to leave, but the chief put up his hand.

"You stay where you are. He isn't able to have any visitors and I want you in this meeting so we can get some straight talk out of you. Sit down." The chief waited until Winston was back in his seat. "That information on Moorehead is for all of you. I called the bank

169

last night and told him I wanted him in my office first thing this morning. Seems from the information obtained from the two bank robbers last night, the money bags they absconded with from the bank were waiting for them when they arrived. Also, the alarm was sounded well before they ran for the getaway car. They had been told they would be captured and were to be paid $20,000 for their effort. However, the one thing in particular I would like to know about is that they said someone high up in the police department would take care of them. Know anything about that, Winston?"

"Why should I know anything about what they were told?" Winston's face paled as he spoke.

"You were one of the people who released them and I don't know of anyone else in this department who had any dealings with them." The chief leaned back in his chair with his fingers laced. He appeared as if he were stalking a prey.

"It was Moorehead who insisted they be released. I was just there because he asked me to be. You need to ask him about anything unusual, not me." Winston's color hadn't gotten any better; in fact, he was almost white as a ghost.

"That is the reason I wanted him in my office this morning. OK Captain, we'll see what we get from other sources before we nail anyone to the cross." The chief turned to Snyder, "I want you to make sure these two detectives get the support they need. They have a full plate and I don't want them to be disturbed. Also, when will we have four radio equipped patrol cars?"

"I got the money to Jay Stevens late yesterday and he said he would be ready to install the radios in the cars by the weekend. He will notify us when to bring the cars. He has been assisting Childers and Tankers with the lie detector being used on the felon from Star City, but he should be free from that after today."

"Is that true?" He turned to Rad.

"Yes, sir. We will be finishing up the interrogation as soon as we leave here. There is one other thing Jay has in the mill for us which I would like to keep confidential for a while."

"I'm going to leave that up to Captain Snyder since he is now in charge of these special functions. You brief him on what you want and I will leave it up to him. OK, that's all for now, I'll be back in touch later today." The chief rose, making it evident to everyone that the meeting was over.

"Chief, I want to be on record that some of these things Childers and Tankers are up to may be illegal. I'm sure the councilman will not condone anything which may put this department in jeopardy and I know he won't overlook all the money being spent on radios and other contraptions." Some of Winston's color was coming back into his face.

"It shall be noted, you are on record, if that makes you feel any better." The chief gave him a scowl. As the rest of the people departed, the chief turned to Rachel, "Get me the notes on this meeting as soon as you can."

Things were active in the interrogation room as Rad and Rabbit connected Allen to the lie detector. This time the recording device was located behind the prisoner, out of his direct sight. They had barely started the questioning when Captain Snyder walked into the room. He nodded at the two detectives and motioned for them to continue.

"Before we turn on the machine, let's review what we know from our last meeting. Your name is Allen Jenkins. You were born in Atlanta, Georgia. And, on the night in question you were at the train station at the bottom of Ninth Street. It also wasn't the first time you had been to Hill City. When asked if you had stabbed the man found in the station, you said no, maybe, yes and then added there were extenuating circumstances. Now we need to get to that Yes and the extenuating circumstances."

"The stabbing was an accident. I didn't mean to hurt the man, I only meant to scare him." Allen appeared calmer than during any of the previous meetings.

"You didn't mean to hurt him? When I saw him he had three stab wounds in his chest. If that's your way of frightening a person, I would hate to see what you would do if you meant to kill him. Let's get to the questions, then if need be, we will talk." Rad switched on the machine and waited until all the proper lights glowed bright. "Were you hired to kill Alvin Clement?"

"No!" The needles immediately went from side to side on the scroll. "I didn't know his name, we just ran into each other at the train station." The needles continued their gallopade.

"Remember, only Yes or No answers." Rad looked at his notes.

Jay, who had slipped into the interrogation room right behind Captain Snyder leaned over and whispered in Rad's ear. "I think the machine will work with regular answers as well as if we only used Yes or No ones. Let's give it a try and see what we get."

"Good," Rad looked directly at Allen, "my advisor tells me we can use any answer, so we will not require you to just answer Yes or No." Allen nodded his understanding as Rad continued. "Now, you claim you just ran into the man at the train station. Were you sent there to meet him?"

"No, it was just a chance meeting." The needles danced wildly.

"Did he try to grab your money?"

"Yes, that's what he did and I had to defend myself." The needles moved from side to side creating a large black mark on the paper.

"No one sent you to meet the man?"

"No, no he just showed up while I was waiting there to catch the train." The answer caused the needles to do their wild dance. It was evident Allen wasn't going to tell the truth about what occurred at the train station.

"Allen, you are within ten minutes of going back to that cell in the basement of this jail and I don't care if you ever get out. We've given you every chance to be truthful with us, but it seems you are incapable of telling the truth. Now, I'm going to give you one more chance." Rad paused and looked slowly around the room. The pause only lasted a minute, but it must have seemed like ten to the prisoner. When Rad's gaze came back to Allen, there was a noticeable change in his demeanor, "We know someone hired you to meet Alvin Clement at the train station. Whether your purpose was to scare him or kill him, only you know. We also think someone paid you to do the job, otherwise, you wouldn't have had all that money on you when you were picked up in Star City. Now, you can either tell us what occurred, or you will be back in that basement cell before the big hand on that clock points straight up." Rad pointed to the large clock on the wall of the interrogation room, which showed the hour hand only three clicks away from twelve.

"I can't go back in that cell with those rats, I'll go mad. I don't really know much, but I will try to tell you the truth if you give me one more chance." Allen was twisting his hands and shaking in his chair.

"OK, one more chance. Were you told to exterminate Alvin Clement, and do you know who gave the order?"

"I don't know who hired me to make the hit. I was contacted by phone and the voice, which was very husky, told me what he wanted done. He said there would be ten thousand dollars in a luggage locker at the train station. I was to get the money, make the hit, and leave town." The needle on the machine only moved slightly. It looked like the true story was finally coming out. "I really didn't mean to stab him. I only meant to put the fear of god into him until he tried to rush me. I told him he had been setup for a hit, and if he were smart he would get out of town. He wouldn't listen and tried to go for my knife. I stabbed him in self-defense. When I left on the train I wasn't sure whether he was dead or alive." The needles only flickered until the very last statement, then they moved to the edge of the paper roll.

"What made you so lenient? Your record doesn't indicate that ever happening before."

"I really can't explain it except to say, his eyes had the look of a trapped man. I think he knew I was there to kill him and he pleaded with me. He told me he had been hired to put the strong arm on an individual and things had gone bad. He claimed he had killed a man by accident and now he needed money to get away. That's when he tried to jump me." From the looks of the machine, the first part appeared to be truthful, but the very last words made the needles dance.

"Some of your story tracks, but I think you know who hired you. You've been seen around town; who have you been in contact with?"

"I was only in this town once before and that has been days ago. I didn't meet anyone; I was visiting an old friend up on Fourth Street. I used to know her when we were growing up in Atlanta.

She had told me to drop by for a freebie if I was ever in town. I was passing through and thought it would be nice to collect." The needles only flickered.

"Who else was at the house?"

"There were several people in the place, but I didn't have anything to do with them. They were having a separate party, completely apart from where I was in the house. One well-dressed guy did try to make conversation, but I brushed him off and went about my business. There is one thing I haven't mentioned and that is the guy on the phone sounded familiar. He said if things didn't go well, I better not come back to this town." From all indications, he was still telling the truth. "My life could be in danger, I need protection."

"What is the name of your friend up on the hill?"

"Her name is Sarah. She said she wasn't going to stay in this town very much longer. Said she was going to head on and find some new pickings. She didn't tell me where she might be going." Another true statement.

"Very well, we'll unhook you now and put you on ice for the time being. I want you to give Detective Tankers Sarah's address. We might want to talk to her."

After Allen departed with the jailer, Captain Snyder, the two detectives, and Jay Stevens waited for a moment. Rad said, "I think he tried to make us think he only killed in self-defense, but the machine caught him in a lie. I do think he was telling the truth when he said he didn't know the name of the man who hired him. But, he gave us a name and place we can follow-up on to find out who the individual may be." They all agreed with nods of their heads.

Jay turned to Rad, "I believe we've got this lie detector working well. It was easy to see when he was telling the truth and when he was lying. Once you had him, he came clean."

"Yes, plus the threat of being with those rats again certainly helped get the truth out. I wish he could have put a name with the person he saw on Fourth Street, but maybe we can get something from Sarah. Rabbit, why don't you check with her. They could be regulars at her place; there aren't that many houses in the red light district. If not, maybe one of the other girls will know who they may be. Once we find out, we will meet with you, Captain, and see where we are."

"Sounds good to me. As the chief said, I'll be working with you from now on." Snyder smiled then turned to Jay. "Jay, I will be getting the first of the patrol cars to you this afternoon. The chief wants to get four of them equipped as soon as possible. You will be at your place, won't you?"

"Yes sir, I've purchased all the equipment I need and will be able to do the job when the cars arrive." The group moved towards the door.

Before Rad could get out the door, Jay grabbed him by the arm; "I have that wiretap in place. I can check it tonight to see what we have. Do you want the tape checked that soon?"

Rabbit held up his hand, "I'll pick up Jay later today after he's finished a couple of cars. Then we can check the tape together," he looked at Rad and got a nod. "If there is something worthwhile on the recording, we'll have it first thing in the morning."

Rad and Rabbit saluted Captain Snyder as he departed. He yelled back, "Don't forget to vote; it could mean our jobs."

The intensive care unit at the Hill City Memorial Hospital was like a tomb when Captain Winston walked up to the nurse's station. No one was in sight so he leaned over the counter trying to see if Moorehead's name showed on any of the charts. He wasn't having much luck looking at things upside down, so he went around the counter for a better look. There right in front of him was a chart saying Moorehead was in Room 312. He was just rounding the counter when the head nurse entered the hallway from another room.

"Is there something I can do for you, sir?" Her voice was steely and she drew out the 'sir' to add emphasis to the fact she wasn't happy to find him behind the counter.

"Oh, hello nurse, I didn't see you when I came in," Winston smiled nicely, attempting to use all his charm to soften her icy comment. "I'm Captain Winston of the Hill City police and I'm here to see Mr. Moorehead."

"Mr. Moorehead isn't able to have visitors, doctors orders." Her voice hadn't softened any from her first statement.

"Well, this isn't police business, I'm a personal friend. The doctor called me earlier today and told me Mr. Moorehead was asking to see me." Winston's voice was almost in a plead mode; he could see the head nurse wasn't about to go against the doctor's orders.

"You say the doctor called you?"

"Well, he actually called Councilman Brenner, who asked me to visit Mr. Moorehead since he was tied up until later this afternoon. He notified the doctor to put my name in his place."

Let me contact the doctor to see if he will authorize your visit. He gave me strict orders not to let anyone in to visit him." She picked up the in-house phone and asked for the doctor by name.

Winston couldn't hear her conversation; she had cupped her hand over her mouth and turned her back to muffle her voice. All he could see was her head bobbing up and down as she spoke to someone on the other end of the line. Finally she put the phone back on its cradle and turned to him.

"The doctor said you can see Mr. Moorehead for three minutes. I'm to time you and if he starts to labor before the time is up, you are to leave immediately. Is that understood?"

"Yes, I'm sure it won't be any longer than three minutes. He had some important information he wanted to pass on. When I get it, I will leave at once."

The nurse rounded the counter and started down the hall. She passed two doors and came to a third, which was partly open. "This is his room, I'll be looking at my watch."

Winston entered the room slowly; the curtains were half closed which put the room in semi-darkness. He could barely see Moorehead propped up in the bed next to the far wall. There were several tubes and wires attached to his upper torso. Two of the wires led to monitors, one for blood pressure and the other to check his heart. The monitors were hanging from a metal stand near the head of the bed. The room reeked of the typical hospital smell, clean and antiseptic.

Moorehead's eyes were open and he beckoned for Winston to come forward when he saw him. "Come close, I don't want to have to speak too loudly. Where is Brenner? I wasn't sure they would let anyone in."

"He was tied up, so he gave my name to the doctor. However, getting by the Iron Maiden out there wasn't easy, she checked with the doctor to make sure it was OK. How are you feeling? What happened? You weren't having problems last night."

"I haven't been feeling very well for the last few days, ever since the bank robbery. Then last night I got the worst pain I've ever experienced in my life," he pointed to his chest, " and I knew something was wrong." Moorehead wheezed as he spoke.

"We need to get you out of here. Things are coming to a head and we may have to leave much sooner than planned."

"Is Brenner winning the election? We need for that to happen or things will really be in a bad way." Moorehead passed a small piece of paper to Winston, "Here is the phone number of the person with the money. Get in touch with him as soon as you leave here and make sure the plans are firm for our departure when the time comes."

"I'm not sure of the election results. I did hear the turnout was heavy. I also heard Brenner was pressing at the polls. The rumor was he was trying to influence voters by speaking to them inside the restricted area around the voting booths."

"Leave it to that idiot to screw something up, that's one of the reasons I wanted to talk to him," Moorehead started to cough. "I don't know why we bothered with him. He has about as much of a chance as a polecat to get reelected." The cough deepened and the heart monitor started to squeal. "But, without him many of the things we've planned for this one-horse town will be difficult to accomplish. Let's take the money and run." Those last few words were difficult to understand. Moorehead's eyes closed and his head drooped forward on his chest.

The door burst open and the nurse and two orderlies were on the dead run. "Get out of here!"

As Winston reached the hallway he could hear the high-pitched sound of the heart monitor as it went into a steady monotone. He knew they wouldn't have to worry about arranging departure plans for Moorehead. Their friend had departed more than the town; he had left this world.

Mathew Clement and his passenger, Kyle Brady, walked causally into the interrogation room. There was a smirk on Mathew's face when he spotted Rad. "My lawyer will be here within the hour, and I ain't saying nothing until he comes."

"Fine with me, Mathew, but you may want to revise that position since you are being formally indicted for murder and/or accomplice to murder. We have a witness who can put you in the car outside the house in White Rock at the time of the murder. We have a tire print from that car when it was parked outside the house. You were driving that car then and it is also the same car you were driving when we pulled you over this morning. The car is registered to Mr. Worthington who you say you drive for on occasion. Now, you can take the rap for murder all by yourself, or you can tell us who was with you on that fateful day. Kyle, maybe you are the other culprit?"

"No sir, I wasn't anywhere near White Rock the day Mathew was driving that car. It was he and his brother. They were the ones who went to see Clyde Bishop, not me." Kyle jumped back as Mathew made a lunge for him.

"You dumb ass! Can't you keep your mouth shut for two minutes? I'll wring your neck when I get my hands on it." The officers assisting Rad pulled Mathew back into his chair and threatened to put the cuffs on him if he didn't calm down.

"Mathew, it seems we can now put you at the scene of the crime, for sure. Our other witness didn't really get a good look at you. Your size and color were the only identifying features we had, until Kyle helped us out. Would you like to tell us what happened?"

"I didn't murder nobody and neither did my brother. Or at least he didn't intend to. He was sent over to have a talk with Clyde Bishop. Seems Clyde had been mouthing around about the bank being in some sort of trouble. He was one of the tellers there, you know. Well, my brother was hired to let him know he'd better quiet down or else."

"Who hired him?" Rad leaned forward to make sure he heard the answer. This could be key.

Mathew paused and looked over at Kyle with a look that could kill. He then turned to Rad. "Mr. Moorehead, the bank president, hired Alvin. He knew he had done some strong-arm work before, so he said he would pay him a thousand dollars to go over and tell Clyde he'd better keep his mouth shut. However, things went sour when Alvin confronted Clyde. Clyde pulled a gun and threatened to shoot. There was a struggle and Alvin was able to grab the gun. The gun went off during the ensuing tussle. Unfortunately for Clyde, the bullet hit him in the stomach causing a fatal wound. He was dead before Alvin left the house."

"What happened to the gun?"

"I knew something had gone wrong before Alvin got back to the car. There wasn't supposed to have been any gunfire, so when I heard the shot, I knew we were in trouble. I was relieved when I saw Alvin come out of the house. He didn't have a gun when he went in, now he had one when he came back to the car. He held it in his lap, just staring down at it as we drove off. We drove around for almost half an hour before we went down to the river. I threw the gun as far out into the water as possible." Mathew seemed to slump back in his chair, exhausted from his tale of woe.

"So your story is your brother was only supposed to talk to Clyde Bishop, and the killing was in self-defense?" Mathew nodded in the affirmative. "Seems like a thousand dollars is a lot to pay a person just to have a talk with someone. Are you sure that the instructions didn't go further?"

"You can always ask Mr. Moorehead; he could confirm what he told Alvin to do."

Rabbit, who had entered the room in the middle of Mathew's story, leaned over and whispered to Rad. Rad's face went solemn, he looked up at Mathew and said, "Unfortunately, Mr. Moorehead won't be able to help us. He just passed away at the hospital. A heart attack."

"Well, that's too bad, but I'm telling you the truth. I don't have any reason to do otherwise."

"Your use of Mr. Worthington's car, is that an everyday affair?"

"Yes, I usually keep the car and have it on call for Mr. Worthington. That way, he doesn't have to worry about any upkeep. He does pay me for what I spend on the car. It is about thirty dollars a month."

"Seems someone may have paid for your brother to be killed. Do you know anything about that?"

"No, but I understand you might have the killer here? If so, why don't you put us in the same cell for an hour or so? Could remedy any problems you might have in keeping him."

"Would you believe your brother was killed in self-defense? Seems a lot of that is going around these days." Rad looked for any surprise in Mathew's face; there wasn't any. "OK, Mathew, and you, too, Kyle, we are going to send you back to your cells until we can put some of this together. In the meantime, if your lawyer ever shows up, we'll send him to you." Rad's smile was more sinister than gleeful.

As the two detectives walked down the hall towards their office, Rad turned to Rabbit and said, "Did you get to see Sarah?"

"As a matter of fact I did. She wasn't sure of the name of the man Allen had talked with, but she did say that several of the big wigs in town spent more than one evening at her place of work. They were there every Wednesday night, and they did more than smoke cigars and play cards, if you know what I mean."

"Did she give you any names?"

"Yes, she mentioned Worthington, Winston, Brenner, Russell, Moorehead, Coleman, and Willard. She said they weren't all there every time but there was usually a majority on the regular party nights." Rabbit used his notes when he gave Rad the names.

"I know most of them, but who are Coleman and Willard?"

"That's the beer guy and his lawyer. She also said the manager of the country club attended the gathering a few times, usually when he knew there would be extra girls available."

They turned into their office and closed the door. Rad looked very serious as he spoke, "It appears one of the murders could have been accidental. However, I believe the one at the train station was a planned hit all the way. Allen Jenkins is a born killer and would do anything for money. Also, the bank robbery appears to have been staged. But, I can't believe Moorehead was behind all this without some help from somebody else. But, who?"

"We've got several to pick from including our very own police captain. There could have been help from more than one. We could have a conspiracy on our hands." Rabbit looked at the names in his notebook as if one might jump out at him. "Maybe when I review the wiretap with Jay tonight, someone will become our number one suspect."

"Let's hope so." Rad moved towards the door, "I need some lunch, want to join me or are you going home today?" Rabbit rubbed his stomach, indicating the need for food. Rad continued, "Good, but let's not forget we've got to vote. We can do that after lunch." Both detectives were out the door before another word was spoken.

The bank was officially closed to business as soon as notification of Moorehead's death was made public. However, the chief didn't have any trouble gaining entrance. While most of the employees had already departed, the chief teller and a few others were at the beck and call of the bank examiners who had come up immediately from Richmond when notified of Moorehead's death.

Mr. Skinner, the head teller, approached Chief Stoddard as soon as he entered. "Too bad about Mr. Moorehead. He had his faults but he was too young to die. We won't know what will happen here at the bank until after the board of directors meet. And, that won't be until after the examiners finish their investigation."

"How are the examiners doing? Have they been able to establish how much money is actually missing? You said you put the amount at close to three million."

"They haven't had time to determine the exact amount as yet. They feel they will be able to give us a pretty fair estimate by this time tomorrow. We've been lucky not to have many depositors wanting to withdraw their money. I'm sure the bank will remain solvent, so there is no reason for them to worry. Is there anything I can do for you, Chief?"

"No, I actually came over to see Moorehead's secretary. I want to take a look around in Moorehead's office and she will probably insist on me having a search warrant. Is she in?"

"No, she left when all the other employees departed. His office is wide open, so be my guest. You won't need any warrant as far as I'm concerned." The chief thanked him and headed for Moorehead's office.

The shades had been drawn so the room was almost dark when the chief entered. He walked directly to the window and raised the shade to let some light into the room. He didn't want to use the overhead light if possible. The desk was his first point of inspection, which appeared in pristine order. There weren't any papers on top and only a pen set and lamp cluttered the smooth mahogany surface. The drawers were locked, which was to be expected. The locks could easily be forced, but without a warrant he decided not to jimmy them. There was a piece of scrap paper in the wastebasket which when smoothed out showed three telephone numbers. He would check those out later.

He strolled around the room but didn't see anything else of interest. His thoughts varied: *The bank president was a very neat and orderly person. Come to think of it, there was no reason it shouldn't be that way. The secretary probably made sure everything was in its proper place before she departed. It was part of her job.*

Chief Stoddard waved at Skinner as he headed for the front door. "I'll check with you tomorrow."

Winston's voice was laced with fear when he spoke to the person on the other end of the phone line. "Things have gone sour. We need to get out while we can; if it's not tonight, then no later than tomorrow."

"You may be correct, but don't panic just yet. Let's wait until after we see what the election results will be. I've also learned the bank examiners won't have any positive account of how much money is missing from the bank until late tomorrow, at the earliest. We've got time to stick around. There is always an outside chance we won't have to go if Brenner comes through. So, stay calm and I'll tell you when it is time to run." The voice was firm and the word 'run' was the last thing Winston heard as the phone went dead.

182

CHAPTER ELEVEN

Officer Patrick was leading Councilman Brenner towards the rope barrier, which designated the boundary of the voting restricted area. "You must know you aren't allowed to be within the restricted area unless you are voting, Councilman."

"You had better take your hands off me, officer. Do you know who I am? I'll have your badge for this." The councilman was trying to pull away from Officer Patrick's grip, but wasn't having any luck.

"Yes sir, I know who you are and I know the law. When it comes to persons allowed in the restricted area, only the person voting can be there. And, you weren't voting, you were disturbing the people who were voting." Patrick's voice was calm but firm. He wasn't letting the councilman browbeat him with his arrogance. "Now, I would advise you to stay out of the restricted area, or I will have to take you to jail."

The councilman finally shook his arm loose from the officer's grasp, but not until they were beyond the designated rope barrier. "That will be the day. As soon as I can contact your erstwhile chief, you will be looking for another job." Brenner stomped away from the voting area, continually glaring back in Officer Patrick's direction. He crossed the street and headed for the bus station, which was located on the opposite corner.

Officer Patrick made a beeline for the callbox halfway down the block. He was due to check in and it wouldn't hurt for him to

183

pass his side of this incident with Councilman Brenner to the desk sergeant.

Several blocks away, in fact almost at the other end of Church Street, Coach Webb was standing outside the Armory. The voting poll at this location had been seeing a steady stream of voters since its break of day opening.

The coach had just tipped his hat to three people who were checking voters prior to them going into the booths. One, a former player, had come over to shake hands with the coach when a patrol car drove up to the curb. The officer driving leaned out the car window and said, "Understand there has been some disturbance at the polls. Seen any of that here?"

"Not here, but I understand Councilman Brenner has been causing a nuisance earlier this morning at more than one of the polling places. Thank goodness he hasn't shown up here. If he had, we would have called for your assistance."

"Well, that's good to hear. If he comes around and gives you any trouble, let us know." The officer started the car, then leaned out the window again. "Coach, what are you doing here?"

"I was down on Main Street having lunch and thought I should do my civic duty and vote. This is my voting place, otherwise, you wouldn't be seeing me here, it isn't my plan to hang around the polls. I will be bringing my wife to vote later in the day, then I will go home to wait and see what the results will be, just like every other sane individual."

"All I can say is good luck. We need someone who will look at police problems without thinking the chief is trying to steal all the money in the city budget." With that, he drove off in the direction of the fire station at Fifth and Church.

The chief's phone was ringing as he entered his office; it only took him two strides to reach the instrument. "Chief Stoddard speaking."

"Chief, this is Skinner at the bank. I think I have some information that will be of interest to you."

"Fine, Skinner. What is it and can you give it to me over the phone?"

BLUE RIDGE JUSTICE

"I can tell you this much, in checking on Mr. Moorehead's estate, it appears he was dead broke. There wasn't a penny in either one of the accounts he had here at the bank. As of now, I can't tell when they were cleaned out, but I'm almost positive he had money in them as late as last week. It also appears he had liquidated all his other assets."

"When do you think you will be able to tell what happened to his money? He was reported to be one of the richest men in Hill City."

"Wait a minute, here is an entry cutting two checks which depleted both of his accounts. They were dated day before yesterday and the checks were made out to a Mr. Smith and a Mr. Jones."

"They certainly sound like upstanding citizens. Any addresses or ideas on who Messrs. Smith and Jones might be? If Moorehead was giving his money away, I'm sure he knew where it was going."

"Can't answer any of those questions now, but I will keep digging and get back to you when I can." Skinner's tone was one of despair. He had his hands full with the bank examiners and now this revelation.

"OK, Skinner. Maybe it's time for me to get a search warrant for Moorehead's office. Could be something in his desk that might shine some light on things. I'll put the paperwork through and we'll see what we can find."

"Good, I'll make sure his office is secure. The bank examiners don't seem interested in it. Will be in touch later." Skinner was off the phone and the chief was out his door.

The jailer was bringing Allen into the interrogation room as Rad and Rabbit were coming down the hall. He had called earlier to tell the detectives Allen had insisted on speaking with them before he was to appear before the city magistrate for indictment. He had told the jailer he might be able to identify the man who hired him to take care of Alvin Clement. This had been the trigger that got the detective's attention.

Looking directly at the prisoner, Rad spoke, "We aren't going to waste your time nor are we going to let you waste ours. You've now stated to the jailer that you know who hired you for the hit on Alvin Clement. Who was it?" Rad was getting right to the point, he didn't

185

plan to fiddle around with someone who wasn't prone to telling the truth.

"I told the jailer I thought I knew who hired me. I've been running different conversations through my mind trying to remember what various voices sounded like when I was visiting Sarah. I've been comparing them with the voice I heard over the phone when I was hired. I ain't saying I'm sure, but I think I can narrow it down." Allen's voice sounded forceful like someone who was sure of his facts. However, his eyes were shifting back and forth, which didn't support the impression he was trying to project.

"You think you've narrowed it down? You've been trying to remember names? I don't think you can remember what you heard yesterday, much less several weeks ago. I think you're playing for time." Rabbit leaned into Allen's face as he spoke. "Let's get out of here, Rad, we've got better things to do than listen to this tripe."

"Hold it a minute, my friend. Let's hear what he thinks he knows." Rad appeared more patient than his partner. "Tell us what comparisons you think you've made."

"Well, for one, I've said all along the voice on the phone was husky. When I think of it, the man who came over to me at Sarah's had a gravelly voice in a husky sort of way. He must have been an executive or owned his own business. He was too smooth to have worked at a day job. He was one of two decked out in a coat and tie. The others were dressed more casually."

"I hear you, but you still can't put any names with the faces. Your recollections won't do us much good. We need positive identifications." Rad stood and made a move towards the door.

"Wait, wait. Is there any way I could get another look at a couple of these people? If I could hear them speak, I might be able to nail one down for sure. The one who I think might be the guy, the one who called me, was a very distinguished looking individual. He must buy his clothes at one of the more expensive men's stores. He looked like butter wouldn't melt in his mouth." Allen was rubbing his hands trying to dry his sweating palms.

"I don't think there is much chance of you being around these people anytime soon. However, if the opportunity does occur, we'll let you know. In the meantime, we'll know where we can contact you."

Rad couldn't stifle a smile as he motioned for the jailer to take charge of the prisoner. Rabbit laughed out loud.

"Chief, Moorehead's secretary came back to her office about fifteen minutes ago and we caught her trying to destroy some of the contents in his desk. We stopped her but she is raising the very roof and threatening to call everybody from the governor on down. What do you want us to do?" Skinner sounded at his wits end.

"Hold her right there. I've just this minute gotten the search warrant. I'm on my way and I will deal with her."

Skinner's sigh of relief could be heard over the phone, as could the ranting of Moorehead's secretary in the background. The chief couldn't hang up fast enough as he motioned for Rachel to follow him down the hall.

Rad and Rabbit had just returned to their office when Rachel walked in. Her first words were about the chief dashing over to the bank after receiving a call from the Mr. Skinner, the head teller. Her next comments were his instructions telling them to come over as soon as she could contact them.

"What's going on at the bank that he would want us there?"

"I'm not sure, but the chief got a search warrant so he could see what was in Moorehead's desk. It sounded like Moorehead's secretary had come back to work and was trying to destroy some papers before they could be seen. Mr. Skinner had her restrained and the chief ran out of here on the double." Rachel had to catch her breath after her rapid-fire answer.

"Well," Rad looked at Rabbit, "we'd better get over there."

"Before you go, I've got some interesting news I'm sure you will want to hear." Rachel paused to make sure they were listening, "I received a call from my girl friend who works at the travel agency on Main Street between Tenth and Eleventh. She told me she had just issued a train ticket for Captain Winston to go to Cincinnati this coming Saturday night departing at seven o'clock. She called me because she thought I transacted all police department travel and she thought it was funny that Captain Winston booked this trip

187

in person. Also, she was surprised he didn't use the usual police voucher; instead he paid cash for the ticket."

"Did she say if anyone else was going with him?"

"No, that information isn't usually given out, but I could call and ask her. She is a good friend and if I told her how unusual it was for police travel not to go through me, I'm sure she would tell me if anyone else was involved."

"Rather than call her, why don't you go to see her? That way you may be able to tell if there is more than one person planning a trip to Cincinnati this Saturday night even if it wasn't booked in conjunction with Winston." Rad got a nod from Rachel ensuring him she would find out any information available. "If you find out something you think is time sensitive, you can get me at the bank. Otherwise, I'll check with you when I see you tonight. We are still on for dinner?"

"We certainly are. I've been looking forward to it and I will be ready by six-thirty. I want you to see the new garment I bought for the occasion; I think you will like it. See you then."

Rachel was on her way back to her office as Rad and Rabbit headed out of the building for the bank. As they reached the bottom of the front steps, Rabbit touched Rad on the arm and looked directly into his face, "Seems like you are seeing a lot of her recently. Anything I should know about?"

"If and when there is, you will be the first to know," Rad's glare didn't leave any room for further questions and Rabbit was smart enough not to offer any.

The election committee's main office was on the first floor of the city hall. The committee chairman was on the phone with the main polling place in the Fort Hill area, which was located on the premises of Fort Early. "How do you expect me to get all the way out to your location? I don't have any transportation and if I did, it would take me almost half an hour to get there. If you are having trouble with Councilman Brenner, call the police."

"We've called them but they haven't responded yet. I'm ready to have a couple of the big men here restrain him if he doesn't leave the polling area." The voice on the other end of the line was almost screaming into the telephone.

"That would be a good idea. He may yell bloody murder, but you will be in the right. I'm sure the police will be along any minute now. However, we can't wait for them, so do what you have to do to get him out of that voting area. I'll back you in whatever occurs."

Mr. Skinner opened the side door of the bank for the two detectives. He pointed the way to Moorehead's office and then went back to assisting the bank examiners.

As Rad and Rabbit entered Moorehead's outer office, the first thing they noticed was a uniformed officer standing behind Moorehead's secretary, who was sitting quietly at her desk. At closer look, they saw that her wrists had been handcuffed to the chair arms. Her tranquil appearance was shattered when they glanced at her eyes, fire and malice leaped out when her glare focused on them. They both nodded as they proceeded into the inner office. Luckily looks couldn't kill, or surely they would have been liquidated on the spot.

Rad motioned his head towards the outer office when the chief looked up, "What happened there?"

"She wouldn't quiet down so we had no other course. We'll let her go when we finish here, but until then, she stays put." The chief motioned them over to Moorehead's desk.

"Find anything of importance, Chief?" Rad looked at the mess of papers the chief had on top of the desk.

"Not as yet, seems he had a bunch of papers in this lower drawer, but it is difficult to tell if any of them mean anything. Here, Tankers, take a look at these while I dig a bit further." The chief handed Rabbit a large folder. "Childers, you take a look in that filing cabinet against the wall and see if you can find anything of interest."

The room fell quiet for several minutes except for the rustle of papers and the occasional sound of a drawer opening or closing. Suddenly the silence was broken by a muffled shout from Rabbit, "Look what I found in this folder!" He was in the process of laying out the pertinent papers on the desktop.

"What have you got?" The chief was bending over the desk.

"Well, it looks like Mr. Moorehead had kept a timetable of the happenings of the last few days. Look at this first entry," Rabbit pointed to the top paper he had placed on the desk. "It has the time and date of the bank robbery. Then there are three phone numbers with a note saying, call these after the two robbers have been apprehended. It has a check mark by it as having been completed. Hey, one of these numbers I recognize as Captain Winston's. It's only two digits off our number, Rad."

"Yeah, and one of them is Councilman Brenner's number," added the chief. "I've had to call it enough times to remember it. However, the third number doesn't look familiar to me. Either of you know who it belongs to?"

"No sir, but here it is again with an entry about securing the money. It says to call it after the money has been secured. It also has a check mark showing it was completed." Rabbit was rapidly running his finger down the page trying to scan the items noted by Moorehead.

"Here is an entry about getting the robbers released, with a check mark. Then look down here," Rabbit's voice was reaching a level of excitement, "something about arranging transportation. Wonder what that was about? There isn't a check mark beside the entry."

"I don't know, but hand me that phone." Rad picked up the receiver and waited for the operator to come on the line. It was only seconds before he heard, 'Number Please'. He spat out the number and waited. It was a good thirty seconds before the operator came back on the line to say there was no answer. "Give it another try, operator, I need to get through to this number." Rad drummed his fingers on the desktop while he listened impatiently.

After what seemed like an eternity the operator was back with, "I'm sorry, sir, but there is still no answer."

"Can you tell me whose number this is?"

"Sorry, sir, but I can't give out that information without proper authorization."

"This is the police, I need to know who has this number." Rad was trying to keep his voice calm, but he was having difficulty keeping a low tone.

"I'll connect you with my supervisor, sir, please stand by."

Rad listened to the void of a blank telephone line until finally a gentle, but stern voice, said, "Sir, this is the supervisor, what can I do for you?"

"I'm Detective Childers of the Hill City police department and I need to know who you have listed for phone number 882."

"Just a moment, please." The pause lasted less than five seconds, "Sir, that number is unlisted. I am unable to determine the owners name or even the location of that number. I can tell you it rings simultaneously at two different locations, which is unusual. In fact, I've never seen a set-up like this before. Must be somebody special."

"Unlisted, someone in the phone company must know who has that number?"

"Only the main office would have that information, sir."

"Thank you for your efforts, operator, I'll contact the main office," Rad gradually returned the phone to its hook. He turned to the chief and Rabbit slowly shaking his head, "Whoever it is, has gone to some effort to keep their identity unknown. An unlisted number, which rings simultaneously in different locations does insert a bit of mystery."

"Well, it's getting late and I think we've gathered all the information we need from here," the chief was closing up the right drawer as he spoke. "This timetable you found, Tankers, should give us enough to follow up on. I'll go by the phone company on my way to the office and get a name for us. Then we can have a little talk with whoever it is. I also want to talk to Captain Winston, he has some explaining to do."

"Did you know he has recently purchased a train ticket for Cincinnati, supposed to be leaving this coming Saturday night? Paid for it with his own cash." Rad made his comment sound as casual as possible.

"No, I wasn't aware of that, even more reason to have a talk with him. I'll leave word with dispatch for him to contact me in the morning. When you arrive tomorrow, come to my office and we will try to determine where we are and what course of action we need to take." The chief didn't hesitate; he was out of the office stopping only to tell the officer to release the secretary and escort her to her car after everyone had departed.

Rabbit still at the door, turned back towards Rad, "I'm getting with Jay to see if we got anything on the wiretap. I should have the information for us in the morning. See you then, have a good time tonight."

"Oh, I plan to, but if you need me you know where to find me."

As they were passing the shackled secretary, they gave her a departing smile. Her glaring demeanor hadn't changed from when they first arrived. "Don't think you will get away with your high-handed tactics. As soon as I can contact my lawyer, you will be hearing from me. The police had no right to restrain me and you will answer for it." Luckily Rad and Rabbit were moving rapidly, but her ranting was still in hearing range until they were outside the bank.

The news broadcast was on the radio as Rad entered Rachel's apartment. She held up her hand and pointed towards the radio. "The election for the first district council seat is still too close to call at this time. Councilman Brenner has the slimmest margin on Coach Webb with only 10 percent of the polls reporting. It will be late tonight before a final count will be available since many of the polls are complaining of some difficulty in tallying the vote. There is an unconfirmed rumor of voter fraud which this station is investigating as we speak. More at eleven o'clock."

"Sounds like the councilman could be involved with some dabbling in the vote count. I heard he was causing problems at several of the polling places earlier in the day. If that is the case, he could have more of a problem than just losing the election. He could be setting himself up for a bit of jail time." Rad took off his coat and took a long look at Rachel's outfit.

Rachel wasn't dressed in what one would consider eating-on-the-town clothes and Rad noticed it right away. He had never really seen a negligee in person, but he was sure Rachel's attire must be one. It revealed more of her than he had ever seen. He was about to say something to that effect when she beat him to the punch. "Do you really want to go out to eat tonight? I thought it would be more fun to stay in and have the entire evening on a more casual basis. I can throw something together if we get hungry, which could occur after awhile. What do you say?"

"Suits me fine, in fact I'm all for it. I do wonder about what you have on, looks more like a dressing gown than a dress." Rad relaxed back on the sofa.

"It is, thought you might like it. It is easy to get into and out of if there is a reason. Why don't you get more comfortable while I get us something to drink?" She leaned over and gave him a short kiss before departing for the kitchen. "I'll be right back."

The shrill ring of the phone shattered Rad's anticipated thoughts, "Are you expecting someone to call?"

"No, not tonight for sure. I'll get it, the phone's right around the corner." Rad watched as Rachel rounded the corner, her dressing gown flying, which was a sight to see. She grasped at the instrument as if to strangle it, "Hello." As she listened, disgust slowly began to spread across her face. She turned to Rad and extended the phone, "Here, Rabbit says he must talk with you."

Rad put the phone to his ear, "Yes?" For a full minute he listened and then said, "I'll be right there. Don't let anyone know what you've heard. When we are sure we have the facts correct, we'll let the chief know. I'm on my way."

"Sorry, my dear, but duty calls. I may be all night. This could be the answer to all our problems. I'll give you a call if I get through sooner than expected." Rad had his coat and hat on and was at the door.

Her voice wasn't pleasant at all, "Don't bother with calling, I'll be asleep. Maybe I'll see you at the office tomorrow." Rachel forcibly closed the door behind him. Rad could hear the thud of the dead bolt slamming shut all the way down the hall.

Rabbit and Jay were in Jay's workshop when Rad entered. They were bent over an odd piece of equipment, which resembled a record player but stood upright with two spools and a dial. Rabbit looked up as Rad laid his coat on a vacant chair, "You've got to hear this recording. Jay picked it up only an hour ago."

Jay motioned for Rad to have a seat while he threaded the tape between the two reels. "It will take just a minute to get to the best part, since there is a lot of leader on this tape." Everyone watched as the tape fed through the machine.

Suddenly a voice was heard, "I thought I told you to never call me at this number unless it was important."

"But it is important. The police got a warrant to search Moorehead's office. They were there this afternoon, his secretary called me after they let her leave. Did you know he kept notes on the recent happenings?" The voice paused for effect. "Well he did, and he also had copies of telephone numbers and this is one of them. They are bound to find his notes and all of our participation in this scheme will be common knowledge by tomorrow, if not before. We'd better move up our plans to get out of this city, and do it quick."

"I just can't up and leave without some preparation. I'm an important man in this town and my reputation would be ruined."

"Your reputation won't be worth two cents when this information hits the streets. The best we can do is make a run for it. When can you get the money together? It had better be before tomorrow night."

"We said we would wait to see how the election turned out. Is there any chance Brenner could win? If so, he could cover for us."

"There isn't a chance in the world of Brenner winning the election. In fact, he could be arrested for trying to unlawfully influence the election results. He could very probably have to stand trial for fraud if what the rumors say is true. He could be in jail by tomorrow."

"I've had the money in a safe place since I got it from Moorehead, and I will have it at the house before noon tomorrow. I'll meet you at the train station. Isn't there a five-thirty train we can catch?"

"Five-thirty is correct. Make sure you are careful; those two detectives are smarter than I thought. They've almost put all the pieces together."

"OK, Winston, you can count on me. Too bad Moorehead won't be with us, but that only means more for us. See you tomorrow." A click was heard and the tape went silent.

"Is that all we have? Whose phone did this come from? The voice sounds familiar but I'm not sure. You have any idea, Rabbit?" Rad was out of his chair as he looked from Rabbit to Jay.

Jay motioned for Rad to return to his seat, "Wait a minute, detective, there is more." He let the tape continue for another couple of turns on the reel.

A voice came on, "Federal Storage, how can I help you?"

"I have a ticket for two packages, the numbers are, 856-uv and 856-uw. I need those delivered to 245 Peakland Place by ten o'clock tomorrow morning. Can you do that?"

"Yes sir. I see that the storage has already been paid. The packages will be there on time." The tape went silent again.

"That's Charles Worthington's address. And, it was his voice on the first part of the tape talking to Winston. It all makes sense now; those two at the murder scene in White Rock were using his car. Sarah also mentioned he was in attendance at her place on Fourth Street. He must have been the one who fingered Alvin Clement for assassination." Rad's mind was racing as he slowly looked around at the cluttered workshop.

"I could pick Worthington up at his home after the packages are delivered. They must contain the money. Then we could get Winston if the chief hasn't already put him in custody." Rabbit had a pleased look on his face.

"It appears there are only three people masterminding this crime wave: Moorehead, Worthington, and Winston. I thought for sure Brenner played some role, but it looks like he was only a pawn in their overall scheme. I'll bet he nearly chokes when he learns how much of a palooka he has been," Rad looked directly at Rabbit. "We'll contact the chief and Captain Snyder first thing in the morning, they will want to be there when Winston comes to his office. Should be a welcomed scene to see that traitor get what he has coming to him."

Rabbit looked over to Jay, "Great work, Jay. Make sure those tapes don't get lost. I'm sure the district attorney will be able to use them when these crooks come to trial."

Rad spoke quickly, "I'll see you both in the morning." Jay looked surprised, "Yes, you too, Jay, we want you there. You've been as much a part of this solution as Rabbit and I so you deserve to be in at the end." Rad started to get his coat back on but stopped to look Rabbit directly in the eye, "I think you've helped ruin what was to have been a wonderful night. However, to have these scalawags dead to rights has been worth it. Let's hope there will be other opportunities."

The continual ringing of the phone was a mournful sound to Rad's ears. Rachel was certainly home and she should have answered her phone by at least the sixth ring. Rad clicked the lever to get the operator's attention. When she came back on the line, he said, "I'm sure my party is at home; are you sure the phone is ringing?"

"Yes, it is ringing. Maybe the fact it's two o'clock in the morning might have something to do with the fact no one is answering." The operator's voice sounded like she was half asleep herself.

"Very well, operator. I'll wait until the sun comes up, then I will give it another try. I didn't realize it was so late or early; I guess it depends on how one looks at it. I appreciate your help."

"Don't mention it. Have a good morning." Then the line went dead.

CHAPTER TWELVE

The chief was pacing the floor of his office when Rad and Rabbit arrived. Jay was also accompanying the two detectives as they entered a very strained atmosphere. The chief's voice virtually leaped out at them immediately as they crossed his office threshold, "Where is Captain Winston? He hasn't arrived in his office yet. I want him in my office as soon as possible; he has a lot of questions to answer."

"He might have more than just a few questions to answer after you hear what we heard last night. Jay, set up that tape so the chief can hear it firsthand."

As Jay went about getting his machine set and the tape ready, the chief said, "Check and see if Captain Snyder is in his office. I want him to hear this so he won't have to be briefed later."

Jay nodded that the tape was ready just a few moments after Captain Snyder joined the group. "OK, Jay, let it roll." Rad had a grin on his face, which contrasted the look of concern on the chief's face.

The group listened in silence until after the first part of the tape went quiet. Thinking it had ended, the chief said, "Do we know who that is talking? The voice sure sounds familiar to me."

"Patience, Chief, you need to hear the last part." Rad held his hand in the air in an attempt to calm him.

They all watched and listened as the tape continued to roll through the machine. When the chief heard the Peakland address, he shouted out, "Worthington! Why he is one of the most respected men in town. It is getting so you don't know who is playing an honest hand." He paced back and forth behind his desk before speaking again, "We need to nab him with that money. He said he wanted the money delivered by ten o'clock. We need to be there to make sure he doesn't go anyplace after he gets it."

"Rabbit can have his place staked out and be on hand to arrest him when the money is delivered. I can wait here with Captain Snyder and make sure Captain Winston doesn't get off before we can nail him. How does that sound to you, Chief?"

"Fine with me. It is evident Captain Winston didn't plan to come in today. It would be nice if we could pick him up before train time, if in fact he still plans to depart by train. Do either of you know any of his hangouts?" All he got were blank stares.

Finally Captain Snyder rose from his seat, "Maybe I know someone who might give me a lead on Winston. He once told me of a contact he had over on the east side of the river. As I remember, there was a house on the bluff that overlooked the river. He spent some time there with a friend, a lady friend."

"Do you know the friend's name?"

"No sir, I'm not sure he ever mentioned it. Anyway, I can check out the location just in case he might be laying low there until time for his departure." Captain Snyder pulled a small notebook from his pocket and began looking for an address. "Here it is, it is just off County Road 103. Elm is the street name; I know its approximate location. Want me to check it out, Chief?"

"I think that would be a smart thing to do. You take one of the radio patrol cars and see if he happens to be at that location. If so, apprehend him. Better take a couple of officers with you in case he won't come voluntarily. If he isn't there, let the dispatcher know and head back here on the double." As Snyder departed, the chief looked towards Rad and Rabbit, "Tankers, you take a patrolman and stake out Worthington's place. You should make sure you are in position so you will be there when the money arrives. When you see the money delivered, catch him red handed, then bring the entire kit and caboodle back here. I want to personally put him in a jail cell."

BLUE RIDGE JUSTICE

"Right, Chief. I'll take Officer White with me. He is a good sturdy type in case Worthington tries to get physical." Rabbit departed the office, leaving Rad and the chief alone.

"Chief, what if Captain Snyder doesn't find Winston? We had better be ready to cover the train station in case he decides to go for an early departure."

"Let's check and make sure we know when any trains depart from Hill City and from which station. He could be making a run for it well before the five-thirty train headed for Cincinnati." The chief paused and then yelled out, "Rachel, come in here a minute, please."

As Rachel entered the office she hardly glanced in Rad's direction. "Yes, Chief. What can I do for you?"

"We need to know the schedule of every train scheduled to leave this city for the next eighteen hours. From the information Detective Childers was able to secure last night, we think our suspects could be trying to get out of town well before their planned departure. Thanks to some diligent late night work by Childers, Tankers, and Jay Stevens, we may catch the people responsible for all our troubles."

"I wasn't aware last night's work turned out to be so important. I may have done an injustice to someone I know." Rachel made her statement in a muffled voice and sounded like she was mumbling to herself. The chief looked up questioningly, which seemed to bring her back to the present. "I'll get right on the information you want, Chief." She departed the office after a longing glance in Rad's direction.

The phone was picked up before the third ring. A guarded voice, which could hardly be heard, said, "Yes, who's calling?"

"It's me, we need to make some emergency plans. We should lay low until our train departs this evening because I think they are on to us. There were several calls made to my phone this morning, but I didn't answer. I'm not going in to work this morning; in fact, I've severed all contact with the police force." Winston's voice sounded tight and less than enthusiastic. "Have you gotten the money yet?"

199

"No, remember it is to be delivered at ten o'clock. When it gets here I intend to leave the house and hide out someplace. Got any ideas where a good place would be?"

"If I were you, I wouldn't wait for the money to come to me. By ten o'clock, they could have your place staked out."

Worthington sounded secure when he said, "I don't think they know I'm involved, I've kept a pretty low profile. Moorehead got all the publicity with the bank robbery and all."

"You could be surprised. I heard some talk about a recording device, which could be used on private telephones. That young guy, the one who's been hanging out with Childers and Tankers, Jay Stevens, has some things that surpass anything I've seen before in police work. Why, they could be recording this conversation right now." Winston paused and then said, "I know a place where we can lay low until the five-thirty comes in. If we play our cards right, we can sneak on the train without being seen from the station."

"Maybe I had better get out of here right now. I'll try to get the money early. Where can I meet you?"

"There is a vacant warehouse just up the tracks from the passenger station. It is for sale but as yet no one has been interested in it. You can get to it by going to the bottom of Eighth Street. Park your car behind the building; it won't be seen from there. We can stay out of sight until train time. I'll get some burgers from the Texas Tavern, which will tide us over until we are on the train. You get the money and meet me there. Better move fast, I don't think we have much time."

"Suppose I can't get the money?"

"Let's hope you can, but if it means being arrested, what we have will have to do. I've got a couple of thousand with me and you should have more than that."

"I do, but I will do my best to get the bank's money. I'm on my way, see you there."

"Don't forget to leave some lights on in the house so it will look like you are still at home. However, don't answer the phone again because I won't be calling again. If you don't see my car at the warehouse, don't worry for I plan to leave it in a safe place. I'm outta here, good-bye." Winston eased the phone onto its cradle as he prepared to make himself scarce.

Sergeant Stevens, who had been monitoring the radio dispatch section, came running down the hall to the chief's office. When he saw Rachel, he said, "Is the chief in? Captain Snyder wants him on the radio."

Rachel didn't have to make a move; the chief was out of his office and hurrying past the sergeant before the sergeant could start back down the hall. He reached the radio dispatch room a good ten steps ahead of the sergeant.

"Patrol Two, this is the chief. Do you read?" Silence answered his transmission. He repeated the call and waited for a reply.

Static crackled out of the speaker, then, "Roger, Chief, I read you loud and clear. How me?"

"I read you fine, Patrol Two. Have you located your party?"

"Negative, no one was home and there aren't any signs he has been here. I'm on my way back to headquarters to pick you and Childers up. Heard anything from Patrol Three?"

"Nothing since he departed, but he just left a few minutes ago. He hasn't had time to get in position. When you arrive we can go over and see how he is doing."

"Fine, I should be back at headquarters inside of twenty minutes. See you then. Patrol Two out."

The chief turned away from the mike and said to no one in particular, "Isn't this two-way radio something?"

Sergeant Stevens, who had resumed his seat at the desk, said, "When do you think we will have all our patrol cars equipped?"

"Shouldn't be too long now. With advances like this, we are on our way to becoming the top police force in the state, if not the entire East Coast." The smile on the chief's face attested to the fact he was pleased with the money he had spent on this new capability, despite Councilman Brenner's objections. "Stay on that radio, Stevens. It might be the key to us capturing those renegades before they get out of town."

Rad and Rachel were waiting for the chief when he returned to his office. They were holding up the morning newspaper for him with

201

the bold headlines showing, COACH WEBB DEFEATS FORMER COUNCILMAN BRENNER BY THE SLIMMEST OF MARGINS. In a smaller caption below, the banner read, 'Councilman Brenner Demanding a Recount.'

The chief looked surprised, "Boy, there is something wrong with that headline. The word I was getting was Coach was winning by a landslide. Get in touch with the election chairman and see what's going on."

"I called him right after Rachel and I saw the paper. He says there appears to have been some false ballots cast at several voting stations. In each case, Councilman Brenner had caused a disturbance throughout much of the voting period. They are in the process of recounting the ballots from four locations. He says they are the places where the biggest discrepancies appeared. He will let us know what he finds out, but for sure, Coach Webb has won the election."

"Rachel, see if you can get Brenner on the phone for me. Childers come on in the office and let's see if he can be contacted. We can't do anything until Snyder gets back here or we hear from Tankers."

It was several minutes before Rachel called on the interphone to say she had Councilman Brenner on the line. "Hello, Councilman. I understand you think there ought to be a recount. Is that true?" The chief's eyes rolled up as he listened. Rad could hear a part of the conversation coming over the line, simply because it sounded like the councilman was screaming. Finally the chief broke in and stated, "Councilman, I suggest you come over to my office before this situation gets out of hand. If what you say is true, we will see that everything is straightened out. However, I'm getting a different story from the election people, so I insist that you come over." The pause lasted only a matter of seconds, "Fine, I'll be waiting to see you."

The chief turned from the phone and said, "I think the councilman may be our guest while we put him under indictment. I can't think of it happening to a more deserving person." The smile on the chief's face was bigger than Rad had ever seen before.

Rabbit and Officer White pulled their patrol car to the curb on the opposite side of the street, about a half a block from Worthington's house. Peakland Place had a median strip, which divided the tree-lined street. Their location gave them a good view of the residence without highlighting their position.

As they waited, Rabbit reached for his watch and said, "My piece says nine-thirty, how about yours, White?"

"Mine's the same. We should be here in plenty of time if the goods aren't to be delivered until ten. You did say ten o'clock, didn't you, Detective?" Seeing Rabbit's nod, Officer White leaned back and stretched out his long legs so he could get comfortable.

Stakeout had never been a favorite pastime for Rabbit, but surprisingly the time went by quicker than anticipated. It was just a couple of minutes to ten when Rabbit and Officer White realized there was no delivery person insight. "Wonder why the delivery guy hasn't shown up? Those people are usually right on time. His truck should be in sight, if he's coming at all. Maybe the delivery has been cancelled. Let's find out if anyone is home." Officer White nodded his agreement and Rabbit started to open the patrol car door. "You go around back while I knock at the front door. Someone might want to make a fast exit out the back way."

"Don't worry, I'll have it covered. Let's do it." Officer White was trotting toward the rear of the house as he spoke.

Rabbit attempted to look into a front window before knocking at the door. He didn't see any movement in the room, although there was a light burning on a side table, but the area looked unoccupied to him. He moved to the door and rapped hard, hearing the echo of his pounding resounding down the hall inside. He waited for at least a minute and knocked again, still no response. He was about to knock a third time when Officer White came around the corner of the house.

"Doesn't look like anyone's home. I could hear you knocking all the way out back. For sure, no one came out the back way."

"I believe you are right. Seems Mr. Worthington has flown the coop. Let's get on the radio to headquarters and see what they have in mind." Both Rabbit and Officer White headed back to the patrol car.

It only took a minute to get the radio warmed up and the first words they heard were, "Patrol Three, come in. Patrol Three, come in."

"Patrol Three, dispatch. We haven't made any contact at our location. The delivery was not made. Repeat, the delivery was not made."

"Understand. The chief wants you to check with the storage company on your way back to headquarters. See what information they can give you about the delivery or non-delivery. Then return to headquarters."

"Roger, dispatch. Will be in touch. Out."

The scene at the Webb residency was close to a three-ring circus. The newspaper and radio people were crowded around the front door while Coach was attempting to keep them from entering his home. "All right guys, back up a bit. If you will give me some room, I will try to answer all your questions."

The local newscaster from the radio station was attempting to act as chief spokesman as he held his microphone towards the coach, "Now that you have been elected, and we hear after a recount it was by a landslide, what are your plans? Doesn't the landslide vote also give you the mayor's slot? Is it true that former councilman Brenner is going to have to face charges? Give us an insight, Coach."

The coach pushed several of the reporters who had edged around to his side back off the stoop. "Let me take one thing at a time. First off, I'm not sure of what has or will happen to Brenner. I understand he is paying a visit to the chief of police as we speak. I have been informed he had something to do with the original close vote. But, that's all I know about his situation at this time. I'm sure you folks will know more than I will, and well before I do."

The star news reporter for the morning paper jumped in and said, "Give us some idea of what you plan for the police department. We had previously been told by Brenner he was planning to cut the force."

"Any cuts are far from my mind. Contrarily, we need a strong police force and if anything, it will be improved even more than it is today. You will see an increase in the number of detectives. The two now on duty have been overworked. They have almost single-handedly been responsible for solving the worst major crime wave, involving capital offenses, that this city has ever seen. While things are not exactly finalized, they are on to the culprits and should have things wrapped up before the day ends. To aid them, we will add a crime lab to the department. A Mr. Jay Stevens, who has already been working closely with the detectives, will head it. There will be other items but it is too early to say what they will be. Also, we look to make improvements in our city government structure."

"Mayor, will you and your wife be moving to a bigger house?"

"My wife and I have done very well here in this house for ever so many years. We see no reason to move. We aren't trying to impress anyone; we are the same people you've known for all the years we've been here in Hill City. Being an elected official won't change my outlook on life. Now, that's all I have for you today. I'm sure we will be seeing much more of each other; let's hope we will all be as happy as we are today."

"One more question, Coach, I mean Mr. Mayor. How do you and Chief Stoddard get along? It was a known fact Councilman Brenner was ready to relieve the chief."

"The chief and I get along just fine. In fact, I have the greatest confidence in our police force. It is good today and it will be even better in the very near future."

The crowd of reporters slowly ebbed away, however reluctantly. It was the first time in a long time they got some straight answers without having to badger the person they were interviewing.

A wide-eyed clerk was responding to Rabbit's question, "Mr. Worthington picked up those packages an hour or so ago. We had planned to deliver them at ten like he asked, but he came in early and made the pickup."

"Do you recall how he carried them out of here? Did he have a suitcase?"

"He had two suitcases. There were ten well-wrapped packages, each being almost the size of a shoebox. He was in a big hurry and kept dropping the packages as he tried to put them in the suitcases. One broke open and there was money in it. Don't know how much was in each package but it looked to be a pretty fair amount. He scooped up the one that broke open in a hurry; he tried to keep us from seeing the contents. We helped him get the suitcases into his car after he finished stuffing them. They were very heavy. He didn't seem to be the strongest person in town."

Rabbit paused, and cocked his head to one side, "Did he make any comments about where he might be going? Was he driving a black Ford?"

"He didn't say where he was headed, but yes, as I recall, the car was a Ford. I'm pretty sure it was black. I haven't seen too many other colors these days."

"OK, if you hear anything from Mr. Worthington later on today, be sure to give us a call at this number." Rabbit handed the clerk a slip of paper with the telephone number of police headquarters on it. "It is very important that we make contact with him. Did you notice the direction he took when he left?"

"Not really. If anything, he headed for downtown, but he could have made a turn after going a few blocks."

"Thank you for your help. Remember, if you hear from him again; be sure to give us a call right away. We'll have an All Points Bulletin out on that car in a matter of minutes. Thanks again for your help."

Councilman Brenner strolled into the chief's office as if he were still responsible for the conduct of the department, but before he could sit down the chief slapped handcuffs on him. "What are these for? Do you know who you are accosting?" The councilman's face was beet red and he was screaming at the top of his lungs.

"Sit down before you blow a gasket." The chief almost slammed him into a chair. "You are under arrest for fraud and manipulation of votes during the election yesterday. We have confirmed the facts with the election officials. You were seen adding ballots to more than one voting place. And, we have other witnesses to the fact you interrupted voters during the time they were at the polls in more than one location."

"I want a lawyer; you can't lock me up. When I get out of here, you'll wish you never touched me. I'll sue you and this sorry excuse of a police department for everything you and this city have."

"You can call your lawyer, but before he arrives you will be spending a bit of your time in one of our finest accommodations. I don't know if you have seen our fine jail from the inside before, but I'm sure the furnishings will be to your liking. You are the one who directed that the cells be as austere as possible. You'll be happy to know you are getting what you asked for." The chief could hardly suppress his smile.

As the jailer led Brenner away, he was still yelling at the top of his lungs. Hopefully he wouldn't disturb the rats when he got to his cell.

Rabbit was almost at a trot when he entered the office he shared with Rad and was removing his coat as he moved. Before he could shed his coat or reach his desk, Rad said, "So Worthington had already picked up the loot? What did the storage people have to say?"

"The clerk said there were packets of money that would barely fit into two suitcases. He knew the packets were filled with money because one of them broke open. He said Worthington tried to scoop up the contents before it could be seen, but he was a bit slow in his attempt."

"Could he estimate how much there was? If it took two suitcases to carry it off, it must have been quite a sum?"

"No, he didn't even try. But the amount must be in the millions." Rabbit looked up as Rachel walked into the office. She always got a long stare from Rabbit whenever she made an entrance. Of course, Rad wasn't completely unaware of her presence, particularly when her gaze zeroed in on him.

Without blinking she said, "The chief wanted to let you know there is a train scheduled to leave the Ninth Street Station at twelve-thirty. It is a special mail train with a couple of passenger cars added on. He wants you to check it out in case Worthington and Winston try to leave town earlier than they had planned."

Before Rachel had hardly finished speaking Rad's phone rang. He picked it up quickly and almost immediately said, "Roger that, we are on our way." He put the phone down almost as fast as he had picked it up and immediately looked at Rabbit, "Do you still have that patrol car?" Rabbit nodded to the affirmative. "That was the dispatcher saying Worthington's car had been spotted going down Eighth Street. Rachel, tell the chief we are on the way to the bottom of Eighth Street and we will also check out the twelve-thirty train."

The door to the vacant warehouse creaked when Worthington used his shoulder to open it. He was having a difficult time trying to maneuver the two suitcases and open the door at the same time. The room he entered was dark with very little light coming in through dirt-streaked windows. He looked around, finally spotting Winston in the far corner. He had been looking out a window towards the train station, but turned when he heard the door.

"Looks like you got the money. Good going. Can we get it in anything smaller than those two suitcases?"

"Not if we want to take it all with us. I was barely able to get it in just two suitcases. Three million takes up more room than I thought it would." Worthington seemed relieved to put the two cases down.

"It is good you arrived when you did, a train just pulled into the station. It appears to be made up mostly of mail cars. But there are two passenger cars tacked on to the tail end. Must be a special because it didn't show up on any of the schedules I looked at. It could be a positive omen for us, I think we should try to get onboard and get out of town, now."

"I'm ready if you are. Just let me catch my breath and we can make a run for it. You will have to help me with these suitcases. Do we want to wait for the train to start moving or do we try to get on now?" Worthington pulled out his handkerchief and mopped his brow.

"The door over there," Winston pointed towards the east side of the building, "opens on the railroad side. We'll need to move quickly towards the far side of the tracks, and then we can get on the first passenger car without being seen from the station. Hopefully we can time it so we will get aboard just as the train starts to move." Winston lifted one of the suitcases, "Boy, these are heavier than they look."

They both headed towards the door, each dragging a suitcase by its handle.

Captain Snyder and Officer Johnson had just stopped their patrol car in the parking lot and were getting out when Rad and Rabbit came running out of headquarters.

Rad yelled to the captain, "Worthington's car has been spotted going down Eighth Street. Follow us and maybe we can corner him near the train station. Also, there is a train due to depart from the station at twelve-thirty. He and Winston may be trying to catch it." Rad leaped into the driver's side of Patrol Three while Rabbit took the passenger's seat.

The two patrol cars almost skidded sideways as they spun out of the police parking lot heading towards Eighth Street with sirens blaring. It was amazing how traffic gave way for them, although they got a lot of questioning stares as they zoomed up Main Street between Ninth and Eighth. The townspeople weren't used to seeing police cars racing at speeds of twenty plus miles per hour, especially around the noon hour. A common thought was; there go the police, late for lunch again.

Both cars turned down Eighth in close trail. And, as if in unison they slowed and cut their sirens as they crossed Commerce Street. The two short blocks to the railroad tracks were void of any traffic, however, Rad could see a black Ford parked next to the warehouse at the bottom of the street. He pulled in beside it.

While he and Rabbit waited for Snyder and Johnson to join them, they moved to the corner of the warehouse; that's when they spotted Winston and Worthington moving along the double tracks toward the front of the train. They were dragging the two suitcases rather than carrying them. It appeared their load was more than they could handle.

"Halt! Halt!" Rad cried out. "You are under arrest."

Both culprits stopped for a moment, like two deer caught in a car's headlights. The four officers didn't hesitate, but headed on a dead run towards the fugitives just as the train started to move out of the station.

Winston and Worthington appeared to be confused, but finally began to move in an attempt to cross the tracks in front of the on-coming steam engine. Worthington stumbled and fell before reaching the first track when the suitcase he was dragging slipped from his grasp. Winston paused when he heard Worthington yell out, but for only a second. The steam engine was almost on top of him when he jumped clear leaving his suitcase on the tracks. Worthington fell to his knees with his arms wrapped around his suitcase and went into a praying position. The snorting monster contacted the suitcase Winston had dropped, cascading money into the air like confetti on the stroke of twelve at a New Year's Eve ball.

As the group stood looking down at Worthington with the money flying in all directions, the train gathered speed and left them behind. Winston wasn't in sight on the far side of the tracks, so he must have boarded the train as it moved past him.

Rad leaped into action. He grabbed Rabbit by the arm and started towards their patrol car. He yelled over his shoulder as they ran, "Captain, can you and Johnson take charge of Worthington and the money? Rabbit and I are going to catch that train at its next stop. We'll try to let the chief know what we are doing."

CHAPTER THIRTEEN

As Rad and Rabbit raced out of town, traffic hadn't really been a problem. They had been slowed going up Fifth Street hill, but once they cleared the city limits they were on an open road. Approaching Forest the roadway almost paralleled the train tracks, but there weren't any trains in sight as they went flying through that small crossroads. They could see some smoke in the distance, but was it from the train they were chasing? They were hoping to get to Medford before the train cleared the station. They certainly didn't want to attempt a chase all the way to Star City because the needle on the gas gauge in their patrol car was fast approaching 'E'.

When they talked to the chief on the radio before leaving the city limits, he hadn't sounded too happy about Winston getting away and them having to chase trains, particularly to Medford. But, they told him they had no other choice but to continue. The chief had perked up when he learned the money had been recovered, or at least most of it. To their benefit, the radio connection didn't last too long, reception weakened to the point that understandable conversation ended. They were on their own.

Rad had the car full out, but just as they topped the crest of an uphill portion of the road, a very large hay wagon straddling the roadway suddenly came into view. It wasn't more than two hundred yards in front of them and it didn't appear to be moving any time soon. It took all the skill Rad had to swing the car off the road and miss the wagon by only inches. The maneuver, however,

211

didn't solve their total problem; their tires were caught in the ruts forming the shoulder of the road, which kept Rad from immediately steering the car back onto the pavement. To add insult to injury, a large tree was staring squarely at them less than a quarter of a mile ahead. Only through exceptional dexterity was Rad able to bring the machine past the tree by using the sloping embankment to safely return the car to the hard surface of the highway. Visions of their earlier motorcycle ride flashed before their eyes, in fact; maybe it was their whole lives.

The dispatcher was busy working the dials of the base radio set in an attempt to regain contact with Rad and Rabbit. The chief was leaning over his shoulder urging him on.

"It appears they have gone out of range, sir. We just don't have enough wattage to maintain contact that far away." The dispatcher held his hands out in despair.

"What were their last words? It sounded like they said they were going to chase that train all the way to Star City if they had too. Did anyone hear it any different?" The chief looked around for confirmation.

"I thought they said they were headed for Medford and hoped to catch the train there." Rachel was looking at her note pad as if she were reading from something she had jotted down at the moment.

Not getting the answer he wanted, the chief continued, "Well luckily, I got through to the Medford sheriff before I came in here. He said he would try to get some people over to the station to see what they could do to help out. However, he also said the train was due in less than five minutes, and they were a good ten to twelve minutes away. I guess those two detectives are going to be on their own if they can make it in time. Let's get over to the interrogation room and see what Captain Snyder and Officer Johnson are doing with Worthington. I hope they have the money with them."

The conductor was standing in the foyer between the two passenger cars. He had one of the half doors open and the sight of the countryside rushing by made it appear the train was traveling double its speed. "You haven't found the felons you were looking for yet, Captain?"

212

"Not yet, but I know they are on the train someplace. I've only had time to search the first car back there." Winston nodded his head towards the last car on the train, " But I see we are getting close to Medford. How long will we be in the station?"

"Not more than a few minutes. It's only supposed to be a water stop, but there's at least one person getting off in Medford. We could have one or two who want to get on, but it would be kind of unusual for this train. Since you didn't want me to call ahead to authorities, you won't have any help while we are stopped."

"That's OK; I'll be able to cover anyone trying to get off. I'm sure I'll have them cornered before we get to Star City." Winston tried to look as confident as possible. He was glad to see the conductor depart for the other end of the train. He hadn't been sure the conductor had bought his story. It was a bit odd, him jumping aboard the train just as it was rolling out of the station in Hill City. Luckily he had his badge with him, which did the trick when he flashed it. Now he would try to lay low, particularly until the train got out of Medford. The only bad thing was, he didn't have the money. He could do without Worthington, but the money would have been nice. His thoughts changed as he noticed a slight grabbing of the brakes, which indicated the train was slowing. Houses were visible alongside the right-of-way so, the station couldn't be far away.

"MEDFORD, MEDFORD, all passengers for Medford." The conductor's voice rang out through the cars.

Captain Snyder had placed Worthington in a chair with his wrists handcuffed to the chair arms. The one suitcase with money was open on the table. There were also several large gunnysacks on the floor with the contents from the destroyed suitcase.

Worthington looked up when Chief Stoddard entered the room. "I demand to be released. I want to see my lawyer."

"Oh, you will get to see your lawyer, but before you do, you will have the honor of spending a little time with us. You should enjoy being in an adjacent cell with your friend, ex Councilman Brenner." The chief looked away from Worthington and focused on the money. "Did you recover all of it?"

"I'm not sure, Chief, since we aren't positive of the exact amount. I know some of it blew in all directions when the locomotive hit the suitcase that Winston dropped in his escape attempt. There were several railroad employees in the area who got an early bonus. But, I think we got most of it."

"That was good work you four pulled off. Now if Childers and Tankers can catch up with Winston, it will be perfect." The chief paused and looked back at Worthington, "Do you have anything you want to say at this time? Now is your chance to lighten your guilt."

"It was all your captain's idea. He is the lone instigator. He contacted Moorehead and me with the plan. I will be happy to testify against him. You also might look around, there could be other corrupt people in your police department." Worthington had a smug look on his face.

"I'm sure he had to twist your arm. Not only were you involved in robbery, but there are two deaths you will be accounting for." The chief looked at Captain Snyder and said, "Put this disgusting person in one of our better cells. He and his friend deserve the best we have, rats and all."

Heavy steam belched from the engine as it started to inch forward out of the Medford station. The words, 'ALL ABOARD,' were still ringing in the air and the conductor was swinging from the station platform onto the train.

Rad skidded the patrol car to a stop as close as possible to the platform. He and Rabbit leaped out and raced towards the metal steps of the last car. Rabbit had just cleared the steps when a shot rang out. They both ducked into the alcoves of the vestibule on each side of the car.

The conductor, between passenger cars, looked inward towards the rear of the train just as Winston fired his second and third shots. He was hit in the shoulder and fell back out of sight. Even though wounded, he managed to reach up and pull the emergency cord. Immediately the train ground to a halt.

Winston had been halfway up the aisle of the second car when he fired his last shots. When the train came to a stop, he moved further up the aisle. He turned to see Rad and Rabbit advancing rapidly up the passenger cars towards his position. He fired his fourth shot.

The two detectives reached the vestibule between cars and saw the conductor leaning against the wall of the car. A spot of blood was on his jacket but it didn't appear his condition was fatal. "Don't worry about me, I think it's just a nick. Get that maniac up there. He sure conned me when he came on board. The train won't leave here until you get him."

"Good. How many passengers are in the second car?"

"Only five and they are mostly at this end."

"That's fine because our shooter is already halfway up the car. Can he get through into the mail cars?"

"Not unless he breaks down the door. And I don't think he is strong enough to do that."

"OK, you lay low and we will see if we can get to him." Rad waved at Rabbit so they could position themselves closer to the door leading into the second car. When they were in place, Rad signaled to Rabbit so he could cover him as he went through the door.

One shot was all it took to keep Winston's head down. Rad ducked safely behind the first seat. Rabbit followed quickly by easing into the seat across from him. Winston, three quarters of the way up the car, was also using the seats for cover. They could see three of the passengers all scrunched down behind the seats just in front of them; most were flat on the floor.

"Give yourself up, Virgil; you can't get off this train before we get you. We don't want to shoot you if we don't have to." Rad's voice was strong and left no doubt they would shoot if he didn't surrender.

"You two couldn't hit a fish in a barrel if you tried. Tell them to get this train moving or I will kill these two passengers I have with me."

Rad whispered to Rabbit, "He must have the two missing passengers up there with him. I don't think he would kill anybody, but you never know. We need to get a good shot at him or he may try." Rad looked at Rabbit as if to say, 'got any ideas'? Rabbit tried to peek up above the seat, which drew another shot from Winston.

"That's his fifth shot, I think he only has one more bullet. When he fires it, we can rush him." Rabbit's face brightened with the thought.

"Not so fast. He once told me how he always carries additional bullets with him. So, him being out of ammunition is out of the question. I think our best bet is for both of us to rush him. We can fire a couple of shots over his head and then dash up the aisle. When he comes up to shoot, one of us ought to be able to get a good shot at him. The main thing is to make it count."

"OK with me. Give me the nod when you are ready." Rabbit had finished reloading his pistol and seemed ready to go.

Rad held up his hand for Rabbit to wait and said, "Virgil, this is our last warning. Come out with your hands up; we don't want to hurt you."

"You two stumble bums couldn't hurt a fly. If you don't get off this train and get it moving in one more minute, I will shoot one of these people. One more killing won't mean that much, and quit calling me Virgil."

"OK, Virgil, but I don't think you will kill either one of those people."

"Oh yeah, you've already used up ten seconds of your minute. I mean what …"

He never got the rest of the sentence finished. Rad and Rabbit were up and running towards his position. When he realized what was happening, it was too late to do anything but run for it. He tried to fire a shot as he turned for the end of the car, but it went wild.

Rad hit Winston in his firing arm, which caused his gun to fall to the floor. Rabbit dashed forward and pounced on Winston before he could retrieve the gun.

The ordeal was over.

Cautiously, two heads rose from behind the seats at the far end of the car. A man and his wife, very white faced, were hugging each other.

Only the conductor and Winston had been wounded; none of the passengers had even been scratched.

It was a miracle.

As the two detectives were placing Winston into the patrol car, a waving conductor yelled, "Don't worry, I'll be fine. I've got to keep the N&W on time." He quickly grabbed hold of the handrail of the second passenger car, shouting at the top of his lungs, "ALL ABOARD."

They waited until the train was out of sight and turned the patrol car in the direction of Hill City. Hopefully the ride back would be less stressful.

Epilogue
(Two Months Later)

Things seemed to be back to normal in Hill City. The new mayor had the town moving forward. The newly elected city council had been seated and was working well with hardly any dissention among the entire group.

The police department was still under the watchful eye of Chief Stoddard. Since Captain Winston had his badge ripped from his tunic, he was no longer on the roster. Now only one assistant chief position was needed, and Captain Snyder filled that slot. Rad and Rabbit had been promoted to detective sergeant, and looked dapper in their civilian attire as they moved around the city in one of the new radio equipped patrol cars. Jay Stevens had been appointed and was well ensconced in the special crime labs unit. New and better ways to improve police work were happening everyday. To no one's surprise, there hadn't been a major crime in weeks.

Rachel and Rad had been seen together in the White House restaurant and they appeared to be more than just friends. Their closeness in the back booth wouldn't have left room for an extra napkin to be placed between them. Word was wedding bells were not too far from becoming a reality.

The board of directors at the bank had appointed Mr. Skinner as the bank's new president. It was no surprise when he fired

Moorehead's former secretary and replaced her with one of the younger ladies from the front reception desk.

Trial results for Worthington, Winston, and Brenner reinforced the fact that Blue Ridge Justice was being conducted in the courts of this hilly town. The dastardly trio had been convicted for their various crimes and would soon be put away for a large chunk of their remaining years.

The so-called bank robbers / extortionists had already exchanged their names for numbers in Richmond's big house. In fact, they had been making little stones out of big stones for well over a month.

And finally, Allen Jenkins must not have liked his chances with the state's justice system. Rather than face trial in Hill City or be extradited to the Tidewater area, he decided to go for a swing by using one of his bed sheets. The jailer found him with his feet missing the floor by only a matter of inches.

And as luck would have it:

Rad and Rabbit were walking down Main Street after finishing breakfast at Old T's. Rabbit was asking Rad about any future wedding plans. Rad was hemming and hawing his answers as they made the turn up Ninth Street towards police headquarters. Just as he started to make sense, his voice was suddenly drowned out by the piercing sound of a bank klaxon on the corner of Tenth and Main. The sound shattered the morning calm.

They turned to face each other with questioning looks and said, **"Here We Go Again!"**

Printed in the United States
83309LV00003B/1-108/A